PALLID LIGHT

THE WAKING DEAD

PALLID
LIGHT

THE WAKING DEAD

WILLIAM JONES

2009

FIRST EDITION
10 9 8 7 6 5 4 3 2 1
Published in December 2009
ISBN: 1-934501-11-5
Printed in the U.S.A.

Published by Elder Signs Press
P.O. Box 389
Lake Orion, MI 48361-0389
www.eldersignspress.com

For my wife

The author wishes to thank Chuck and Kevin for their keen insight, and Stewart and Rick for helping to keep the gang organized.

The End of the Day

In all its raucous impudence
Life writhes, cavorts in pallid light,
With little cause or consequence;
And when, with darkling skies, the night

Casts over all its sensuous balm,
Quells hunger's pangs and, in like wise,
Quells shame beneath its pall of calm,
"Aha, at last!" the Poet sighs.

"My mind, my bones, yearn, clamoring
For sweet repose unburdening.
Heart full of dire, funeral thought,

I will lie out; your folds will cling
About me: veils of shadow wrought,
O darkness, cool and comforting!"

—Charles Baudelaire

CHAPTER

1

THE ROOM DISAPPEARED IN a flash of blackness, hiding the apartment in a heavy gloom. I smiled. Dark places never bothered me. I've lived most of my life in them—sitting in cells, hiding in the shadows. No, the light had always been my problem. No matter where I went, I needed to bring my own darkness.

But tonight it wasn't the city-wide power outage that sent something cold crawling up my spine. It was the strange lights.

A hard storm rolled in from the west, bringing with it streaks of lightning, booming thunder, and a thick curtain of rain. It also brought red and blue lights—neon heavens.

"Rand, you there?" The voice was followed by a hammering on my apartment door. Fat drops of rain exploded against the window. I waited a moment, watching the sky, the lights, the streets. Sensing the strangeness.

"Rand!" The apartment door rattled again. "Let me in."

"Turn it down." I dropped off the wooden stool before the window, and moved toward the door. My pace was slow, really just to taunt Cada. She lived in a constant *State of Emergency*. I thought about that. Funny how people lose it when anything unusual happens. But she was like that before the storm.

"What do you want?" I opened the door, leaning to the side, avoiding her fist as it missed its target. "Pretty good swing."

Her blue eyes widened, eyebrows forming a hard line. "Why the hell didn't you answer?"

"Just did." I pulled the door wide, waving her inside. "You know, you look like one of those fish that inflates when you're angry. Maybe a little cuter though."

"I've been calling," she said.

"Ha. Guess the phone is dead. Or maybe I threw it away." I shrugged.

She hoisted a finger at me, then pointed a different selection at the window.

"Have you seen what's going on out there? No power and half the city's flooded. And you're sitting here, playing hermit and joking."

"Who's joking?"

Thunder shook the apartment. Another wave of rain tapped against the windows like a million anxious fingers. And the strange lights glowered above the storm.

She stomped across the floor, running shoes squishing with each step. "While you're here doing . . . doing—" she threw her hands in the air— "doing God knows what, everyone else is sandbagging, trying to keep the town from washing away. Think about it, Rand. No power. No lights. No alarms. And you . . . here . . . in Temperance. Alone. If anything happens, *anything* . . . you're taking the fall."

After I'd moved to Temperance, Cada Finch befriended me. She was one of those types who thought loners needed friends, when really she was the one in need. Always the hero of some lost cause. This time the cause being me.

Cada just wasn't made for Temperance. I wasn't either. But a small town in Illinois, skirting the edge of Lake Michigan seemed like the perfect spot for an ex-con. Yeah, I still don't get the "ex" part. Once a convict, always a convict. Jackson, Temperance, choose your prison.

"So you're saying the town thinks I'm going on a killing spree?" I flashed a smile, strolling to the fridge. *Flattering.*

"No," she answered abruptly. It seemed like the rest of her sentence caught in her throat. "No, not *that.* But really weird stuff is going on and they'll pin you for it."

I laughed, pulled a beer out, twisted it open. "You think I give a damn?" Took a swig, and returned to my seat.

Water flowed down Bridgeway Drive. It already crested the curbs and was swelling onto the sidewalks. I looked at the sky, it still glowed in unnatural colors. Hues of blue and green with jagged red lines of lightning.

"Does that look like an aurora to you?" I pointed the bottle at the sky.

"It's just lights reflecting off the clouds." She approached me. Wet, short strands of blonde hair clung to her face. The sweatshirt and jeans she wore repeated the trick but with her rangy body. "I saw Gordon Cleary tonight," she said matter-of-factly.

I gave it some thought. For a few seconds, I wondered which was stranger: lights reflecting off clouds during a power outage, or Cada seeing a dead man.

◆   ◆   ◆

"I was at Greene's store buying some Marlboros when the power died. Figured I'd need some batteries. Dave brought out a flashlight to help me find them, and that's when Gordon walked past the front window." Cada dug into her pocket, pulling out a crumpled pack of smokes. Water wrinkled fingers rifled through them. "Jesus, Rand, he was still dressed in his suit from the funeral home."

She patted her pockets. I pulled out my Zippo. Her hands and face trembled as she tried to align the cigarette with the flame.

"Thanks." Cada pulled deep and exhaled a stream of smoke, spilling out like dragon's breath. "Dave didn't see him, but I did. And he really wasn't walking. It was more like someone was pulling him along like a puppet." She took another drag. "Something's wrong out there."

Something did feel wrong, but I couldn't put my finger on it. Not quite yet. And I didn't want to mention it to Cada until I knew what it was. That had always been my thing. All of my life, just before things went sideways, I sensed it. Handy, sure. Handy enough to get me locked away for murder. But thanks to a fucked-up system, I got out on a mistrial. That one I didn't see coming.

"It was probably somebody pulling a joke," I said. "Dead men don't walk . . . except in prison."

As if to counter my words, glass crashed downstairs.

"What's that?" Cada asked. Her *State of Emergency* just went up a notch.

"Sounded like a window." Plenty of experience with breaking windows. And whoever broke this one didn't care about being quiet.

Cada started pacing again, puffing like a train. "Where's the guy downstairs?"

"Eric? He's mostly not home." Actually, I didn't care for the prick. He always eyed me. Definitely had an itch to see me locked up again. I wouldn't be surprised to find newspaper articles about me hanging in one of his bedrooms, accompanied by thumbtacks with strings stretching back and forth showing my whereabouts. I knew his kind. *They* were the fucking crazy ones.

Mixed with the rumble of thunder was the crashing of furniture. Maybe a yell or two.

"Shouldn't we check on him?" Cada asked, halting.

No. "Yep. Right," I sighed. I went to the door, Cada trailing. "You stay here." I gestured at the couch. "Keep a spot there. And if you hear me tell you to run, you move."

Temperance was a small town. Certainly not big enough for this much mystery in one night. Hell, it wasn't big enough for more than one apartment building. When I moved in, I hooked a second floor flat on a side street. It'd been a boarding house years ago, back when trains existed. I guess it's what most people would call cozy. I called it fucking inconvenient. Dorothy Ford owned the place. And she wanted it to stay just the way it was in the 1800s—it's that old. No cable, no satellite. A phone, and a useless rooftop antenna was as high-tech as the place got. Of course, I understood why an ex-con lived in Dorothy's historical museum of dead thrills, but why Eric Walker? A man with an expensive car, nice suits, and enough money to vanish for weeks—why would he live there?

Like I said, I knew the type. He was hiding something. And as I marched down the narrow stairwell, I hoped his secret didn't decide to pay a visit.

When I reached his door, it was slightly open. I peered through the crack. Glimpses of furniture, paintings on the walls, and shadows were visible in the sickly glow cast through the windows. Now and then, a brilliant flash of lightning uncovered a darker recess.

Pushing gently, the door opened with a creak that was quickly swallowed by the marching of the rain. To my left, one of the bay windows was shattered. A stream of water rolled over the jagged edges of glass, pooling on the hardwood floor.

From the bedroom I heard the tumble of something hard— muffled by the ceaseless rain.

"Eric?" Calling for him went against my every fiber. But I wouldn't put it past him to be sitting on the other side of the door, shotgun leveled. Waiting.

He knew my history, like most people in Temperance. And like most, he didn't like me. No problem, I didn't like most of them.

With soft steps, I moved across the room. The only weapon I had was a pocket knife. Mostly useless. And if I pulled it, I was on shaky ground—prowling through a flat in the dark, uninvited. Not worth it.

I halted at the bedroom door. It too stood ajar, but the angle was wrong. Couldn't get a view inside. I rapped on it once, and waited. I thought I heard mumbling, but in the roiling rain it was hard to tell.

Slowly, I pushed open the door. There lay Eric. Flat on his back, sprawled across the floor, blankets spilled over the bed, folding beneath him. At his sides were two locals. Teenage punks who wanted to be tough, but who were afraid to leave the protection of a small town. They liked to mouth-off at me, knowing all the while they were safe. And I'd never seen them when their eyes weren't glazed. I'd dubbed them *Stoned* and *Stoner*.

They ignored me. Hunched over Eric's body, they pawed at what remained of Eric's insides. His gut was split—clawed open. And the two punks unraveled his intestines, gnawing and chewing them.

A knot formed in my stomach. *And I'm the monster?*

Blood glistened on the floor, gushing outward. Their wet faces shone in the greenish light of the storm.

This was seriously fucked-up.

Then one turned his gaze toward me.

CHAPTER

2

IT WAS *STONED* WHO clambered to his feet first, swaying back and forth. The other continued working on Eric's eviscerated corpse.

The world spun for a split-second as I tried to understand what I saw. It wasn't the blood, or the gore. I was used to that. I came from a world of darker horrors—decapitated heads in a bag, butchered torsos, knapsacks filled with limbs. And the agonized wails of the mothers and wives who discovered their loved ones. No, butchered bodies didn't bother me as much as the horror-struck face of a mother who'd found part of her son in a bag, sent as a message.

And somehow this was different.

Stoned stumbled forward. A vapid gaze set on his face. Sneering lips revealed crimson teeth. Without him saying a word, I knew what he wanted. Another meal.

"You can't be serious," I said, pushing the door wide open. It bumped against a wall stop. "What a bunch of sick fucks. What the hell are you high on?" I wondered if Eric's secret was some sort of designer drug.

A tepid growl came from *Stoner*. Maybe he was trying to talk, maybe not. I didn't much care. What I did know was the guy downstairs who didn't like me was dead, and was being eaten by two brain dead punks. Somehow, *this* was going to come down on me. That's the way the world worked.

Then Eric sat up.

"*Shit!*" I stepped back. "You're alive?"

A thick red liquid spilled from his mouth, dribbling down his chin, stringing into his open abdomen. Guess that answered my question.

None of this fit together in my head. Everything inside me screamed, "Get out!" But there was that feeling. That dark chill touching my spine. There was also a thick stench.

I raised my hands. "Ok fellas, I'm leaving. Have at it." I stepped backward, eyeing *Stoned,* who seemed to finally get his footing.

With Eric upright, the second teenager turned his attention to me. He struggled to stand, slipping on the slick floor. With each move, gore spewed from his mouth, followed by a guttural hacking.

I backstepped into the living room, already knowing how this was going to play-out.

Stoned bolted forward, as though spurred by an electrical shock. His arms reached outward, fingers clawing the air.

I sidestepped, lifting my booted foot and pushing it against his knee. It made a crunchy sound, then he squeaked. I grabbed his shoulder and pushed, sending him down, face first on the floor.

Keeping my eyes on the other two, I planted my boot on the back of his neck. "Stay there," I said to *Stoned,* "or I'll put you down."

He gurgled. The others made growling sounds.

I pushed with my boot, thinking *Stoned* might warn the others away. Instead, he uttered nonsense sounds. Eric and his new pal kept coming.

In the ghoulish light they looked dead. And Eric, innards drooping to the floor, dark blood washing down his legs, by all rights should be dead. It made less sense with each passing moment.

My thoughts whirled as though the storm outside had entered my head. Things had become so unreal, I had no choice but to accept them. I knew how the cops would explain them later, and that explanation involved me.

I started to lift my foot from *Stoned's* neck. Then I thought it over. Eric ambled toward me, guts dragging on the floor, a stupid half-smile on his face. *There's no good ending here.*

"Fuck it," I said. "Never liked you anyway." I stomped on the kid's neck. It popped as my foot pushed into the soft flesh.

In two steps I was on the next teenager. Maybe if I kept him alive he'd talk when he came down from his high. *No. It didn't work that way for you.*

I grabbed his throat, pulling him forward, and clocked him on the head with my elbow. He dropped like a ragdoll. Meanwhile, Eric was still taking robot steps across the floor. He plodded ahead, one foot in front of the other, swaying from side-to-side like walking a ship in a storm.

Saving him time, I stepped forward, and hammered a fist into his nose. The bone cracked. Blood oozed. And he didn't blink.

I looked at his blue and bloodied face. There was something more than emptiness there. I wasn't sure what. Maybe a little bit of Eric. Maybe a little bit of what he was hiding. His lips turned upward ever so slightly into a snarl. And for the first time, I'd noticed a faint glow in his eyes.

"Not happening," I said.

He reached out—arms slow and stiff.

I grabbed his thumb and twisted, expecting him to drop to his knees in pain. Instead, he clawed at me with his other hand, coming closer, teeth snapping.

His guts dangled from his abdomen. And he kept moving. Obviously, my mind was muddled. Of course he wouldn't feel any pain—he was beyond that.

I didn't know what Eric was hiding, but I had always sensed a darkness in him. Drug dealer, serial killer, kidnapper—didn't make a difference. I saw it there, and despised it.

"Bad day for you," I said. With a free hand, I clamped onto his collar, pulling his head back. He gurgled, red spittle seeped from his mouth. I released his thumb, locked both hands on his head, and twisted. His neck snapped. Finally his body stopped squirming. I pushed him away, letting what was left of him tumble to the floor.

This was not how I'd expected my visit to go. *Thought I might help the asshole.* Maybe *this* was his secret, I decided. Some kind of cannibal and drugs scene. But it didn't make sense. He was a traveler. He'd keep his secrets far from Temperance.

I knew something was up before I'd arrived. I knew it the minute the storm started. And something told me this was just the beginning.

I had a few minutes before Cada started worrying and decided to go looking for me. I scanned the flat. There was no use trying to clean up. And all of this was still going to land on me, unless I found something pointing in another direction. I had the one teenager who might tell the truth—doubted that. Figured I'd look around the place. Maybe find whatever Eric had hidden. The situation was beyond the point of getting worse.

Knowing the tricks, I headed to the bedroom, skirting the macabre decorations on the floor. Checking the dresser drawers was a waste of time. *Amateur stuff.* I didn't bother. But I did take his car keys sitting in a bowl on top of the dresser. I had to hoof everywhere, and it looked like I might need to move a bit faster unless things turned around.

Outside the storm persisted. Loud cracks of thunder shook the building. The rain continued its ceaseless dance upon the roof and ground. It created a constant thrumming.

I opened the closet. On the top shelf there was a shoebox. It was too obvious to hold anything damning—but I still hoped. Inside I found a 9mm Beretta, three magazines, and a half empty box of cartridges.

Probably has a permit. I took the pistol, pushed in a clip, and stuffed the rest into my pocket. Just then, a familiar feeling settled over me. How many times had I followed this path? Getting ready to run. It was supposed to be over when I was locked up. And I'd told myself it would never happen again when they let me out.

Like I said, I bring my own darkness with me.

Right now, things needed to keep moving. I had to keep those thoughts at bay. One after another, I yanked clothes from the rack in the closest, tossing them aside. Eric wasn't going to make this easy.

Mixed with the tattoo of the rain was the sound of a footfall from behind. I turned. In the doorway stood *Stoner,* eyes hollow, jaw slack. His face was painted in blood, as was the hoodie he wore. One foot plodded forward. He burbled some sounds. Maybe they were words. I sensed a rhythm. A shape to them. It wasn't English. Regardless, his intent was clear.

I pulled the pistol from my belt and chambered a round.

CHAPTER

3

I AIMED THE BERETTA AT the punk's head. I was waiting for another roll of thunder to cover the sounds of the shot. I knew if Cada heard it, she'd be down in an instant.

Stoner lumbered closer. Rain snapped against the building as though expectantly tapping fingers. The pistol remained leveled.

It seemed as if I was lost in time. The blasts of thunder came every other minute. A few more steps, and *Stoner* would be on top of me. Looked like I'd be hammering him with the 9mm instead.

An odd question danced at the edge of my mind. I'd seen these two kids many times over the last year—but never at Eric's. They roamed downtown, hung-out on corners. Both were the same height and size, and both perpetually wore caps or hoodies. Now, as *Stoner* approached, I wondered if he wasn't *Stoned* instead. Yep, a stupid thought, but what else could I do while waiting to put two in the punk's head.

"Rand!" Cada's voice sounded.

Finally a snarl of thunder rattled the building, and I squeezed the trigger three times in quick succession. *Stoner* dropped like a rock. Or maybe *Stoned*. Didn't much matter.

I snugged the pistol underneath the back of my belt. In seconds,

I passed through the flat, reaching for the door just as Cada opened it.

"Nothing here," I said. "Let's go back."

"You look outside?" Cada asked. "We gotta leave."

"Sounds good." I planted my hands on her shoulders and turned her around. We took the stairs quickly. "Before we plan anything, we need to talk."

She laughed, but the sound was weak. "We can talk while we leave."

I guided her into my flat, closed and locked the door. She stood before me, clothes soaked, blond hair pulled back in a short ponytail.

"You need to put on some dry clothes," I said. "There are some sweatshirts and pants the bedroom. Oversized for you, but the drawstrings should help."

She planted her hands on her hips. "Look out the window." Her voice was calm, but it was the type of calm that came before panic.

"All right," I said, pulling my T-shirt over the pistol stuffed in the back of my belt. I turned and looked out the front window.

Nothing tonight made sense. In fact, it was the kind of nonsense telling me something important was going down. Wasn't random. I was just blind to the pattern, to the entire picture. It was beyond my reach, but in the recesses of my mind, I felt everything lock into place. Understanding it was the problem. Nonetheless, I felt it.

As I gazed out the window, I saw a parade of people marching past Dorothy Ford's museum of dead thrills. A group better suited as cast members in a movie like *Carnival of the Damned*—a horrible flick Cada introduced me to. All of them were rain-soaked, clothes sagging, hair stringy. All of them stumbling as through they'd forgotten how to walk. All of them deathly pallid in the eerie light of the storm.

I stood and watched in silence.

"Uh-huh," Cada muttered. "That's what I said."

"What the hell's going on?"

"Got me," she answered. "Looks like everyone's had a brain flush. And look—" she moved to the window, pointing— "they all look like Gordon Cleary. It's like they're puppets being pulled along."

She was right. And after seeing Eric, I was starting to think Gordon Cleary wasn't a small town prank. Not unless everyone plodding down Bridgwater Drive was in on it.

I turned my gaze toward the sky, watching the aurora-like lights slither across.

"We've got to leave," I said.

"You think?"

"All right. You can make fun later. Right now grab some clothes and food."

Cada folded her arms. "There is no way I'm going out in that crowd. I don't care how tough you are or act."

I'm not going out there either. "Eric was gone," I said. "So I borrowed the keys to his SUV."

"You're holding back. Something else is up. I can read it on your face."

She was right. Most people avoided looking me in the eyes. But Cada was different. The minute she'd heard a convict had settled in Temperance, she was at my door, sizing me up and asking questions. And she had an eerie sense for when I was hiding something.

"What happened downstairs?" she asked.

I shook my head. "You don't want to know. But it was along the lines of what's going on out there." I jerked a thumb at the front window.

Her face lit-up as though she'd been struck by lightning. "Do you think it's in the rain? Some kind of virus or something? I've seen shows where storms have pulled dead fish and frogs out of lakes and rained them down on towns. Christ knows what's in Lake Michigan. I'm sure there's something out there that could make all of Temperance sick . . ." She let the words fade as her eyes dropped to her soggy clothes.

"It's not the rain," I said. And I believed it. "Your theory is scary enough to be true, but you'd be like the rest of them already." I ushered her into the bedroom, grabbed a duffle from under the bed and started handing her sweats. "I don't know what it is, but I think it's got to do with those lights."

I went to the closet and retrieved another duffle. Quickly, I dropped the two extra clips and box of cartridges in it. Then I stuffed it with clothes.

Mechanically, Cada crammed the sweats into the duffle bag, moving around the bedroom picking up random clothes I'd pulled from the closet.

I watched her for a moment. Anger burned in my muscles. I grabbed her by the arms, and gave her a quick shake. "Don't try to make yourself like that. If you were like them, I'd know it. You wouldn't just be standing around. There's more to it than wandering the streets in the rain and staring." I pulled a pair of pants out of the bag, placing them in her hands. "Go in the bathroom and put them on. I'll pack, and then we'll leave."

"How can it be the lights?" she said softly.

"You're asking me?" I laughed.

A knock sounded at the front door. I stepped into the living room, pulling the Beretta.

"Where'd you get that?" Cada asked.

They didn't seem like the knocking type. Then it came again. It was soft, not like a cop's knock—determined, urgent. There was no authority behind it. Those were the type of knocks I'd learned to dread. They were usually followed by the door bursting open and a band of police officers yelling.

"Eric gave it to me," I said to Cada. "Get in the bedroom."

"Cada, are you in there?" The voice was weak, but definitely male.

"Nate!" Cada yelled. She turned to me and repeated it. "That's Nate."

I shrugged. "Yeah. Right. Nate. Who the hell is Nate?" I didn't trust strangers showing up with all of this weirdness going down.

Hard blue eyes fixed on me. "He's my friend," Cada said. "And you've met him before. He's come here with me a couple times."

The wimpy knocking returned. "If you're in there, Cada, you got to let me in."

Cada continued staring at me. There was no amount of hard façade she couldn't penetrate with her gaze. "All right," I said, stuffing the pistol behind my back. "But if he starts to act like one of them . . ." I jerked a thumb at the window and let the sentence hang.

"Hold on," Cada yelled to Nate. She trotted across the room and opened the door.

Nate stood there, a gangly six-two or more, glistening midnight blue windbreaker pulled taut over his frame. He was all angles—elbows and shoulders and knees. Rain saturated jeans slipped from narrow hips. And a sopping mop of hair covered his eyes and face making him look like an emaciated Saint Bernard, or a far too thin John Lennon.

With spider-like fingers he parted his hair, adjusting his round glasses. Then I definitely remembered him. He was the John Lennon wanna be. Sometimes he played in small time bands, always impersonating Lennon—although most of the locals thought he was original.

Cada led him into the living room, tossing towels at him as she went.

I'd spent nearly a third of my life in prisons. Not much by most convicts' standards—being thirty years old. But when you live the life I did, everyone looks old. Everyone except *Nate.* I'd never asked, but I guessed Cada to be around twenty-four or twenty-five. I knew she wasn't jailbait, and that was all that really mattered. Not that we ever did more than talk and watch videos. Doing anything more than being pals just didn't feel right. And even though I teased Cada about eating popcorn and watching old movies, I enjoyed it. Most people steered clear of me. Being with her made me feel human. In the end, there was nothing between us. Still, I didn't like Nate. Given the present situation, I liked him even less.

"Can he borrow some of your clothes?" Cada asked. "He's really soaked."

A smile played across my face. "Sure. Whatever you can find . . . that fits. But not the leather jacket."

"You guys seen what's happening out there?" Nate shifted his gaze between us. "The whole town's lost it. They're pulling each other apart in the streets."

"What are you talking about?" Cada asked.

Fuck. I saw the panic looming on the horizon. Didn't need that now. Just wanted to get out of town.

"Oh yeah," Nate continued. "People are gnawing on each other and walking around like they've been drinking Drano. Christ, it looks like most of Temperance has become zombies or something."

"All right, put a plug in it," I said. Out of the corner of my eye I saw Cada pacing. I turned to her. "We're going to leave. And once we're away from Temperance, we'll figure out what's happening. For now, pack and get moving." I waved them into the bedroom. "Change in there with whatever fits you, John. And then finish packing those duffels."

"Nate," he said, ambling toward the bedroom. Cada stayed behind.

"The name's Nate," he followed up.

"*Pack*," I snapped. *Nate* vanished behind the door.

Cada looked at me wide eyed. "You saw it too, didn't you? You saw them killing each other."

"Saw some teenagers acting strange. Doesn't matter. We're leaving."

For the most part, there was only one emotion alive inside me. The same one switched on for most of my life. Anger, or variations of it, were all I needed. On the streets of Detroit, or in prison, nothing else was necessary.

She wasn't the hard as nails type. Most of the women I knew had two kids by Cada's age, and either went for adoption, or sold them. They were hard. Their world made sure of it. Along the way, a few of them got lost in drugs, others escaped. Coming to Temperance showed me not everyone was empty.

Something rattled on the roof. It tumbled a few times, then faded into the wash of rain.

"Let's get moving," I said, adding some urgency.

"What was that?" Cada asked.

"Probably a branch or a shingle. Noting to worry about."

"So we're just leaving? That's it? Driving away?"

I knew Cada didn't have family in town. Although, I never bothered to ask why. Just seemed natural. But now I wondered. "Does Nate have anyone here?"

Worry lined her face. She swallowed. "No. He's alone."

A sharp resentment slashed through me. I didn't care about these things because I traveled without baggage. What I should have done was simple. Walk out the door. Alone. All of this other shit was rotting my brain. It felt like I was watching the world through dark glasses. Blind and not sure where to go.

"They died when he was sixteen," she continued. "Left him the house and enough money to play *Rock Band* for the rest of his life." She clasped her hands, rubbing them as though they were cold.

Go. Leave without them. Not your problem. Just baggage to slow you down. The emotion I understood kindled inside me. I knew what Cada wanted to hear, and against my better judgment, I said it. "He can come with us."

She smiled. "Thanks." Then she ran into the bedroom.

None of this made any fucking sense to me.

CHAPTER

4

STANDING IN THE FOYER, I watched through the narrow wood-framed windows as the ragged mob thinned. Cada and Nate waited behind, duffle bags slung over their shoulders.

The air was damp. With the heavy rain, it was tough to know if the lightning strikes had slowed. The sky still shimmered a bluish-green.

"Anyone getting a cell signal?" Nate asked.

I glanced over my shoulder. The display from his cell phone glowed in his hands.

"No," I said. "And turn that off before the light attracts attention."

He gazed at me flatly—probably how he thought John Lennon would respond.

"How do we get past them?" Cada asked.

I turned back to the door. Most of the people looked half alive, or half dead. They shambled down the center of the street. Some barely moved, dragging a broken foot or a leg behind them. None of them approached the driveway where Eric's Traverse was parked.

"Hopefully they won't see us," I said. "If they do, we're faster. All we need to do is get to the car. Then we're safe."

"Unless they break a window," Nate said under his breath.

"They're not that strong," I said. "I've already dealt with a few."

"Don't have to be strong. Just need a tool."

I spun on Nate. We nearly matched height—maybe he had a little on me. But I had at least one-hundred and twenty pounds on him. "Listen, if you'd rather head out on your own–"

"Rand," Cada said, placing a hand on my chest, holding me back. "I know you're right. Nate's just trying to help."

"Stop helping then."

Nate shrugged boney shoulders. "Just saying, if they can use tools the windows aren't protection. No need to get hot over it. We just need to–"

"Shut-up." I raised a finger to silence him. "I do not want to hear you mention *peace,* or *love,* or *working together.* Right now I like John Lennon. Don't change that for me."

Before he replied, I opened the door. "Let's go." I pressed a button on the SUV's remote. Headlights flashed.

A few, five or six, people shambling in the street turned toward the Traverse. A couple had to hop-skip in order to change direction. Others, those who looked more lively, twisted about, heading for the driveway.

Cada pulled the sweatshirt hood over her head. "Don't let the rain touch you," she said, bolting across the porch and down the stairs.

Tugging a knit cap over his head, Nate followed. The cap was mine, of course. As were the clothes. The only thing that actually fit him was his shoes and windbreaker.

From the doorway, I watched as the pair climbed into the SUV. In one hand I held the keys, in the other the Beretta. Except for the few people who turned toward the driveway, the rest of the line continued down Bridgeway Drive. Didn't know if they had a rally point or were just walking in circles. Didn't much matter. I just wanted to leave.

I moved down the driveway, water pelting my leather jacket. Inside the SUV, I saw Cada motioning for me to cover my head. Her infected water theory was good, but if it was the cause then either we had immunities or it wasn't taking.

I climbed into the driver's seat, pulling the door closed. The engine rumbled to life just as three of the townsfolk arrived at the passenger side window.

Two men and a woman. All were dressed as though they'd been indoors before deciding to roam the streets in the rain—another reason not to buy Cada's theory. One man wore a sweater and jeans. The other in a white dress shirt, with slacks made shapeless by the water. The woman wore a nightgown. All color disappeared from their clothing as the rain continually washed their outfits making everything a sodden gray.

Hands clubbed at the windows. They gurgled and sputtered as water drained down their faces into their mouths.

"Let's get going," Cada said anxiously.

I shifted the SUV into reverse, guiding it down the driveway. The glow of the taillights attracted more people.

"What's wrong with them?" Cada asked. "Wake up!" she yelled. Her voice reverberated inside the Traverse.

"Whoa!" Nate complained from the backseat. "Roll down the window before you do that again."

"It's like they're all sleep walking," Cada said.

"More like they're zombies," Nate replied.

"And how would you know that?" Cada turned to face him.

"He doesn't," I said.

A group stumbled up the driveway as though pulled toward the SUV's headlights.

"All right," I said. "They're acting like zombies." Images of Eric and the toasted teens flashed through my mind. If Eric wasn't a zombie, how did he get up after having most of his guts pulled out? "Doesn't matter what you call them. It's how they're acting that's the problem."

"Zombies explain Gordon Cleary," Cada added. "Oh my god, we have to go to Greene's. Dave's still there."

I hit the horn. Cada jumped, her seat belt the only thing holding her down. There were two people—zombies—behind us, bouncing against the rear door. They ignored the horn, and continued to paw at the rear window.

"Enough of this," I said, shifting into drive. I wheeled the SUV across the lawn and into the street, swerving around the shamblers.

The suspension took the curb well. But the street was overflowing with water, making me wonder how many roads were washed out. Most of Temperance used drainage ditches. That meant most of the roads were under water.

"Where were they putting up the sandbags?" I asked Cada. The SUV sluiced down Bridgeway Drive, splashing arcs of water.

"Ashland and Bay," she replied. "Just down Main Street from Greene's store. Dave said the lake already flooded most of downtown. They were trying to dam it up."

I was beginning to dislike Temperance. Main Street was the only road out of city, and it cut through the center of downtown. I slammed a fist against the steering wheel. "We need to hit higher ground until this rain stops. There's no way I'm washing out this engine on a flooded downtown street."

"High ground would be Height Street," Nate said. His smugness had returned.

"Can you swim?" I asked.

"Stop it," Cada said. "He's trying to help. So turn down the macho a few degrees."

I snorted and flipped on the brights. They did little to remove the sickly shimmer painting everything. Wipers pushed away water, making the world a combination of clear and unfocused with each swipe. The headlights did little to cut through the heavy sheets of rain. Each drop sparkled in unearthly colors on their way to the ground.

"Let's head to Greene's," I said. "Maybe see what's going on there." I figured there'd be a town meeting, including Temperance's two cops. No doubt my arrival would delight everyone.

The safest route was Hall Street to Lakeview. Both were asphalt and banked high. Maybe less water, and hopefully no zombies.

The Traverse rolled to the end of Bridgeway Drive, passing through overhanging willow trees. I turned onto Hall, following its shiny surface to Lakeview. The road skirted the edge of downtown. Scattered trees and fields flanked both sides.

Water puddled everywhere. The lights from above reflected across acres of tall grass. And the lightning had returned. Strange streaks of red and yellow split the darkness, snaking downward. A tremendous rumble followed each flash.

"Why is the lightning red?" Cada asked.

I pushed up the speed on the SUV. Suddenly being in the open seemed like a bad idea.

"Maybe particulates in the air coloring it," Nate said.

The guy had plenty of answers.

"It's like the world is coming to an end," Cada said. She shifted in her seat, looking at the sky through each window as though expecting a different result.

"Focus on what we're doing," I said, mostly to prevent Nate from offering something that might put me in an even fouler mood.

Since we'd left my flat, anger was festering inside me. Easy to justify. Cada and Nate. And faulting myself for not going alone. Yet, there was something more. I didn't buy into easy reasons. Something else was there, like someone pushing my buttons just to set me off.

"Still no signal," Nate said. Again he was playing with a cell phone. *Whatever keeps him occupied.*

On the east, Lakeview approached. I followed it, passing a dotted line of mailboxes on the left. None of the houses stood near the road. They were hidden beyond a wall of rain.

The headlights reflected off the slick blacktop. The movement of the Traverse made the shafts of rain seem solid. Telephone poles whooshed by as I accelerated toward Height Street.

Suddenly, Cada screamed. She thrashed against the safety belt, tugging at it, trying to escape.

I slowed the SUV. "What's wrong?"

"Did you see it?" she cried, eyes electric with terror. "Did you see it?"

"See what?" I gripped her arm. "Calm down." I let the SUV slow to a stop.

"Oh god! Don't stop! No!"

Her panic was contagious. Nate fidgeted in the backseat. Pressing the door locks repeatedly, checking the windows. And my heart was slamming against my chest. It was like the electricity in the air was charging us up, pumping fear and anger through our veins.

"Tell me what you saw." I tried to hold Cada still.

She gazed at me with wild eyes. "I don't know. It wasn't human." She looked about, scanning the embracing gloom. "Please keep going . . ."

"I saw it too," Nate said. "It was there but it wasn't. Dark like a shadow. And it was fuzzy. Almost looked like a man." He faced the window, and added, "It was like it radiated darkness."

No help there. Too much was happening. Cada and Nate were flipping out. And one weird thing after another was occuring. I didn't know what to believe.

"Go!" Cada yelled.

I exhaled, and pushed the accelerator. Just needed to focus on getting to Greene's store. *Deal with one thing at a time.*

"Look straight ahead," I said. "The lights play tricks."

"There's no way that was an optical illusion," Nate said sharply. "Talk about weird. It was like I felt it there, but couldn't focus on it. And when I saw it, there was something like a glowing blackness."

"Got it," I said. "Not a flash of light, just a bunch of glowing nothingness. Now how about you keep quiet until we get to the store?"

"I'm not looking out there again," Cada said. A sideways glance revealed her eyes were clamped shut. "It knew I saw it. I could tell."

CHAPTER

5

"WHAT ABOUT THE RADIO?" Nate said. A static buzz filled the interior. In the rearview, I watched Nate study the backseat radio controls. For a moment, I considered locking the console. But the radio was worth trying, and it kept him busy.

The speakers crackled and buzzed as he tuned through the band. Now and then I thought I heard a voice in the static, but when I had Nate tune back, there was nothing.

"If this were a terrorist attack, the Emergency Broadcast System should be transmitting," he said.

"When did we get to terrorists?" I asked.

"Just a thought," he said. "Only fascists don't like ideas."

My fingers gripped the steering wheel, but I remained silent. *Not much longer.*

Then I started seeing things.

I slowed the SUV. In the headlights were several people in the road. They stood, slumped, empty faces, forming a straggling line across Lakeview Road. They ignored the downpour, swaying with the blowing wind.

I stopped the Traverse.

"Now what?" Cada asked.

"A zombie version of a road block," Nate said.

And for once, Nate was right.

It took a moment for Cada and Nate to fully comprehend the scene. When they did, I sensed the panic boiling.

"They're not moving. It's like they're waiting for us," Cada said.

"Can't be," I replied. "Don't seem that smart." Least I didn't think they were. Everyone I'd seen so far had seemed to be as smart as a shoe. A thinking person doesn't stagger toward a man aiming a pistol. And *Stoner* did.

I shifted the SUV into Park. We were at least ten yards away from the line.

"Are you crazy?" Cada asked.

"Yep," I replied.

"Turn around," Cada said. "We can find another way."

"Yeah, not a good idea," Nate agreed.

"Our options are limited. Turning around won't help. We'll just end up where we started. There isn't a way around."

Through the rain-streaked windshield, I watched as a few of them faced the vehicle.

"We'll wait for them to move aside, or we clear a path."

Cada twisted toward me. "I vote clear a path. If we wait here, they're going to mob us. Or that shadow thing will find us."

"This isn't happening," Nate said. His voice was hollow as though lost in some distant land. "It can't be real."

Should have known. He was channeling Lennon.

In my lifetime, I'd learned only a handful of skills. In Jackson Prison, I was taught to make office furniture. The prison sold it to businesses, called it "Freedom Furniture." The name didn't even deserve a bad joke, so most inmates ignored it.

During my time, I learned making furniture wasn't my calling. Sure, I could follow an assembly line. But I didn't have the spirit for it. Didn't care. Always figured someday a suit would be sitting in a chair I assembled and it'd fall apart. That I could get behind, but it wouldn't help sales.

It might have been I was good at some other things. But I never had a chance to find out. What I had a talent for—a clear, gifted talent—wasn't favored by society. When I looked back, I don't think I was born that way. Or miswired from birth. It was a skill I learned, and honed. The same way I learned to make furniture. The world I lived in gave me the tools and training. Mastering the skills was my doing. But it wasn't the type of thing you did as a hobby, and walked away from. It haunted you day and night. A gift and a curse. Guess it really depended upon who you were. And that's why I didn't encourage part-time dabbling.

"Look closely," I said. "Do either of you know any of these people?"

"I don't want to look," Cada said, keeping her eyes locked on me.

She didn't want to look because facing them was more than she could handle. At least with what she was thinking. I understood that much. But then, she wasn't the one who'd have to drive through them—run them down.

"They're not real people anymore," Nate said. "Something changed them. They're husks. Nothing's inside them."

Hiding. That's what the two of them were doing. They were terrified, and grabbing at any justification. Having been there, I couldn't let them take that step. When you did, it was a one way journey.

The rain tapped a rhythm on the roof while I peered at the mob. Nearly all of them faced the SUV. And their mouths were moving. Originally, I took the motion to be their usual snapping. The same as I'd seen in Eric's flat. That wasn't it. It looked as though they were trying to shape words. One after another, they worked their mouths as though speaking.

"Bad news for your *half-empty* theory, Nate. This bunch looks like they want to chat."

As though compelled, Cada turned forward. She craned her neck, seemingly trying to read their lips.

"Habit," Nate said. "They're mimicking, not speaking."

"Look again," I said. "Either there's more to it, or they just broke into a rendition of *Singing in the Rain*. Either way, their mouths are trying to form words. And that's got to be more than old memories."

Cada dropped back, letting the seat catch her. Her face was distorted with horror. Hugging herself, she inhaled and exhaled deeply. "We have to leave," she said between breaths.

"Go back? Or run them over?" I asked.

"I *get* your point. Okay, I recognize some of them. Don't know their names, but I've seen them plenty of times. Maybe they were mothers and fathers once, but not anymore. Now they're monsters." She tightened her arms, and started rocking back and forth.

"If they're not the people you knew, then what are they?" I pressed.

"I don't fucking know. Look at them." She freed an arm to point. "They're no longer human."

So much for my morality lesson. I looked at the gaunt and dough-faced people, scanning their lips.

"I don't really care if they want to talk," Nate said. "I've seen them biting each other and ripping skin away. They want to do more than strike up a conversation."

I popped open my door, and stepped to the street. "Lock it behind me," I said.

"Rand, no!" Cada lurched across the armrest, clamping hands around my arm. "You can't go out there."

"Yeah," Nate added. "We're not people to them. We're carry-out."

"I need to be sure," I said, pulling from Cada's grip. The safety belt kept her from crawling over the armrest.

Heavy drops of rain snapped against my leather coat. Leaning against the doorframe, I looked at her. "Don't worry." Then I closed the door.

Even in the downpour, I heard the voices. Didn't understand a bit of it. Sounded like random noises—almost words, but incomplete. Together, their voices were raucous, growing in volume as though there were urgency. Even though they faced the SUV, I wasn't sure if they were speaking to it or among themselves, or maybe just making noises like a baby did.

I walked to the rear of the Traverse. Inside Cada and Nate frantically gestured for me to return. A few of the zombies started shuffling toward me.

"Hold on." I waved a hand at the mumbling mass. "I need a few tools. Or maybe just one." I pulled open the back door. "Told you to lock it," I said to Cada.

"Get in here," she snapped. "They're going to kill you."

Beneath a carpeted floorboard was a recessed storage compartment with a spare tire, jack, and stubby lug wrench. I was envious of Eric. This vehicle had more hiding spots and storage places than I'd ever seen. Shame it was forever beyond my price range.

I stepped back, lug wrench in hand. Nate was pushing Cada into the front seat as I pulled down the rear door. "Lock it this time," I said. "Just be a minute."

My boots slapped against the wet asphalt as I walked toward the haggard crowd. They weren't in a hurry.

I gripped the lug wrench in one hand, and checked the Beretta snugged into my belt with the other. Stopping a few paces away from the meandering townsfolk, I listened.

The rain hissed and spat. Each person before me shone in a greenish cast. Soggy sleeves stretched, covering hands, flopping as they moved about. Then I saw their eyes.

Only the whites shone. Not really the whites. There was a pale green tint in them like they were glowing. *Definitely something wrong there.*

They jabbered, spitting out sounds.

"Haaaah-thimm . . . Kak-kak . . ."

Jibberish. I didn't want to admit it, but Nate seemed right. It was like they'd lost their minds. They were zombies. Talkative zombies. But pretty much not the people they used to be.

The sounds repeated, growing louder. It sounded like a chorus of frogs attempting to croak out words.

"Can you understand me?" I asked.

Sunken eyes passed over me. The mindless sounds continued. Then the absurdity of the situation landed on me like a heavy weight. Of all the people in Temperance, I'm the last who should be standing in the rain trying to help a group of people who in their right mind despised me.

Several staggered closer.

"Stand still if you understand me," I said above the rain.

The real reason I was out here was to prevent nightmares. Cada and Nate might not be bothered by killing tonight. Days from now, the memories would lurk in their thoughts, growing darker and heavier with each year. That was what broke most people. The regret. The self-torture. The lingering darkness inside them.

I stepped out of the headlights. The group of walking dead fell silent. One after another, they started toward me.

Waving the lug wrench, I said, "Over here. Keep to the shadows. Form a line."

Unwittingly, they obeyed. Maybe it was the motions I made. They always seemed to move in a direct path. I'd picked an angle, forcing them to reorganize, pretty much bringing them one at a time to me.

"If you can understand me, stop." I said.

Throaty gurgles came in response.

As they neared, I saw cuts and bite marks, flaps of flesh snapping in the wind. All of these were slow. Back at my apartment, at least a few of them were fast.

"Stop," I said.

They repeated their own mantra of sounds and coughs.

Slashing rain popped against my leather jacket as I waited. Cada had called these people "monsters." She didn't know, but I was too. It was the thing I was good at.

CHAPTER

6

EYES CLOSED, I HELD my face toward the heavens, letting the rain wash away the blood and gore. Five mutilated corpses encircled me, with two other bodies still moving. Shattered bones pushed through skin, arms and legs were twisted at obscene angles, and they continued to wallow about.

Even though every film I'd watched informed me as to what I needed to do, I hadn't accepted it. In Eric's flat, my actions had been instinct—it hadn't occurred to me that every neck needed to be snapped, or every skull smashed. The brain needed to be severed from the body.

These *things* didn't feel pain. As I lured them away from each other, I'd quickly put them down. Yet, they continued to crawl, or pull themselves along. That made them very dangerous, slow or not.

My experience centered on pain as a weapon—the instrument, a knife, gun, fist, or lug wrench was just a means. Pain was what controlled people. That's why I'd taught myself to endure it, embrace it, focus on it.

Water raced along my jacket. I pushed a hand through my cropped hair. Cold water swathed my face. I welcomed it.

After I'd tangled with the first group of zombies, the others shuffled away. They fell silent. And now they stood statue still, eyes on the black horizon. Not a peep came from them.

I let the lug wrench slip from my hand. It clattered to the blacktop, the sharp sounds quickly blunted by the soft flow of water. Opening my eyes, I saw a flashlight wink on inside the Traverse. A narrow beam jerked about, shining against the interior roof. I started walking. Needed to get there before they spotted me and the corpses on the road.

The flashlight formed a brilliant line, reaching from the windshield into the darkness. Slowly it glided one way, and then reversed direction.

I rapped on the driver's window.

A muffled scream came in reply, followed by a blinding light. I lifted a hand shielding the light. "It's me," I yelled. "Turn off the light, and open the door."

Locks snapped and blackness shrouded me. I crawled into the SUV.

"Geeez, I thought you were dead," Cada said. There was an edge in her voice, but it was different from before. "You okay?" She popped on the overhead lamp.

I stabbed the button, turning it off. "Can't see outside with that on." *And they can see us.* "I'm fine. Just got a few to follow me away."

In the periphery of my sight, I spied Nate carefully observing me.

"I wasn't bitten," I said.

"Just making sure," he replied. "You'd do the same."

"Don't think it works that way." I snapped the safety belt in place. "Right now there's a bunch of them standing still. It's like someone was using a remote to control them, and suddenly turned them off."

During the time I was away, something had changed with these two. Maybe they had a conversation and came to a conclusion about me. Or they glimpsed what I'd done and it pushed them over the edge. Didn't know what it was, but they were different. Mostly quiet and calm.

I cranked the engine, shifted into gear, and let the tires roll.

"We still heading to Greene's Store?" I asked. The answer didn't matter. I wanted to hear them speak. Get a measure of their mood. Maybe figure out what changed.

Both agreed, but said little else.

How long the remaining zombies would stay locked in place, I didn't know. And regardless of what they were, in my mind "zombies" definitely described them.

I guided the Traverse down Lakeview, angling away from the circle of bodies. The route remained clear.

"What do you mean someone turned them off?" Cada asked as we gained speed.

"Pretty much that. Some of them stopped moving. And speaking. They just stood still like I wasn't there."

Cada stretched forward, looking at the sky. "What could do that? Control people?"

"Nate?" Figured I'd give him a chance to speak. Get both of them talking.

"How would I know?"

Great. He has an answer for everything, except when you want one.

"Thought you might have a theory." Occasionally I stole glimpses at him in the rearview. He seemed sullen. He'd dropped back in the seat, and had even put away the cell phone.

"No idea," he said.

"Can you control people with radio waves?" Cada asked. Her gaze returned to me. "I mean I saw a TV show about it once. But that doesn't mean anything."

Cada was good for at least one television show on every topic. A part of me admired that.

The mailboxes and trees lining the sides of Lakeview disappeared. In their place were two-story, clapboard houses. Dark windows gazed at the road. I slowed as the road angled upward.

"Height Street is right up here," Nate said.

I braked, but didn't stop. The SUV rolled through the intersection. I cut left, onto Height.

No more than one-hundred yards away stood Greene's Store.

Guess it was called Greene's General Store a decade or so ago. Had been a family business. When the older Greene passed away, Dave took it and removed "general." A facelift, I guessed. All of the large chains were flipping names, so Dave probably followed along.

As we approached, I didn't see what I'd expected. Dave had a generator, and he was on high ground. Even with the town black, I anticipated Greene's to be glowing. Lights inside and out. People moving about, picking up batteries and supplies.

Instead the place was dark. A handful of pickups and SUVs lined the parking lot, and three men stood outside the place.

"Looks like the cops are here," Cada said. An undercurrent of concern carried her words.

I let the Traverse roll to a stop, gliding into a parking space.

The Temperance City Police SUV wasn't here, but standing at the entrance in a slicker was one of the town's two officers. I recognized the other men, although I didn't know their names. I tended not to mingle with the locals much.

"Let's go inside and see what's happening," I said.

"You want to go in like that?" Cada's eyes moved over me.

I looked down. Even in the dull light, I saw faint blood stains. Sighing, I pulled off my leather jacket. Figured I'd look softer without it.

I wondered what Cada made of the stains. She had a powerful imagination. She was probably reconstructing something in her mind, picturing how the blood ended up on me. It didn't really require much to figure it out.

Nate opened the door. The overheads flashed on. He climbed out.

I tossed up my hands. "Makes no difference now."

◆　　　◆　　　◆

"So you're coming from Dorothy's place?" Officer Paul Harris asked. "I expect you came across a number of dead heads on your way here."

"Dead heads?" Nate repeated. "You're calling them dead heads? You can't be serious."

Paul fixed a Nate with a stony gaze.

Nate shrugged. "Hey, it's just the name used for fans of the Grateful Dead. Call them what you want."

Officer Harris was difficult to read. Usually cops were tough for me to crack. This one seemed to have a strange sense of humor, or had lived under a rock.

From his stocky build, square shoulders, and shaved head, I imagined him as once being a Marine. His voice carried a little Texan with it. Then again, why would a Texan move to Temperance to be a cop?

I put a hand on Nate's shoulder. "Go inside with Cada. Officer Harris has a few questions for me."

"There's a sign in sheet at the counter," Paul said. "Fill it out. I'm keeping track of who gets here."

One of the other men standing guard at the door stepped closer. A long barreled twelve-gauge was cradled in his arms. "You see Dorothy before you left?"

Cada continued to linger. I nodded. She seemed to mull it over, then led Nate into the store.

Sheets of plywood covered the windows. And several planks had been anchored over the entrance door. The never ending deluge had already caused the larger pieces of wood to warp. The squat building seemed desperate and lonely. Memories of the film *Alamo* jumped to mind.

Beyond the edge of the parking lot, the hazy illumination of the storm revealed the sharp slope of a hill that rolled into downtown. The streets near the lake were dark with water. Crowds of people streamed around buildings in no particular direction. I guessed they were at least a mile away. Further out, an angry Lake Michigan churned, reflecting the bluish-green light from above, sending wave after wave up the beach, flooding the lakefront buildings.

"Are all of those people . . . alive?" I asked. I wasn't sure how to describe them. *Dead heads* was certainly out. And *zombie* didn't quite seem to work with these guys.

"Hey, I asked you a question." The man with the shotgun said curtly.

And he had. Thought about complimenting him on his impressive memory and astuteness. *Not going to help.*

"Dorothy wasn't there," I said. "She doesn't live there. Just rents out the place."

The man grunted as though he'd expected a longer answer and hadn't prepared a follow-up yet.

"What about the other tenant?" Paul asked. "Did you see him?"

There was no good answer to that question. So, I did what usually worked for me. "Didn't see him. Then again he doesn't stay there much."

"You mean you didn't check on him?" The man with the shotgun finally came up with something.

With his bushy beard, orange cap and coat, and round shape, he reminded me of a Teddy bear dressed for hunting. Figured he was just as dangerous, but quite a bit more annoying.

I turned sharply, meeting his gaze. The rain pattered a moment as he probably wondered what I was thinking. "What's your name?" I extended a hand. "I'm Rand Clay."

He stepped back, gripping the pump action shotgun tightly. "I know you're the convict. And that's all both you or I need to know."

I lowered my hand and smiled, then spoke to Paul. "Those people down there—" I gestured toward the lower streets. "Are they coming *for* us or *to* us?"

The officer repositioned his hat. Clear plastic covered the fabric. His shifting caused beads of water to roll off the edge. "*For* us," he said flatly. "Trying to gather a few more people before that."

This *was* the fucking Alamo.

CHAPTER

7

"YOU'RE NOT GOING TO trust him are you?" The local with the twelve-gauge pump ventured back into the conversation.

"We need all of the people we can muster," Paul said. Then he motioned between us. "Franklin Preston, this is Randall Clay."

"Rand," I said. "If you don't mind."

Franklin's furrowed brows greeted me. The second introduction had gone no better than the first.

He repositioned the long-barreled shotgun in his arms. "Guess all of this is just a big party for you."

"Not the type of party I'd normally attend."

He snorted. "Laugh at it." He turned to Paul. "Tell me you're not giving him a gun."

"No. No gun." Paul turned away from the hillside view of downtown. He looked at me. "There is no law prohibiting Mr. Clay from legal possession of a firearm. He's not a convict. But I think things would go better if he didn't have one right now."

I pulled my swampy T-shirt down, making sure to cover the Beretta tucked beneath my belt in the back. My plan had been to stand next to them as the rain washed away the remaining blood from my clothes. Hiding in plain sight was always the best approach.

"Um . . ." I scratched my head, glancing at Franklin then at Paul. "Technically . . . I've been charged and served time for other felonies." I let my words fade into the rain, doing my best to taunt Franklin. "I don't know much about Illinois gun laws, so I'm not sure if the State would allow me to possess a firearm." I shot a fast smile at Franklin. "Never really came up before."

One thing I didn't miss from my life away from the urban sprawl was the small town mentality of Temperance. In Detroit there were clear cut reasons to dislike a person—wrong gang, killed a friend or family member, worked someone's territory. The reasons were always along those lines. No one really tried to stand on moral high ground.

"Look at what's goin' on," Franklin continued. "Can't contact anyone by radio. Phones are down. Television's dead. We're locked in here, and we have to be the law. We can't go lettin' a convict having a weapon. Don't care how convoluted his past is."

"*I* . . ." Paul exhaled, "I am the representative of the law in Temperance. Nothing's changed. And until I hear otherwise, that's how it will remain." He nodded toward me. "Mr. Clay was legally discharged from prison—however many times." He shook his head and eyed Franklin. "Now settle down."

"Good Lord!" Franklin whined. "We both know he's a murderer. Gettin' off on a mistrial doesn't change that, legal or not."

Cada appeared in the store's front door, half behind it. She waved me toward her. I figured I'd stood long enough in the downpour to wash away the blood or cover it in dampness.

"Be back," I said, and abruptly departed. I saw Franklin hurriedly working to string together another series of thoughts before I got out of earshot.

Impatient, Cada waved, hurrying me close. "I don't know that we want to stay. Things seem pretty screwed-up."

I looked up at the sky, letting water splash against my face. "I see your point. But we need a place to stay and some supplies. Looks like this storm's bigger than everyone thinks."

"What are we whispering about?" Nate asked from behind Cada.

She rolled her eyes, and pushed open the door. "Nothing now."

"What'd they want?" she asked, nodding toward Paul and Franklin.

"Nothing much. Just wanted to remind me of my place."

"What?" Cada said indignantly.

"Nevermind." I stepped inside.

There was a small gathering near the back of the store. A battery powered lantern shined down the aisles filled with jars, cans, and boxes. People sprawled across the far end of the store, resting on blankets and sleeping. The familiar buzz of someone tuning through dead radio stations sizzled in the air. Two other electric lanterns hung from strings, illuminating parts of the store, leaving thicker shadows in others.

"Anyone here knows what's going on?" I asked Cada.

"Nope," she said. The sleeves of her wet sweatshirt partially covered her palms, reminding me of the zombies on Lakeview Road. "Dave said most people think it's a terrorist attack."

Nate nodded as though to say, "I told you so."

"He's handing out guns," Cada said. "Dave, I mean. But you need Paul Harris' permission."

"Wouldn't worry about that for now," I said, shuffling past. The place smelled like a laundromat. Ropes were strung across aisles with wet clothes hanging on them.

I stopped at the counter where Dave Greene played with a portable radio. He switched it off and straightened to his full height.

"Rand," he said in a hushed tone, "Cada said you were here. Figured you were getting the third degree outside."

"Something like that. How you doing?"

"If I were charging, business would be booming." He leaned back, rubbing a hand against his neck. He was tall and skinny enough to be Nate's twin in height. A tangled mop of brown hair covered his head. He'd mastered the messy hair look. Always wondered how long it took him to do that each morning.

"You know, I heard a few things on the shortwave radio." Dave leaned forward. "Before everything went out that is. From what I can tell, this storm is covering most of North America."

"That's not possible," Nate said, pushing himself closer to the counter.

"And zombies are possible?" Cada said tartly. "Where have you been, Nate?"

I ignored them. "You staying here, Dave? Waiting for it to clear?"

He was quiet for a moment, eyes drifting down in thought. "Don't know," he shook his head. "If this is happening everywhere, then is there any place to go? There was a lot of traffic on the shortwave. People saying biochemical weapons were in the rain. Terrorists. Claimed the water was melting brains." He grunted. "If that's the case, then right here seems as good as any. Maybe better."

"Don't know about that," Nate said. "We saw some weird stuff on the way here."

I gave Nate's foot a slight kick—hoping he'd remain quiet.

"What?" Nate asked.

I shot him a stern look. There was enough panic without adding to it. Most likely he was going to mention the figures of darkness that he and Cada did or *did not* see. At the least, he'd bring up the line of chatting zombies. Both topics would have me locked in another conversation with Paul and Franklin. Didn't need that.

"We've all seen some peculiar things. But I'd bet Temperance is safer than someplace like Chicago," Dave said. "Oh," he picked up a clipboard. "Need you guys to sign in. Paul is making a checklist." His words were followed by the clatter of several cans at the back of the store.

Dave peered in the direction. "Then again, I won't have much left if everyone stays here." He put one hand to his mouth. "Please use a lamp if you're walking around. Don't want you to get hurt." He straightened, lips forming a narrow line. "Be my luck to get sued after all of this is over."

I looked in the direction of the sound. A man clad in a wool overcoat stumbled across the tile floor. He slumped to the left as though the entire floor was slanted at an angle. His shoulder slid along the aisle as he moved forward.

"Who's that?" Cada asked. "He looks . . . sick."

Stretching his lean frame across the counter, Dave grunted. "Oh. Glen Waller. Came here about an hour ago. Drunk. Been sleeping it off back there with the others." Dave called in a louder voice. "Glen, go take another nap." Dave waved dismissively. "They want guns or booze. My guess is he's coming for another bottle."

I watched Glen as he stagger-stepped toward us. He looked drunk, except there was something else familiar about him.

"Do you have a baseball bat?" I asked Dave.

His eyebrows arched. "Planning on some strike-out?"

"Might say that." I inclined my head slightly, following it with a faint smile and a "just between you and me" tone. "I'd feel better with one. Given my history . . . you know . . . police won't let me carry a gun."

"Gotcha," he nodded. "There's some over in the first aisle. Cheap ones. Mostly sell 'em to the people heading to the beach. Have your choice."

"Thanks." I looked at Nate. "Put our names on the list, Nate. Bet you're pretty handy with a pen."

"Rand," Cada chided.

"At least I can write," Nate said.

"Nice," I replied. "All you need is a playground and a few kids to make that one work."

"Geez, guys. Stop it," Cada said. Then she glanced at Glen Waller again, and said to Dave. "Do you remember how Gordon Cleary looked?"

I started walking to the front of the store.

"I didn't see him, Cada."

The words were swallowed by the growling storm.

Thunder rumbled outside. The sound was so violent it pushed through the floor, and every other direction. Even after the roar had faded, it felt like it was still pressing against my body, burrowing into my bones.

Sitting among the inflatable beach balls and various plastic animals, toys, badminton boxes, and grills, was a tall cardboard box filled with baseball bats. I grabbed the first, and quickly returned to the counter.

"No-no," Cada said fervently. "I know I saw him. And biochemical anything can't make dead people walk."

Nate had moved alongside Glen, attempting to assist him. "Take my arm, Mr. Waller."

I let the bat slide through my hand until the top tapped against the tile. The sound echoed, causing Nate to look up.

"Come over here," I said.

"What? I'm just trying to help him," Nate replied. Lamp light caught in his round glasses, adding a sparkle to the lenses. He'd bowed down, trying to push his shoulder under one of Glen's arms. "If he falls and cracks his head open things will be a lot worse."

"He's not drunk." I stepped forward, slinging the bat over a shoulder.

"Whoa! Whoa! Hold on a minute!" Dave called. He dashed around the counter, halting before me. "Glen's drunk. I spoke to him when he came in. Sure, he's out of it. But he's not one of *them*."

Nate jumped backward as Glen slowly spun to face him. "I don't know about that. He looks a little more than drunk."

"Eaaassh . . ." Glen spluttered. Spittle jetted from his mouth. A streamer of drool dangled from his lip, slowly stretching downward like a spider descending on a line of silk.

"Get over here," Cada said to Nate. She was backpedalling.

"Let's not get paranoid here," Dave said excitedly. He approached Glen. "You need to sleep this one off, Glen."

"Eeeaaaaasssh-taassh . . ." Glen moaned.

Dave grabbed him by the arm, trying to spin him about.

"Kwooop!" Glen grabbed Dave with both hands, an open mouth sinking into his throat.

CHAPTER

8

C ADA SCREAMED.

"Pull him off!" I bolted forward with the bat.

Dave squirmed, clawing at the zombie's arms. In the electric lantern glow, blood gushed from Dave's neck, glistening. He staggered backward, slamming into the rack. Pickle jars fell, exploding on the floor, the clear liquid mixing with the dark blood.

The zombie gurgled, and shook its head like a dog—teeth still buried in the pulp of Dave's neck.

I sidestepped, trying to get reach on the zombie.

"Someone help him!" Cada screamed. She ran forward, slamming both fists against the zombie's body.

Then I caught the expression on Dave's face. Recognized it at once. A shadow passed across his eyes. It was an expression that stayed with you, haunted you. The face of a dying man.

Moving closer, I grabbed the zombie by the hair, started to pull, but felt the resistance. Teeth gnawing on muscle or something else kept it locked in place. If I pulled, whatever the zombie was biting would come along.

Again I glanced at Dave. Dark circles surrounded eyes with no sparkle of life. His arms dangled. The only thing holding him up was the zombie's weight pressing Dave's body against the rack.

Cada continued hammering with her fists. "Stop it! Stop it! Someone help!" Sobs punctuated her words.

I released the handful of hair, and gripped Cada instead, pulling her back. "It's too late–"

My words were cut short by the glare of flashlights.

"Everyone move away!" Paul called.

Cada struggled against me. I wrapped both arms around her and carried her away, one hand still holding the bat. "It's not us," I called. "That guy's chewing on Dave."

Two beams of light sliced through the gloom. One landed on Cada and me, the other on Dave and what once had been Glen Waller.

"Glen, you need to move away," Paul ordered.

"Look at him for Christsake, Paul. He's biting Dave. Just shoot the bastard." I recognized Franklin's voice. Decided it was best to usher Cada farther away in case that twelve-gauge fired. She struggled to break free.

"Nate's all right too," I called to Paul. My hands were full with Cada, but I managed to peek over my shoulder. Nate was bent over, heaving up everything inside him.

"Move away," Paul repeated. He had the cop voice down.

"He ain't moving," Franklin said. "If you're not gonna shoot, I will."

The *snap* and *click* of the twelve-gauge loading a shell sounded.

Cada stopped fighting and sank to the floor. Head hung low, her sobs were thick and agonized. She repeatedly slammed a fist against her knee.

"This is the last–" The blast of a twelve-gauge drowned-out Paul's warning. Cans and jars flew from the shelves, hitting the floor with a crash. Behind it came the heavy *thump* of a body—maybe two.

I looked. Dave lay in a mutilated heap. The zombie twisted and rolled, trying to return to its feet. To the left, Nate was hunched over coughing.

The back of my head thrummed as though a million volts were running through me. This was the pressure I'd felt before, but more powerful now. In fact, I realized I'd been feeling it all night. It had been steadily getting worse.

Over the clamor, I heard several groans come from the back of the store. I already knew what was happening.

Hunkering down, I put an arm around Cada, using the bat as a brace. "We're leaving," I whispered.

She gasped, struggling to inhale between sobs. I knew Dave and she had been friends. How close, I'd never asked. Dave had always been an easy guy to get along with. Building a friendship with him wasn't difficult. For an instant, I wondered if they had been more than friends.

"Cada," I said, "we have to leave now."

Swollen eyes looked at me.

"I'm sorry," I said. Not sure why I said it. Maybe it was the pressure at the base of my skull. Maybe it was Cada's worried eyes. Or maybe I honestly felt sympathy for her. The words tasted odd as if I'd never uttered them before.

Pulling Cada to her feet, I guided her forward. A light splashed in my face. "Don't you move," Franklin said.

"I'm all right," I shouted. My heart tightened. Anger brewed inside me.

"The hell you are!" Franklin pumped another shell into the shotgun.

"Put the weapon down," Paul said. A beam of light wiggled about, settling on Franklin.

My head throbbed as the weight at the base of my neck increased. Wave after wave of vibration stormed flesh and bone. Meanwhile, booming thunder rattled the building.

"More are coming," Nate said, voice hoarse and raw.

"Mr. Preston," Cada cried, "we're not zombies."

"The hell you're not. I see you cozying up with him—" he thrust the shotgun forward— "and he's a murderer. Now comes a shitstorm and he's not gonna go killin'."

"Officer Harris, *those* are zombies." Nate pointed to the five people milling about the rear of the store. "Or dead heads. Whatever you want to call them."

"Franklin–" Paul started to speak just as Franklin lifted the shotgun to his shoulder, aimed in my direction, ready to shoot.

With one hand, I pushed Cada away. The bat came up,

knocking the shotgun out of Franklin's grip. It roared, spraying the ceiling with buckshot as it flew from his hands. In the muzzle flash, I saw the mix of surprise and rage on his face. It quickly transformed into pain as the bat contacted with his knee making a muffled *pop*.

Franklin collapsed. He curled into a ball, both hands holding his knee. The flashlight spun to a stop drawing a line of light across his body.

"Don't move!" The light from a flashlight stabbed my eyes. "Drop the weapon."

"Shoot the bastard," Franklin moaned.

I looked into the blinding light, and smiled. My head hummed. Fire burned in my muscles. "You're not fast enough."

"What's wrong with you guys?" The glaring light vanished, replaced by Nate's silhouette. "The store is filled with zombies."

Taking advantage of the shadow cast by Nate, I stepped back, into the darkness. I placed the bat in my left hand, pulling the Beretta from my belt with the right. Beyond Nate, I saw Paul's eyes glimmer in the reflected light, and the dim outline of his form. To the side, five zombies moved toward us, each gurgling as though strangling and trying to speak at the same time.

"Can't you feel it?" Nate continued. "It's like the storm's short-circuiting our brains. It's cranking-up our emotions."

He was a punk, but he was on to something. From the moment the storm had started, something had been nagging at me, stirring inside. I'd felt it. It was like watching a shape slithering beneath the surface of a lake. Shifting shadows. Indefinable, but there. Solid.

Headlights slipped between the plywood sheets on the front windows. The growl of an engine followed. *More company. Just what I need.*

Franklin squirmed around on the slick tile. First he grabbed the flashlight, then started scooting toward the shotgun. A decision needed to be made soon.

The front door swung open. Cada stood there, holding it wide, letting the rain splash inside. She raised a pistol.

"Officer Harris, I don't want to shoot anyone," she said. "But right now I'm crazy enough to do it."

"Drop the weapon," he repeated—wasn't sure if he was talking to me or Cada.

His flashlight darted toward her. She remained motionless like a star on the stage in the spotlight.

"Oh fantastic," Nate groaned. "More guns."

"Cada, you don't want to do this," Paul said.

"No shit. I don't. But while you and that Neanderthal Franklin are busy trying to kill Rand, the rest of the world is going to Hell."

"It's the thunderstorm," Nate said. "It's getting us all hyped." He stepped closer to Cada. "And why isn't anyone doing something about those zombies!" A spidery finger pointed at the approaching group.

Although I'd been ignoring it, the mutterings and moans of the five living dead demanded my attention. I watched as they took stiff-legged steps forward.

"Deeeaap . . . Cosmuuh . . ."

Blathering undead. Wonderful.

Even though it made no sense—mostly what they blurted were conversation killers—it revealed something lurked inside them.

A handful of choices were available. From my position, I could put a slug in Paul's head and stroll out the door. Not that easy. I'd forgotten Franklin. Two slugs, then a stroll. Running for the door was another choice. So was striking a deal with Paul. My instincts urged me toward the first choice, but I wasn't sure if that was what I wanted, or a longing inspired by whatever was playing with my mind.

"Rand, we need to work together on this," Paul said. He spun around, bringing the light about on the approaching zombies.

I wasn't sure I understood what he said. Those were words a cop just didn't say to me.

"What do you propose?" I asked, staying in the shadows.

"We leave here and hold-up at the Hanson's farm until we can make sense of things. It's just a few miles away." He glanced over his shoulder. "What do you say, Cada?"

"Any place is better than here."

"I agree," Nate said. "Not that anyone cares."

The shotgun rattled. I pivoted. Franklin raised the long barrel and fired at the zombies.

Two dropped, blood oozing from wounds in chests and legs. The other three wailed, and charged. Fast.

CHAPTER

9

A S THOUGH WORKING IN coordination, or from some previous plan, the three zombies ran directly toward Franklin. They descended upon him, hands grabbing, pulling, ripping, dragging his body toward the back of the store.

Franklin cried out—a hoarse groan.

The suddenness of the attack surprised me. I aimed the 9mm at the nearest one. Like wild dogs, they fought over Franklin, biting and clawing. They scampered about. Crazed, Franklin twisted and swung his fists wildly.

One after another lunged at him, white teeth tearing clothing, ripping flesh. Thick gouts of blood splashed the zombies as gouges of meat were torn from Franklin's body.

I lowered the pistol. Even with a clear shot, I'd probably hit Franklin. For Officer Harris, shooting a man would be an accident. For me, it was a murder charge. *Let the cop do the killing.*

Outside lightning strobed. Cada remained in the doorway, outlined by the blinding flashes of red and yellow beyond. Then the pressure returned. The store's interior wavered before me. It felt as if my brain was pushing through my skull. My gut tightened.

Using the bat as a cane, I stumbled toward Cada. "We . . . have to leave."

Her gaze left the gory scene in the store. She looked at me. Her face was twisted into a cold expression of raw horror. "We can't leave him," she said, seemingly unaffected by the pressure I was feeling.

"Too late," I stammered. *He's buying time.* "You drive." I pointed at my head. "Something's happening. We need to leave."

My mind throbbed with each word. I gulped in lungfuls of air.

An eternal second passed before Cada seemed to understand. Through blurry eyes, I saw her nod. She grabbed my shoulder, and pushed me toward the SUV.

The ceaseless thunder quaked the earth. I stumbled through the rain, climbing into the passenger's seat, wondering if anyone else would leave Greene's store alive.

◆　　◆　　◆

My mind drifted through an ocean of agony. Jumbled thoughts filled my mind. Most of them led to the end of the world.

The future never seemed bright to me. Neither did the past. So the thought of this great, dark world coming to an end never particularly bothered me. Sure, I didn't want to die. But somehow it seemed all right if everyone else went out with me. One big party.

Sitting in the SUV, alone, made it different. Like sitting in a cell. Counting the minutes and seconds and hours until they blurred together. I'd always lived in the moment. Couldn't look back. Had no reason to look forward. *Just enjoy the ride.*

I inhaled deeply, pushing aside the pressure and searing pain boiling in my head. Cada had started the engine and cranked up the heater before rushing back into the store. Hot air rushed into the folds of my lungs, stifling me. Through the windshield, the sky flickered with colors, shimmering through endless curtains of rain, sheet after sheet blowing across the parking lot.

The pistol remained locked in my hand. The bat rested on the floorboard. Reaching across, I grabbed the door handle. Again, a neglected memory pushed to the surface.

Father Devon Worth used to visit my cell. Mostly he wasted his time, although I didn't mind. I enjoyed the company, although I never confessed as much. Hell, I never confessed at all. He persisted anyway, always thinking there was something human inside me waiting to awaken. He'd sit on a metal stool, reading scripture aloud. I always perked-up when he hit *Ecclesiastes.* One of my favorites. Father Devon Worth repeatedly quoted from it— "To everything there is a season and a time to every purpose under Heaven."

I coughed hot air, laughing as I opened the door. Rain slapped against my face as I looked to the Heavens. "I know *my* fucking purpose."

I walked back into the store.

◆　　◆　　◆

I realized the futility in my trying to hide the horrors I'd seen from Cada and Nate. It required me to remain disguised, because I was one of those horrors. My jaw clenched as I thought about it.

I fired the Beretta. Three rapid shots, followed by two more. Each muzzle flash revealed a distorted human face. One after another I put them down. Didn't want to break my stride, so I kept moving toward the back of the store.

Halfway there, a man in a dirty pullover shirt and jeans jumped from the shadows. His feet were bare, and slid along the wet tile. I seized him by the throat, pushed him off balance, aligned the muzzle of the 9mm with his head. The explosion of meaty bits of brain sprayed in the air.

I continued toward the back. It was my way of *praising the dead which were already dead . . .* No doubt, Father Devon Worth would've been pleased.

In the dull glow of light before me another man appeared. He hesitated a moment. Grunted, then scurried back a few steps. As he did, a woman leaped on my back, arms wrapping around my neck. With a swift movement, I bent forward, throwing her to the floor. For a split-second she seemed stunned, then her limbs flailed as she scrambled to her feet. A blood-stained dress clung to her frame— puckering wounds seeped dark blood from her chest and shoulders. As I raised the pistol to fire, a cold hand clawed at my face. Out of the gloom the man appeared next to me, lips pulled back in a savage grin. Cheeks and chin covered in blood.

Fury poured through my body. Reflexively, I swiped at him, making contact with the barrel of the Beretta. His flesh ripped like paper. A small fold flapping as he staggered. Bringing up my left hand, I slammed a hard fist into his nose. Bone crunched. He continued stumbling away—no expression of pain, only a dazed, insane look of anger on his face.

Out of the corner of my eye, I saw the woman scuttling toward me. First she moved on hands and feet, then bounded upward. Cold fingers clamped on my arm, nails piercing flesh. Her teeth sunk into my arm as well. I planted the nose of the Beretta in her stomach and emptied the clip. She convulsed with each slug, eventually reeling backward from the force of the blasts. She double-stepped, and then dropped to her knees howling at the ceiling, sinking fingers into her abdomen, tearing at the wounds.

I spun, flipping the pistol in my hand. With a fast step, I was next to the stunned man. I hammered his head with the pistol's butt. Claw-like hands grabbed at me. I continued until his skull collapsed, and he fell onto the floor, arms and legs twitching.

Somewhere in the distance I heard a voice calling me. It was faint, far away. Then a light flashed in my eyes.

"Rand!"

The blinding brilliance lowered, revealing Cada's face before me. "Please stop!"

Simple words—beyond my comprehension. It was as though she were speaking to me from across some vast invisible chasm. She was near, but seemed so far away, in a remote world where I'd once existed. A numbness swathed my mind.

"Come on! We gotta go!" she screamed. Cold fear lurked in her eyes.

Then another light glided through the blackness. The roar of a gun followed. The brief backlighting revealed Paul Harris. One hand holding a revolver, the other below gripping a flashlight.

He fired again. "Run!"

"Come on!" Cada yelled. She grabbed my elbow. Even through the numbness I felt her soft hands. "The others are coming."

I followed. Each step felt like I was walking on air. Slow, and faint . . . lifeless.

CHAPTER
10

DEAD HOUSES GLIDED BY as the SUV sluiced down the road. Empty doorways and black windows faced the blacktop street, silent and looming.

I ran a hand through my damp, close cropped hair. An icy rock had replaced my heart, pumping cold throughout me, filling me with a heavy emptiness.

The SUV groaned as it accelerated. Cada gripped the steering wheel, pushing the vehicle faster into the darkness. I watched her chest push up and down with haggard breaths. And the world slowly materialized—sound rushing to my ears.

"He's been bitten," Nate said. A light passed over my left arm.

"Don't think it," I growled. "I told you it doesn't work that way.

The SUV jerked as Cada wheeled around a turn.

"Slow it down," I said.

"Thanks for the driving lesson. And fuck you too."

I raised an eyebrow. "Testy . . . I like that."

The pain in my head had nearly faded. It felt like I was coming down off a high—a bad one. My gut churned, and a mild tingling still lurked deep inside my brain.

"Why doesn't it work that way?" Nate leaned forward, wedging his narrow shoulders between the front seats.

I craned my head around. Paul was sprawled behind Nate, head lolling with the SUV's movement. "What's wrong with him?"

Nate looked at me for a moment, then followed my gaze. "Same thing that was wrong with you. Crazy."

"He's not like me," I said. I examined Paul. No broken bones. Couldn't tell if he had any cuts or wounds. "You check him out?"

"Yeah. And now it's your turn." He raised a flashlight, sliding the circle of light across my body.

"Turn that fucking thing off," I said. "Some bandages or a towel would be more useful. Otherwise, don't waste your time."

He glared at me. Had to give him credit. For a stick-man like him to give me a look, it took balls.

"Don't you have to use your inhaler?" I said.

"What?" He aimed the light in my eyes. "I don't use an inhaler." Holding up his forefinger, he continued, "Follow my finger with your eyes."

I faced foreward, sinking into the seat. "Don't piss me off."

"Look, I have to make sure you're not going to flip out on us."

"Leave him alone," Cada said. "And he's teasing you about the inhaler."

"I don't fucking tease."

Tires hummed against the road for several seconds before Nate spoke again. "I don't get it."

"Ha!" I laughed. "I bet you don't, Johnny."

"When you guys grow-up—" Cada tossed the Beretta in my lap— "maybe we can talk about what the hell we're going to do."

She stuffed a hand into the pocket of her sweat pants, and pulled out a pack of Marlboros. With her teeth she nabbed a coffin nail, then tossed the pack on the center console.

"You're going to aggravate his asthma," I said.

The flashlight snapped off. "At least I don't turn into a Terminator when someone shines a light in my eyes."

"Didn't work," I said to Nate. "No edge to it. But keep trying. When you get one that stings, I'll let you know."

The rain shimmered in lines of colors as the headlights cut

through the water. I felt the SUV start to pull as Cada fumbled around the console.

"Geez," she said, holding the cigarette between her lips. "Doesn't anyone have a lighter in their car anymore?"

"Tell me about it," I said.

I grabbed the pack, pulled out a cigarette, and then the *Zippo* from my pocket. I thumbed the wheel, letting the blue flame do the rest.

"Thanks," Cada said, pulling on the cigarette. "Think I need a drink also."

Wind hissed as the rear window slid open. "No problem," Nate said. "I'll just let the toxic rain kill me before the smoke does."

"It's not the rain," Cada said, beating me to it. "I think it has something to do with the electrical storm."

"I don't have to think about that one," I said. "My head was throbbing back there, and all I could hear was the thunder roaring like it was inside me."

"Chimps get excited in thunderstorms, too," Nate said.

"That was better," I replied, leaning around the seat, blowing smoke at him. "Still needs a bit more edge."

"Fuck you," Nate snapped.

"Edgy, but no follow up."

"Listen guys," Cada said. "You can play later. Right now we have to come up with a plan."

"We keep going to the Hanson's place," Nate said. "We have to figure out what's wrong with Officer Harris."

"Same thing that was going on with me," I said. "Remember?"

"I know, dullard. But we don't know what that is."

Dullard? I didn't bother with that one.

"Is the Hanson place on high ground?" I asked.

Cada exhaled a cloud of smoke, and nodded. "It's a farm. The house is on a hill. In the winter kids go sledding down their driveway, so it's pretty high."

"Sounds good." I jabbed the button to lower the window and flicked my cigarette out the opening. "Did either of you feel anything back there?"

"No," Cada said. "Not like you did at least."

"Other than being sick, no," Nate said.

Watching Cada, I knew she was replaying the scene in her mind. Both of them probably were. And I knew it would follow them in their dreams. That pissed me off. Violence and death had been my world. The damage had already been done. But pushing them into the darkness was wrong. Memories wrinkled my mind, and Father Devon Worth returned, babbling Biblical passages justifying the horrors of the world. Like then, I wanted to snap his neck to shut him up. *Justify that.*

◆　　　◆　　　◆

Two circles of light bounced across the encircling trees as Cada rolled the Traverse to a stop in the driveway. The thick canopy blocked most of the rain, and when she killed the engine, a perfect darkness surrounded us. I remembered it from solitary. No light. No hope for light. Nothingness.

Of course, the prison used it to allow inmates introspection. Contemplate their lives. Reduce aggressive behavior. *Right.* Like someone surrounded by violent, aggressive men wanted to find inner peace. Fuck no. The darkness taught me to hone my temper, sharpen my rage. Now the darkness put me on edge.

"Does anyone know these people?" Nate asked.

"Just the old man who lives here. Wife died long time ago," Cada said, unsnapping the shoulder harness. She twisted around, peering at Paul. "Coming here was his idea. Bet he knows this guy."

Although the storm seemed calmer underneath the trees, I knew better. Simply walking up to a stranger's door with everything in the world falling apart didn't seem like a good idea. Dragging an unconscious cop along felt all the worse.

"Nate, keep an eye on him. Me and Cada will check it out. If this guy's like everyone else in this town, he'll answer the door with a shotgun."

"Cada and I," Nate corrected me.

"I'm glad you got the geek thing going. Works better than the Lennon routine."

Nate ignored the remark. He pulled his stringy black hair back, first looking at Cada, then at me. "So you're bringing Cada for protection?"

"Geez, Nate. Everyone knows about Rand. He just can't pop-up on someone's doorstep with all of this happening."

"Then what does he need to go for?"

"Protection," I said. I sensed the fear in his voice. Can't blame him much. If I was him, I wouldn't want to be left alone with a guy who might wake up as a zombie. I knew that's what he was thinking. "Bone-up," I said. "We'll be back soon. Just make sure that *he*—" I nodded at Paul— "doesn't have any more guns on him." I flashed a grin. "Cuff him if you want. You got to like restraining authority figures, Johnny."

"Thanks, Randall," Nate replied.

My jaw clenched. He'd found the sweet spot. Then Cada's hand touched my shoulder.

"Come on," she said. "I don't like being outside."

Funny. I hate being inside.

We climbed out of the SUV. The bright interior lights faded, swallowing Nate and his unconscious companion.

Even though the leafy roof above acted like an umbrella, the wind still whistled, grabbing at my leather jacket, blowing Cada's hair into a frenzy. Leaves sizzled, then hushed.

She led the way—given my rep in Temperance, it was best if I hung back. When we cleared the trees lining the gravel driveway, cataracts of rain washed downward. As we crossed the turn-around cut into the hill, runnels of water streamed through the dark grass. Cada marched uphill with me trailing.

The house was one of those old wooden two-story places with clapboard sides, and plank steps reaching to the porch. A swing rocked back and forth in the stormy gusts, suspended by squeaking chains from the porch roof. Miniature waterfalls gushed over the gutters. The house looked shriveled by the rain, and every window was dead black.

Cada climbed the wooden steps and knocked on the door. I stood at the base of the stairs. Seconds passed, then she hammered again. She had a way with doors.

I figured old man Hanson had probably wandered off into the night, and was lost or dead, or . . . undead. Knocking seemed like a waste of time. But then the door opened. Darkness framed by darkness. Cada stiffened and stepped back.

With long strides, I was beside her in a few heartbeats.

Gazing at us from the doorway was an old man—maybe mid-eighties. Gossamer strands of white hair rested on his head. A baggy wool sweater hung over his wiry frame, dangling like it was strung on a clothes hanger.

"Mr. Hanson?" Cada said, struggling to be heard above the storm. "Hi. I'm Cada Finch." She turned to me. Concern flashed across her face. "This is Randall Clay." Her words were hesitant.

I chewed my lower lip. I hated the name *Randall*. The only thing worse was *Randy*. Neither worked on the streets or in prison. But I didn't expect the old man to start taunting me, so I let it pass.

"What do you want?" he asked in a gravelly voice.

"Umm. Help, I guess. You see, the storm has flooded most of the town. We're kinda stranded. Right now there's no way out–"

"Why'd you want to get out?" Hanson interrupted.

Cada pulled at her hair nervously, knotting it behind her head. "Because people are acting . . . strange."

"Strange? How so?"

That piqued the old man's interest. I did my best not to slot him as one of the old timer prison perverts. They sat around all day with a thousand mile gaze. But if they caught the scent of a story about children, they woke up. *Peppy as hell. Sick fucks.*

Cada glanced at me, searching for words.

"Looting. Vandalism," I said. "You know how people get when the power's out. In fact, we have Officer Harris in the car—" I pointed at the Traverse parked in the driveway. "He was hurt in a fight. We wanted to take him someplace safe. Someplace where we could help him."

This didn't seem like the time to mention zombies and weird lights in the sky. If the old man didn't know about it, I wasn't going to be the one to tell him.

"Paul Harris?" he said. "Is he all right?"

"Yes," Cada said. "Well, we don't know. That's why we're here. He's unconscious, and we can't get him to the hospital cause the roads are flooded."

Hanson squinted into the gloom, stretching his neck like a crane. I didn't know what it was, but something didn't feel right about the old man. His voice was tired and gentle. But there was a hardness beneath it. His actions had a practiced feel to them. Inmates did it all the time at parole hearings. Put on the act. Sometimes it worked. Usually it didn't.

"Bring him in," Hanson said, waving us in. "And your friends. You're welcome to stay here." He stepped backward into the gloom. "I'll get us some light."

"Thank you!" Cada said.

Quickly she trotted down the stairs to the Traverse. I lingered on the porch, eyeing the empty doorway.

My gut told me not to trust the old man. *Put him down now, save the trouble later. I have trust issues. But that's because I never trust most people.*

Maybe I didn't like him because he reminded me of my dad—all smiles for the neighbors and all fists for the family. I thought about it. The geezer wasn't a threat, unless he was a zombie, or part zombie, or whatever mixed-up in between shit there was. That led me back to putting him down. I shrugged off the idea. Maybe he was just regular creepy. Met a lot of those people in life.

CHAPTER

11

YELLOW LIGHT FILLED THE room as the old man adjusted the wick on the kerosene lamp. *Welcome to the new century. We'll be going Green thanks to no electricity.* The thought didn't even entertain me.

"I've got some kindling in the fireplace," the old man said. "And wood out back. I'll get us a rose blossom going."

Paul was stretched out on the couch. I'd watched Cada and Nate struggle with him for a few seconds, but then decided they were just going to end up killing him. So I shouldered the cop, hauling him in. His body was warm, but limp as a wet newspaper. Wherever he'd gone, it was a long way off.

Cada tugged off Paul's slicker and propped his head up with a pillow. I leaned down. "What the fuck is a blossom, and hasn't this guy heard of batteries?"

A stern glance came in response. "You ever wonder why people don't like you?" Cada asked.

"No."

"You should. This is his house. Respect that. We'd still be driving around in the car if he didn't let us in."

I grunted. Guess I didn't see things the same way. We were going to be in the house either way. Asking was polite—normally that's not my thing. In any case, neither the creepy old man nor the sleeping cop were going to stop me from getting inside.

"So we waiting here until someone rescues us?" Nate said. He'd peeled off his windbreaker, and settled into one of the two wingback chairs opposite the couch. The cracked leather covering their frames made them look as old as their owner.

"We're on the east side of town right now," I said. "That means we might get to the highway by foot if we cut through the fields on the other side of the road out there."

"What about him?" Nate gestured to Paul. "He's not walking."

"And we're not leaving him," Cada interjected. "Or Mr. Hanson."

Sometimes a party can get too big. As far as I was concerned, the option wasn't up for a vote. I didn't push it. Catching a nap was higher on my list.

"Who's leaving?" The old man appeared in the living room doorway, a bundle of logs in his arms. His balding head glistened in the light. His sweater and pants sagging from the downpour. Water puddled at his feet.

"Help him with those logs," Cada said.

I let Nate do it. Waking Paul seemed more important to me—not that I was doing that either. Something was unsettling me. I was more interested in figuring that out.

But I did wonder why the old geezer was sitting in the dark until we arrived. That puzzle just returned me to *creepy* again, which chased around to putting him down. *Back at the beginning. Must be tired.*

Nate took the firewood, and as he did the old man's face soured. Looked like he'd just took a swing of bad whiskey. Beneath it, I thought lurked a tempered rage. *Maybe not fond of the young'ens and their new fangled ways. Or too fond of the young'ens.*

"What's the point in leaving?" he asked, eyes narrowing. "There's no hiding."

"You know about what's going on?" Cada asked.

Now's when the make-up comes off and the acting ends. I'd seen it too many times not to recognize it.

Immediately his demeanor changed. The wide-eyed, unwitting geezer transformed into something callous, cold. Watery eyes shone in the lamp light. Thin lips formed a thin smile. Made me feel a lot better.

"What are you talking about?" Nate said. He halted, arms cradling the firewood. "Have you seen any zombies?"

The old man didn't answer. Rain rattling on the roof filled the silence.

Cada slowly rose to her feet. "Are you all right, Mr. Hanson?"

Senility, zombie, or fucking creepy—didn't make much difference to me. Guess I'd have to cut him some slack for senility. But it wasn't that. I saw the meanness there. A cruelty flowing through him. The kind I'd seen in the coldest killers. People like him didn't need weird storms to become monsters. They just were. And he was. Had no doubt.

He glanced at each of us in turn, finally resting on Paul. "I'm dandy. Why do you ask?"

Looking down, he made a surprised sound. A mix of snort and laugh. "I did get rather wet outside. No worry though."

Slowly, with occasional glances over his shoulder, Nate stacked the wood in the fireplace.

Cada and I exchanged looks. "Mr. Hanson, you just said there was no point in leaving. That we can't hide. What did you mean?"

"Yeah," Nate said. Hardly seemed worth the effort to voice it. But I suppose he was reinforcing Cada's point in case the old man disagreed.

"Not too sure what's going on out there," the old man said. "Only know what I heard on the news beforehand. Sounds like most of the state is under the storm."

"Most of the country, or maybe even the entire world," Cada said. "Dave Greene–" her voice shook. "Dave said he'd heard it was happening most everywhere. He had a shortwave radio." Her shoulders slumped as she finished the sentence. Then she rubbed her eyes.

"Reckon leaving is rather pointless then," the old man said. "Sounds like the world has turned upside down. Why bother to hide?"

"Not really," Nate countered. "I mean the world we perceive has changed. But that wasn't real to begin with. It's our daily lives that have been messed-up. The real stuff—love, happiness, sadness, that's a constant. It's still there."

Now Cada and I shot Nate a look. He and the old man were both grating my nerves. I understood where Nate's bullshit was coming from. Doubtless some hippie philosophy. Wonder how fast he'd change his tune if he were trapped in Detroit and not Temperance. As for the old man, he was coming from someplace else. And even though his façade had returned, the creepiness still lurked in him.

"Humans can't comprehend it," the old man blurted. His tone was bitter. "Your structure prevents it."

"No-no," Nate said. "I do–"

"Shut up, Nate." Didn't want these two talking at cross purposes all night. And the old man seemed to be jumping back and forth between *normal* and *weird*. "He's not talking about anti-establishment crap. *He's*—" I jerked a thumb at the old man— "he's talking about what's going on."

"I know," Nate said. His flavor of tone was the type that normally caused me to punch someone. Smartass. I let it slide. He continued, "The world we *think* we see isn't the real world."

The old man laughed. The sound was harsh, and it turned into a hacking cough. He bent, hands on his stomach, coughing until he fell over. He lay in a motionless heap.

"Whoa!" Nate jumped up. "Are you okay, Mr. Hanson?"

I stepped forward, planting a hand on Nate's shoulder, keeping him from approaching the old man. "Hold up. You're too quick to help people. Stop it."

"Let me go!" Nate grabbed my hand, trying to pull it free. It was good to see that not all of the laws of physics had changed. "Are you just going to let him die? Maybe you're a murderer, but I'm not."

I inhaled sharply. Felt my nostrils flare. Tightened my grip on his scrawny shoulder, then I leaned close. "In this new world, you're going to need some murderers, because boneless punks like you can't cut it."

"Release him." The voice was shaky, but I recognized it. I cocked my head to see Paul Harris stretched across the couch, aiming a .38 revolver at me.

"Told you to check him for guns," I said to Nate.

"Guess brains outwit brawn," Nate replied. Although it sounded more like a squeak to me.

"I've had enough of this shit," Cada said. She leveled a pistol at Paul's head. "The rules have changed. So put down the gun."

"Cada . . ." Nate said in a nasally tone.

I released him. This situation had no good ending for me, so I figured I might as well play along. Paul lowered the revolver.

"Put it on the floor," Cada said. "Use two fingers to pick it up."

"Hurray for cop shows." I laughed. "Way to go."

The gun thumped on the floor.

"Pointing a gun at a police officer is a felony," Paul said. "You don't want that."

"Just so you know, Cada," I said, "pointing a gun at anyone is a felony. Don't let Officer Harris fool you into thinking he's special."

"Culled from your own knowledge of felonies," Nate said. He'd moved beyond my reach, but remained facing me.

"Yes," I said. The word was crisp in the air. I followed it with a smile.

"Unless we start working together, I'm just going to shoot all of you." Cada held the pistol in both hands. She stepped back, keeping it pointed in the center of us.

"Looks like a Colt," I said. "A .45, in fact. Where'd you get that?"

Her eyebrows arched. "You don't really care if you die, do you?"

I shrugged, tilted my head quizically. "More yes than no. I'm attached to living. But I'm not afraid of death—think that's what you're sensing. And I know where you're coming from. All of this is fucked-up. I'm just trying to keep us alive." My eyes darted to Nate. "Most of us."

"Screw you," Nate said.

"Chill, Nate. I'm joking. Why do you think I stopped you from going over to Mr. Creepy? Something's wrong with the old man. And as much as I hate to say it, I think Officer Harris might be as normal as he gets."

Thunderclaps shook the house. Stark flashes of light flooded the room as though a million flashbulbs had fired at once. Out of the corner of my eye, through a doorway I spotted the stairwell leading upstairs. It took a moment for what I'd seen to register. Casually, I rested a hand on my hip, letting it slide behind my shirt. Making it easier to grab the Beretta.

Cada lowered the pistol. "Dave gave it to me. Said I might need it the way things are going." She dropped to her knees and started crying, sobs coming in waves.

I always figured her to be an easy-going girl from the suburbs who'd run away to a small town. But now she seemed tougher—well, not right now. She'd flown through a lot of flak tonight, and still had the guts to pull a pistol and tell us all to go to Hell.

Nate gave me a *now look what you've done* stare. Paul pushed himself upright. His hair was tussled and his face glistened from either rain or sweat.

"Let's not get itchy," I said. "Stay put. Cada's right. Unless we knock this shit off, we're all going to end up dead." Just in case, I kept my hand on my hip. With the other, I pointed to the old man. He'd started twitching.

"Why don't we begin with getting Nate away from the creepy guy," I said.

Nate looked at him. "What if he's having a heart-attack? You just want to leave him?"

"Go take a look at the stairs," I said. "After you see the blood there, you can help him if you want."

"What are you talking about?" Cada asked. She climbed to her feet, raising the pistol. Her eyes moist in lamp light.

I gestured toward the doorway. "Take a look, Nate. Maybe I'm wrong."

He stepped toward the wooden coffee table in between all of us. "I'm taking the lantern to check it out. No one move."

"Right. The guy without the gun doesn't say that." I snickered, and inched my hand along my belt, closer to the 9mm.

Shadows slipped along the walls as Nate carried the kerosene lamp to the doorway. He halted outside, glancing back at us, then stepped through the opening.

"Holy shit!"

Guess I was right.

CHAPTER

12

A WIDE TRAIL OF DRIED blood followed the steps to the second floor landing. In the wan light of the kerosene lamp, I looked up. Wooden railings formed an L around the stairwell. All three doors on the second floor were closed.

"Going to need a flashlight," I said. "I'm not going near anything up there with a burning Molotov cocktail." I pointed at the rusty kerosene lamp.

Paul stood in the doorway. "I can cuff Mr. Hanson until we figure out what's going on. Rand and I should clear the bedrooms upstairs. Cada, you and Nathan keep an eye on the first floor."

"Nate. The name's Nate."

Paul nodded. "Sorry, Nate."

I knew how he felt.

"Thanks. So let me understand this. The two guys who flipped out at the store are going upstairs with guns, and Cada and I are staying down here with the possessed dude?"

"He's right. It doesn't sound like the best plan," Cada said. Her words were paced, and she still gazed at the steps.

"I didn't mention giving Rand a firearm," Paul said.

"Hmm . . .. Now I'm starting to dislike the plan." I planted a boot on the first step, listening to the wood creak. "Guess it's a good plan if you just want me to stand and watch. Otherwise, I'm not going up there."

Paul faced Cada, holding his shoulders square. "Do you trust him with a gun?"

"Geez, you are out of touch," Cada said. "First, I trust him more than I do you—yeah I know you're a cop. But I've had more trouble from cops in my life than criminals." She brushed past Paul, entering the living room. "Second," she called out, "Rand already has a gun, so my trust doesn't make much difference. And third, you're not getting mine."

She halted next to the pile of old man. "Can I touch him? Shouldn't we check to see if he's still breathing or something?"

I followed behind her with Nate and Paul trailing. "I have a Beretta, Paul. And under the circumstances, I intend to keep it. What I don't have are many cartridges."

I kneeled next to the old man, resting a hand on his throat. There was a pulse. A strong one. Maybe a bit too strong.

"Yep, I say cuff him, and keep an eye on him. If he wakes again, we might get more information. Or maybe he's just crazy." *Creepy crazy.*

"I guess you two have worked everything out, then," Paul said. Handcuffs rattled as he pulled them from his belt. "Here." He handed them to Nate. "We'll put him in a chair and cuff him to one of the legs."

"Oh, right," Nate wailed. "All he has to do is flip over the chair and he's free."

Paul fixed his eyes on Nate, then on the old man. He nodded. "Correct. But if that eighty-seven year old man flips over a wingback chair to free himself, then Cada needs to shoot him."

"You can always throw that lamp at him, Nate." I slipped my arms under the old man and lifted him, feet dangling like a puppet. My breath caught. He smelled like old man, and worse.

I dragged him to the chair and dropped him in it. The leather cracked. "He did more than pass out."

Maybe it was a stroke. Having to deal with zombies was enough. Adding in demonic possession was too bizarre. Regardless, I still disliked the geezer.

"What do you think is upstairs?" Cada asked.

"From the drag stains, I'd guess a dead body," Paul said, snapping the handcuffs around the old man's wrist and then the leg of the chair.

"Dead equals undead," Cada said.

"Or eaten," Nate added. "Maybe this guy has been chowing down on his dead wife."

"She passed away years ago," Paul said.

"A passerby then, like us," Nate offered.

Speculation wasn't my thing. Most of my of my life I lived off my gut—following instinct. So far it had kept me alive. Maybe incarcerated, but still alive. Didn't really care what was up there, so long as it wasn't moving.

Cada handed me a flashlight. "I don't know what's happening, but I can feel it." She handed Paul's baton light to him, and the Desert Eagle Nate had taken away from him in the SUV. "It's like puzzle pieces strewn on a table. I see the picture, but it isn't put together."

I knew what she meant. The same thing had been nagging me from the moment the storm hit. It was like the world had shifted to the right just a bit, slightly out of sync, and everything was off. Everything changed, but not in a palpable way. Sure, I was ignoring the zombies, weird lights, and people who went insane for no reason—which seemed to include me. Those things felt more like symptoms. The cause, the illness, remained hidden.

Naturally I didn't mention any of this. No doubt it would make Nate feel all the more inferior. A laugh slipped from me, grabbing everyone's attention.

"This is funny?" Cada asked sharply.

"*This* isn't," I said. I mustered a serious tone "I was thinking of something funny."

"Doesn't take much, I suppose," Nate said.

"Touché. Felled me again with the blade of your sharp wit."

"Let's secure this place," Paul said. Obviously not one for banter. He flicked on the flashlight and holstered the Desert Eagle, leaving the holster strap unsnapped. "We need a place to stay. A safe place."

"Is your .38 strapped to your leg?" I asked Paul.

He gave me a level stare. "I have it."

"What? Did you sneak it back when we where in there, looking at the stairs?" Cada anchored her hands on narrow hips. Her hair had returned to the small ponytail it had been in when we'd left my apartment.

"No big deal," I said. "Just pointing out that I'm not the only shifty person in the bunch."

◆　　　◆　　　◆

Paul stood at the base of the stairs, examining the blood stain closely. He moved the flashlight back and forth, bending close at times.

"Whatever's up there is waiting," I said. "If it's able to move. I figure it's either a dead person—dinner, like Nate said—or something waiting for us. I checked the first step. It's old and creaks. No stealthing up there, so we might as well move fast."

Paul faced me. "Got it all figured out, do you?"

It was there, floating in the air. He wanted to make a remark about me having done this before. Probably didn't because smarting-off to the guy who's covering your ass isn't the best idea. Didn't keep him from wanting to do it.

I shrugged. "Been around," I said. "Although robbery wasn't my bag. Learned to check the steps when I sneaked into my girlfriend's place. Her father's room was next door."

"Right," Paul sighed. "Let's get this done." He placed a foot on the step, the wood groaned under his weight, but he continued climbing.

I remained two paces behind, flashlight in one hand, Beretta in the other. Didn't want to get too close in case the Desert Eagle went off. Nearly went deaf once when some joker fired one with a .40 caliber round.

On the stairs, the blood was dry and black in the light. At the landing, it glistened. Thick, and still wet. Too much of it to dry up in this weather.

Again, Paul examined it, inspected a shoe print in the middle.

"We're not solving a mystery here," I said. My agitation was growing. Needed to keep that checked. At the store it took over. And I didn't want to go there again.

"If you want to barge into the room, go ahead. I want to know how many people are up here."

Good point. Normally I didn't overlook that stuff.

"Whenever you're ready," I said.

Satisfied, he took a long step over the syrupy puddle, sidling against the wall. He gripped the flashlight in one hand, and the pistol crossed over the top. The beam bounced down the hall, stopping at each door. The blood snaking around the landing, leading to the first door on the left.

I moved behind him. For the first time I caught a whiff of the blood. It was as thick in the air as it was on the floor. I fought back the urge to cough. If the stench was enough to gag me, there was no doubt Officer Paul Harris had worked someplace else before coming to the small town of Temperance. Because he didn't flinch. My bet was still on the military. Catching a lungful of sour blood and not puking up your guts wasn't taught in night school or any academy.

He focused the beam on the first door, nodding his head. We were on the same page.

Taking quick steps, we moved toward it, flanking each side. The wood floor complained as much as the stairwell. Might as well knock on the door with all of this noise.

I leaned close, listening. There was nothing to hear except the relentless rain and blowing wind. Hopefully that worked both ways.

I pressed closer. Something was there for a brief moment. Maybe. Sounded like whimpering. A female, I decided. The thought froze my bones with dread. I came from a life in the streets where gangs, thugs, and professionals butchered people everyday. It numbed me—or so I'd thought. The idea of finding a mutilated woman on the other side of the door, still alive, spooked me for some reason. Then it lit my fuse. If that old fuck downstairs decided to play serial killer tonight, I was up for the game, and I'd gladly let him play it with me.

Paul flashed his light in my face, pulling me back to the moment. I nodded, and tugged on my ear with the hand holding the flashlight. Don't know if he understood I'd heard something, but at least he acted like it.

"On three," he whispered. He took a step back and counted.

So much for not speaking.

The door cracked open as he slammed a foot against it. It flew so hard it hit the wall and bounced back. Paul was through as it returned, shouldering it open again. His light swept the room.

"Police!" he yelled. "Don't move, hands in the air."

The image of a zombie following his instructions dashed through my mind. Just as quickly, I brushed it away. *Focus*, I chided myself.

I slipped through the doorway, checking the corners. The room was rectangular, no more than ten by twelve feet. Along one wall stood a bed. A stream of dark blood led to it. Both circles of light settled on an unimaginable scene.

Ice formed in my gut, and a dark chill pushed into my bones.

Gazing at us, hollow eyed, was a woman—no more than thirty five—and in her arms were two little girls. The kids were maybe ten or twelve years old. Blood glued down their matted hair, and painted their faces. Raw wounds, puckering gashes, covered the woman's arms and neck. They were clearly bites from child sized mouths. Festering tissue oozed in the wounds with white bones glistening in spots.

"Good God," Paul said. He immediately started heaving.

I kept a light on them, Beretta aimed. My stomach churned, but my rage burned away the sickness. I wanted to blame the old man, but I knew it wasn't him. The storm—the night—had transformed this mother and children into monsters.

Light reflected in the eyes of the girls. Bloody and dark, their empty gaze fixed on me.

"Step out of the room," I said to Paul. "You're no use heaving in here."

He stumbled backward, bumping into the doorway, shoes making smacking sounds in the sticky blood.

I remained facing the woman and two kids. "Stay. Don't move." I knew it was pointless. The three of them were gone. Keeping them in the bedroom wasn't going to work anyway. We needed a place to stay. Sharing with zombies wasn't an option.

One of the little girls grinned. The expression was feral. Together, as though practiced, their eyes widened, and the two shifted to hands and knees, edging around on the blood stained bed.

I watched them. They looked like they were dressed for church—minus the dark bloodstains on the dresses. It was a Wednesday. They could have been returning from Bible study. Guess they didn't know that God was just another word for pain, fear, and want. Anytime I heard someone pray, it was because of those things. As a kid, I didn't waste my time on fairy tales. Didn't as an adult either. But now I desperately wished there was a God. No one gets away free. Not me, not him. Someone owed for this. And I desperately wanted someone to pay for what I had to do.

CHAPTER

13

"ARE THEIR EYES GLOWING?" Paul called from outside the bedroom.

It seemed a silly time to ask. But when I moved the flashlight to the side, leaving one of the girls in shadow, I noticed a faint gleam—as if their eyes were glowing. It vanished when I returned the beam to their faces as if they were glow in the dark toys and not eyes at all.

I remembered seeing it before, but I had no idea why.

"Okay, I'll bite. What does it mean?" I moved backward, bracing against the wall. The children divided, one crawling off the bed on the left, the other on the right. Their movements were jerky, clumsy.

"Don't know," Paul said, his voice hoarse. He gulped air between coughs. "Maybe radioactive?"

Talk about topping off all of this weirdness. It was possible they were radioactive. In fact, *all* of the zombies might be. Not sure how or why. But it wasn't why their eyes were glowing.

The two girls approached. Hands and knees sliding across the blood-wet floor. Then they stopped. It wasn't a normal halt. They were instantly statue still—like a flipped switch turned them off.

I leveled the Beretta at the one on the right, keeping the light centered so both remained visible. Their distorted faces were draped in shadows, eyes a dull white as though they were rolled back in their heads. Strangely, my eyes drifted toward their shoes. I remembered the small footprints on the stairs, and the streaking blood. The old man must have dragged the mother up the stairs, luring the girls behind with the promise of food. Still didn't explain who they were or what happened. But it was good for at least one bullet in the old man's head.

Movement beyond them caught my eye. It was like a shadow shifting through the shadows. Didn't make sense. Shades of black moving. Even so, I wasn't ready to talk myself out of it completely. If there was a shape, it certainly wasn't human. Close enough though to keep my attention. Whatever it was or wasn't, it vanished as quickly as it appeared.

"Coooaarsaa . . ." both girls uttered in unison. The woman made an anguished sound. I remembered when I was a young punk, and the mother who'd opened her door, discovering her son's head in a bag. The cries were alike. Painful and horrified and pitiful. Sounds humans should never have to make. She knew what I had to do, and watched as *something* controlled her children like puppets.

Yeah, some son-of-a-bitch is going to pay for this.

"Nossommm . . ."

I didn't like it when they started trying to speak. Thought it meant they were hungry or something. Deciding not to wait, I squeezed the trigger on the Beretta. It *popped*, and the girl on the left collapsed. Her feet wiggled a few seconds. Fingers clawed at the wood floor. Then, her entire body battered back and forth. She didn't scream. A watery gurgle was the only sound she made.

Cold rage still thrashed inside me. I wanted to turn away, leave. There was no redemption for me, but even the wicked could only endure so much. Accompanying the realization was the familiar pressure inside my skull—something burrowing into my brain.

The girl on the right stepped forward, craning her head, watching the other child with an eerie interest. A glimmer of understanding molded her expression. Maybe she didn't want to die the same way—more of a hope on my part.

The woman on the bed continued her mournful crying. She jerked to her knees, shaking her head, hands clamped over her ears.

"Ooon!" she screamed. "Eespha!"

The wails were unbearable, filled with deep torment. I wanted to say something to her . . .. didn't know what. There were no words I could offer that would make a difference. Even though she made no sense, I knew she was aware of what had happened and was happening to the children.

Before this I was a killer—now doubly so. No wonder *Officer Harris* sat this one out.

"Emuussh!" the remaining girl squealed with seeming delight.

I gave the woman on the bed a passing glance. Hoped she could read my mind and understood what I was doing.

Hot spikes of pain seared my head. Everything blurred, then refocused. I lowered the Beretta to my side.

The little girl shuffled closer.

I dropped to my knees, ready to embrace her. Letting the flashlight fall. It cast a pallid light over her tiny frame, revealing luminous eyes.

There was only one way for me to win—death.

The report of the Desert Eagle roared, sounding like ten pistols instead of one.

The force of the slug knocked the girl backward like a ragdoll. She flopped on the floor, splashing in the viscous blood.

My gaze wandered to the woman on the bed. The ferocious expression chiseled on her face answered my question. She was their mother.

The pain in my head doubled. I bent forward, feeling as though my head were about to split apart. All I had to do was drop the flashlight and pistol. Pressing my hands on my head would make the pain go away.

Or that's what some shadow-like creature wanted me to believe. Figured it couldn't read my thoughts, else it would know the game was up. There was pain. A fucking head full of pain. And that brought a smile to my face. It was like an old friend. Didn't much care to visit it, but nothing to fear.

Behind me came the redoubled hacking sound from Paul. Still had some backbone in him.

With a sudden movement, the woman jumped from the bed. Pale fingers wrapping around the bedrail, propping her ragged body on its feet. She snarled, long strings of saliva dripping from her mouth.

My heart bounced around my chest, rattling against my ribs. I gasped, trying to breathe. A blinding flash of lightning spilled through the window on the far wall, flooding the room with a bluish-green light.

My head throbbed with the hammering of my heart.

The woman jerked at the bed rail, arching her back, twisting her head upward, howling at the ceiling. She was fighting whatever was inside her head. Or trying.

Again, in the corner of my eye a silhouette flickered. This time I didn't follow it. My eyes remained on the woman. In my periphery, I watched the shadow shift through the black corners, moving about the room. Whatever it was, it possessed no solid form—liquid darkness pouring through the night. But it *was* there, no doubt this time. I wondered on how many occasions it'd been nearby, lurking unseen. *Was that what Cada and Nate saw earlier?*

My bet was this blacker than black thing couldn't hear—or at the least, didn't understand English. My gut told me it was the puppet master, lurking in the shadows, forcing others to play out its desires. So much for me wanting a face-to-face with God.

The woman released the rails, spinning about as she slammed boney fists against the mattress, yelling unintelligible words. Words I knew were intended for the elusive interloper.

Shadow or not, it didn't have any friends in the room, and it was trying to play the crowd. The pressure in my head swelled, until it seemed like it was pushing against the back of my eyes.

"You feel that, Paul?" I called over my shoulder, keeping watch on the shadow figure.

"Yes," he grunted. "What the hell's happening?"

"We have a visitor," I said.

I climbed to my feet, and settled my eyes on the dark form. It was like one of those gimmick pictures where you had to concentrate to see it. An image lost in a background of clutter. But once you found it, it was all you saw. Now I saw it.

A million nails pressed into my head. Each one hot and sharp.

Ignore the pain. Use it. Focus it. Prison was a great teacher of the countless ways to handle pain.

I smiled. *Nice trick, but not enough. Not this time.* It also knew how to shuffle my memories, using them to manipulate me. Or maybe possess me.

The woman's cries twisted into howls. Heavy feet thudded on the floor as though her feet were new—or was resisting the order to walk. Regardless, she was coming my way.

My attention remained on the shifting shape in the corner. Didn't know how I was going to stop it. Didn't know if hurting it was possible. And I didn't care. Just wanted to impress my point upon it.

As I moved closer, my pace quickened. It knew I was coming for a meet and greet. A tornado of thoughts swirled in my head. Places, sounds and voices, smells, and a never-ending parade of people washed-up from buried memories. With each, the pressure increased until the pain seemed unbearable. It took every ounce of will to keep my feet moving. Waves of memories crashed down upon me. With each blast, I swept them away, still moving. Then, before I understood what happened, the shadow vanished. The room spun, and the nails piercing my head melted away.

The world was cloaked in a fog. The only sounds were those from my past. Laughing, talking, singing, screaming, wind, doors, cars all splashed about. It felt like every sound I'd ever heard rushed through me at lightning speed.

My legs wobbled. In the haze, I sensed myself falling. Dropping downward, farther into blackness.

CHAPTER

14

I WAS DREAMING WHEN CADA whispered my name. I was with my mom, in our house in Detroit. Maybe it wasn't my mom I was dreaming about. My dad and mom were together, in the living room—like so many nights before. He'd stumbled home. The sound of the front door unlocking always chilled my flesh. Like every other time, he was full of booze and spite.

There they were, together, him holding a glistening hunting knife to her cheek, a thin crimson line proving he was man enough to use it. With his other hand he squeezed her jaw. He liked it when people looked into his eyes. Demanded attention.

When I was younger, mom tried to explain his anger several times. She said he was never the same after being discharged from the Army. Vietnam made him ugly. I didn't buy it. Some place deep inside, I sensed his meanness. It seeped from the marrow of his bones. It had always lived in him. He was just good at hiding. But mom believed the lie she'd weaved to dress-up her husband. Told herself she was waiting for the man who went away to return.

No matter his mood, he always had a laugh and smile for the neighbors. Especially the little girls. And whenever there was an opportunity, he had one sitting in his lap. Teasing, tickling, touching her. When a girl caught on, she became a face on a milk carton. So you could say my old man had three hobbies—drinking, little girls, and beating my mom.

Everything I knew about love, I learned from him.

This time he was burning hot. I never knew what set him off. Always told myself I'd heard mom tell him he was disgusting, and to stop playing with the girls. Whatever the cause, he wasn't going to stop. The slice on the cheek was his way of teasing a woman.

All of this played out while I was hiding behind the banisters on the steps leading upstairs. My mom's eyes were wide, bloated with tears. Her face was flush, lips pressed together in a grimace. She looked at me pleadingly. *Run . . ..* That's what she was thinking—saw it on her face. *Run . . .*

"Look me in the eyes when I speak to you!" he bellowed repeatedly. But she didn't.

She didn't fear him—at least for herself. Her face revealed a worry for her fifteen year old son. Trepidation about what would happen to him after she was planted in the ground. Dad liked to hit disobedient boys. For him, I was the ideal son. A living punching bag. A good time for all.

I wanted to tell my mom not to worry. Instead I remained silent— sneaking up behind him.

He ranted, waving the blade back and forth as though he were conducting a symphony. Never noticed me. Probably never knew what hit him.

If I'd used a knife—one swift plunge in the back of his neck—it would have been poetic. I wasn't a poet. As I lifted the baseball bat above my head, my mom's expression changed. A new dread shaped it.

"Rand!"

I opened my eyes. Light speared my retinas. I bolted upright, throwing out my hands.

"It's all right! You're safe," a woman's voice came.

My head buzzed with memories. Slowly they faded, and I recognized Cada's voice.

"Sorry I yelled," she said, lowering the flashlight. "Didn't know if you were dreaming or if that *thing* was in your head."

I nodded, rubbing my eyes with a forefinger and thumb. "Dreaming."

"Christ," Nate said. "Don't want to be your psychologist."

"Shut-up," Cada snapped.

"Just saying–"

"Some of us don't spend our lives playing *Rock Band*," I said. But I didn't blame him. He had enough to worry about without adding my dreams to it.

"Maybe not," Nate said. "But it sounds like we should. I don't want to share one of your dreams." He stood behind the wingback chair, massaging it, arms stiff.

I nodded. "You're right. But the world doesn't work that way."

After my bearings returned, I dropped my feet on the floor, and sank into the couch. Cada remained nearby, chewing at her nails. Paul stood in the kitchen doorway.

"You looked really bad when Paul dragged you down," Cada said. "Thought you might be in a coma. Then you started talking." She stuffed her hands into the sweatpants pockets as though trying to stop working over her fingernails. "We cleaned you up. Bandaged the old bite mark on your arm—the one from Greene's store." Reassuringly, she added, "You don't have any new ones."

I felt her watching me. Looking for something.

"It's safe," I said. "I mean, I'm safe." I pushed out an exasperated breath. "You know what I mean. Just a dream. And it was my own, not whatever's out there."

"I locked the room," Paul said abruptly. "None of us need to go in there."

The memories of the dream faded, replaced by the scene in the room upstairs. I understood what Paul was saying. The door was locked to hide the horrors inside, and lock away our black secrets— his and mine. My dad would be proud. Obviously, Paul had pitched Cada and Nate some version of what happened, and they bought it. Not even Nate questioned the need to lock the door.

I shook my head, clearing it—trying to brush away memories.

"What about the . . . shadow?" I stammered, searching for the right word.

"You mean the Shade?" Cada asked.

"Is that what it is?"

"That's what we're calling it," Nate said. A spidery finger pushed the bridge of his glasses upward. "What Cada's calling it. I don't think it's a Shade."

"Unless we're talking about the thing that covers a lamp, I've never heard of it." I stretched my back, letting the muscles unknot. Questions poured through my head like sand through a sieve. Try as I might, all of them slipped past. My head wasn't screwed on right. Then again, I wasn't so sure anything about me was ever screwed on *right*, maybe just screwed-up.

I closed my eyes. Snapshots of the bedroom flipped across the inside of my lids—the darkness, the children, the woman . . ..Was she still up there? No. If I were down here, then Paul had stepped up to the plate. Once the shadow disappeared—and I vaguely remembered it vanishing—the woman was easy pickings. *Dad's kinda guy. Not afraid to take out the tough ones, women and children.*

"If we call it a Shade," Nate said, "which is the name for a mythical entity that lives off the energy of humans, then we assume it is an enemy. It also links it with the supernatural. I don't believe in either of those."

"Raising the dead seems supernatural to me," Cada said.

"Doesn't have to be." Nate peered over his glasses. "We don't know if the dead are being raised. "Animated yes. And this creature might be attracted by the unliving."

I thought about telling him to take off the glasses and pull his head out of his ass. But I wasn't sure he was completely wrong.

"Can't tell you if it's supernatural," I said. "But it gives depravity a new high."

Nate gazed at me. "Sounds like it increases vocabularies also."

"You really think I never crossed paths with that word?"

His eyes rolled. "You're right. Probably your middle name."

Paul cleared his throat, stretching an arm across the doorway. His back rested against the other side. One foot raised and the other propped against the inside of the frame. "I think it's safe to assume it is controlling people. Making them the way they are."

He spurred my memory. I scanned the room. Flames danced in

the fireplace. A lantern rested on the coffee table with several cans next to it—all open, mostly beans. "Where's the old man?"

"We cuffed him to a bedpost in the back bedroom." Cada moved to the couch, sinking into a cousin.

I shot a look at Paul. He understood my concern.

"First floor—*this* floor," he said. "The dining room was converted into a bedroom."

"So the Shadow—Shade isn't controlling him anymore?" I asked.

"Nope," Nate said. "When you guys went upstairs, he flipped-out of zombie mode. He struggled with the handcuffs for a while, then fell asleep."

I wondered how many people this creature could manipulate at the same time, or how many Shades were actually wandering around.

"Looks like we had this thing's full attention," Paul said. Then he added as an afterthought, "I helped move the old man to the bedroom. Figured we didn't need him listening to our plans."

"Come on," Nate said plaintively. "Now he's a spy? You know that's the problem with the world. We don't trust each other."

I leaned forward, resting my elbows on my knees. "Bad news, Johnny. The world has a new problem. I don't think this is isolated. And it's not building a case for trusting each other."

"You heard Mr. Hanson earlier," Cada said. "He was obviously possessed by the Shade. We can't trust him right now."

I glanced at Paul. He shook his head. There were three very good reasons upstairs for not trusting Mr. Hanson.

Nate tossed up his hands. "Don't forget to include Officer Harris and Rand. Both of them went crazy at the store. We're running short on people we can trust."

"Now you get it," I said. Leaning forward, I found my boots sitting next to the couch. I slipped them on, pulling the laces tight.

"Look," Paul stepped from the doorway. "We're all tired and not thinking clearly. We need some sleep."

"And who do we trust to remain awake?" I said.

"Cada and I," Nate said. His upper lip curled. "Hate to put a damper on your nihilistic mood, Rand. But so far Cada and I are the only two who've not been *controlled*."

"I can understand why, in your case," I said. "Nothing wants to put up with that 'all you need is love' bullshit." I turned to Cada. "Not sure why you're immune—if you are. But I'm glad."

Paul tromped next to the coffee table. "Before we get into another philosophical debate. Let's figure out who takes first watch."

"How about Nate and me," I said.

Nate started to correct my words. I raised a finger, hushing him.

Cada's eyebrows pushed up at my suggestion. "Are you serious? You and Nate?"

"Yes. Nate trusts me. And I'm not afraid of him. If anything happens, one of us can wake the rest of you."

"Do I get a gun?" Nate asked.

CHAPTER

15

IN TWENTY MINUTES, NATE was fast asleep, curled up in the wingback chair. The fire crackled nearby. He'd tried to fend off the weariness by playing with his cell phone, listening to music and playing games. Unable to recharge the battery, he tucked it away, switching to a book from one of the shelves in the room. That did him in.

Paul snored in the other wingback. It was turned away from the fire. He sat in it, legs stretched across an ottoman. Cada slept on the couch.

The rain continued its tap dance routine on the roof, filling the gutters. The drains outside gurgled and choked with water. Thunder rumbled in the distance. I supposed we were in the eye of the storm or it had moved away.

The first thing I did was riffle through my bag, and reload the three magazines I had for the Beretta. Twenty cartridges remained in the box—needed to find a gun store. *Not going out now, so move along.*

Pacing the living room floor seemed a better use of my time. I walked it, testing with each step for a creak or groan—avoiding them on the next pass. I couldn't shake the caged animal feeling. Occasionally, I tilted an ear upward, listening for faint footsteps. Thankfully there was only the drumming of rain.

What remained inside me, always there, gnawing at my will, was the urge to slip into the night. Being alone was a part of me. The last few months in Temperance had softened me. I didn't like that.

"You're not the hard guy you think you are," Cada said softly.

For a few heavy heartbeats, I thought she'd read my mind. Guess I was used to that happening.

"And you're not sleeping," I replied.

She unfurled the blanket twisted around her body. Soft, weary eyes drank in the room. "How long did Nate last?"

"Fifteen, maybe twenty minutes at the most."

Cada smiled. "I was betting five." She slipped to her feet. "Guys are guys. Five minutes is usually all they last at anything."

"In that case, he probably set an endurance record." Even with the continuous chatter of rain, my voice sounded loud. Years of yelling and smoking had made it coarse. Wasn't a problem in prison. Guess the need to whisper was never important to me. Loners didn't whisper, unless it was to themselves.

"Over here." Cada waved me to her. She'd padded to the front windows, gazing past the porch into the night. "What time is it?"

I looked around the room for a clock. I didn't put much stock in time. Wristwatches were a risk in a fight. Too easy for someone to grab you. And if you threw a hard punch, it was sure to fly off your hand, and tangle.

"Don't know." I shrugged. "Probably around three in the morning. We left my place near ten."

"So why'd you pick Nate as your partner instead of me?" Cada asked bluntly.

"Figured you needed the sleep, and I knew he'd fall asleep. Didn't mind the alone time."

A small laugh sounded. She reached behind her head, tightening the band holding her hair in a small ponytail. "He's a good guy," she said. "You don't need to be so hard on him."

"'Good' don't cut it," I said. "It didn't before and it won't now. Besides, he's too busy trying to be someone else, trying to get anyone to like him. What I'm doing is knocking away the batter to find the real chicken beneath."

"I told you his parents died when he was seventeen, didn't I?"

"Yep." *Mine died sooner. Guess I took a different path.* "Still doesn't give him license to be a punk."

Cada's eyebrows rose in obvious amusement.

"Don't make this about me," I said. "Nate's got this John Lennon routine going. And that's his problem. If he wants to believe in Love and Peace, fucking great. But don't pretend to be someone else."

"Like being a hard guy?"

My jaw clenched. I let the rapping rain reply, biting back my own words.

"Don't get pissed," Cada said, giving me a little punch on the shoulder. "You're a mean bastard. No one doubts that."

She pulled a crumpled pack of Marlboros from her pocket, offered them, then put one in her mouth, hands jittering. She gazed expectantly.

Is this her? Or is she being controlled? I ignored the questions—it was her. But from now on everyone would be wondering about the same thing.

"Got it," I said. Took a moment for me to decipher her expression. "You're trying to quit, so you don't keep a lighter."

"That's the plan," she said, lips clamping the cigarette.

"Not working, huh?"

"Just give me a light. I'll go back to stopping when all of this ends."

I fished out the Zippo, waved the tip of its flame across the cigarette.

She took a long drag, and then blew smoke against the window. "So what happened to your folks? Sounded pretty bad. You kept calling them back there on the couch."

Fragments of the dream wisped past my eyes. I fought down the rise in my throat.

"Didn't think we talked about that stuff," I said.

In the nine months we'd known each other, asking about family had always been avoided. She'd made it clear I wasn't to ask about her family, and in return she repaid the favor. Most surprisingly, she'd never asked me about what landed me in prison. She knew it was murder—all of Temperance did. But the question never crossed her lips. Instead, we met on Thursday nights with rented movies, beer, pizza and popcorn. Staying up into the late hours, nitpicking and laughing at videos had sealed the deal. Or so I'd thought.

"Things change," she said. "Don't want to tell?"

"Probably not what happened to yours," I said.

She coughed, holding the cigarette low. "Mine *didn't* happen, so you'd be right." Something dark moved across her narrow face. *She's feeling her way around, looking for light in the darkness. There's no way I'm the person to help her find it.*

I turned away, staring into the baleful gloom. The SUV sat beneath the trees in the driveway turnaround—looking like it was hiding from the downpour. On the far side of the sloping hill in front of the house was Oakwood Street. Couldn't see its black surface, but I knew it was there. When Cada left the store, she must have skipped off Height and took this road. It led away from downtown.

I returned my attention to Cada. "Your folks break-up or something?" In my mind, I saw the slums of Detroit. A swath of houses surrounded by steel mills, salt mines, oil refineries, junk yards. A rusted metal landscape of poverty. My world, not her's.

"Don't think they were ever together," she said distantly. "Never saw my father. Not even a picture. My mother half-assed raised me until I was thirteen, then she pushed me on my aunt." Cada pulled deeply on the cigarette and spat out a cloud. "Turns out my aunt was just like her sister. Didn't like me cutting into her play time. So I ran away. Been working shitty jobs ever since, touring America. Mostly keeping to small towns. They always need waitresses or cashiers."

"You're doing good," I said. "Look how I turned out. Can't even get a job in a small town. Part-time work is as good as it gets."

Wind whistled past the front windows. Invisible fingers pried at the frames, rattling them, trying to slip inside. The porch swing swayed back and forth as though it remembered what it should be doing.

"You didn't answer my question," Cada said.

"I know." My eyes sifted through the blackness, occasionally following the bluish-green tinted clouds. "Do I look like the kind of guy who talks about his folks?"

"Got me there." She shrugged small shoulders. "But then you don't strike me as the kind of guy who dreams about them either."

"You've been hanging with Nate too long."

"What happened up there, Rand? What happened to you—in that room?"

"Thought Paul told you."

Cada rolled her eyes. "He told us there was a zombie and a Shade. Said that you passed out when you got near the Shade, and that he killed the woman . . .. I mean the zombie." She waved her hands. "Geez, this is so screwed up."

I liked Paul's version better than what really happened. Looked like he wasn't into shooting kids either. Can learn a lot from how a man lies.

"That's mostly what happened," I said. "That Shade prowled through my memories. It felt the same as when we were at the store, except this time it went deeper." I rolled the thought over in my head. The Shade might not be human, but I believed it experienced human memories. It wasn't just watching them. I remembered feeling something strange at the edge of my consciousness, as though it was flinching in pain when the emotions started rolling. If that was true, it wouldn't want back in my head for a while. Might also be why it left so quickly.

"So you think it was trying to control you?" Cada asked.

"That's my take. Don't know how or why. But it felt like it was trying to—" I let the sentence hang. "Possess me. Guess that's the best way to put it. And I think it was doing the same to the woman."

"If so," she concluded, "then one Shade can control several people." Her eyes drifted across the dark fields beyond the windows. The red glow of the cigarette reflected in the glass. "Why just some of us?"

"Asking the wrong guy," I said. "I'd bet it's attracted to certain people, and those are the ones it can work—sometimes. Maybe like a moth, it's pulled toward a flame, even though the fire kills it in the end."

"But the moths are confused. They're attracted to light. The moon really." She grinned widely. "Saw it on a television show. They navigate or something like that by moonlight. But thanks to humans, they get confused. Pretty much, they follow anything bright."

"In this case," I said absently. "It seems the opposite. The Shades are attracted to darkness."

A thought bubbled, but popped before I fully grasped it. Then a grin came to me unbidden. I had a head full of loathsome memories. So maybe I'd be seeing the Shade again, and it would get too close to the flame.

"I still don't get the connection between it and the zombies," Cada said. She exhaled more smoke. "Does it just want to take over people?" She raised a hand. "I know, I know. Asking the wrong guy."

"I can't even guess its motives," I said. "But I do get the feeling that the dead are easier to control. Maybe not physically. But mentally, they're probably free rides. As for the living, unless they're willing it seems like more of a challenge."

Cada nodded, puffing away. "Although the living ones are faster. And there has to be a point where a dead body can't move. That makes it useless."

She shook her head as though clearing it. "This is all so unreal. I mean why take over a living or dead person in the first place? And what are they?"

"I'm more interested in 'where are they?'"

A replied touched her lips, but faded. She abruptly lowered the cigarette to her side. The swift motion grabbed my attention, electrifying my nerves. She leaned near the window. It looked like she was about to kiss the glass. "Rand, do you see something out there?"

I followed her gaze, already knowing what was waiting.

A throng of people shambled through the knee-high grass, partially camouflaged by the murky night. I guessed they were on the far side of Oakwood, but even at a zombie's pace, they'd be knocking on the door soon enough.

"Do you see them?" Cada asked, her voice thin.

"Yep. About thirty altogether." I stretched my shoulders, muscles tight as a clock-spring. "Don't think they're out for a picnic."

"Dammit," Cada said. She stubbed-out the cigarette on the window frame. "Why the hell would they come here?"

"Made an enemy it seems, and it wants payback."

"You think they're after us?"

I looked at her sideways. "Come on. You think the Shade left here with what it wanted?"

"I don't know, you tell me." Her expression was pained and frantic. "I was given the *Rated G* version. Do you have something to add?"

"Paul gave you the details," I said. "I didn't say a word."

"No shit." Her voice was loud and raw. "You were out cold, dreaming about your folks. What Nate and I heard upstairs sounded like a war. Then Paul hands us a line and you keep quiet." She turned to the window. "Now half the town is after us. So you tell me, what did the Shade want?"

The zombies continued up the hill.

I wanted to blame Paul, but I'd have lied too. Somehow I felt like I was being played, locked in a corner with no way out. It wasn't Cada's fault. I couldn't even blame Old Man Hanson—but I wanted to. In the end, my life worked that way. One fucked situation bumping into another and another until they blocked all paths of escape.

"What's happening?" Paul trotted toward us, pistol locked in both hands, pointing upward. Guess Cada's heated voice was enough to wake him. Unless he'd been putting on an act, and not sleeping.

"Wrong question," I warned, stepping away from the storm about to hit.

"I don't know what's going on!" Cada screamed. "Why don't you tell me? And while you're thinking up another lie, take a look out the window." She rolled past Paul like a hurricane. "Don't gawk too long because we have to pack and get out of here before your friends show up."

Paul leaned forward, looking through the windows. Then he faced me.

"Get packing," I said. Then I turned and followed in the wake of the storm.

CHAPTER

16

PAUL AND NATE HUSTLED our stuff into the SUV, also stowing whatever easy food and other supplies they found in the house. Cada insisted on bringing the old man with us. I insisted on getting the baseball bat and following her.

"He was being controlled, just like you and Paul," she said. "So I don't care how *creepy* you think he is. We're not leaving him to die."

She snaked through the kitchen, lantern held high. Shadows dissolved and quickened with her movements. Most of the cabinet doors hung open, and the pantry was gutted. The house already felt empty.

"He's not like me," I said. "The control was temporary."

"It is with him too," she said.

"We don't know that. Besides, the old man is like a beacon for them . . . and a radio. He's probably transmitted everything he hears without even knowing it."

I sidestepped, nearly stumbling into Cada as she came to a full stop. She swung around. The lantern's light temporarily blinding me. "That means you and Paul can be the same thing. Should we leave the both of you?"

Not a bad idea. Thinking of doing just that.

There was a difference with the old man, though. I knew it, just couldn't put a finger on it. I thought I knew what attracted the Shades—and I was certain there was more than one. They didn't seem to have real bodies. So maybe they needed humans, and liked the taste, or feel, or whatever, of vileness in those humans. For them, the ugliest, most debased aspects of people were the lights they followed. I overflowed with those things. But like a junkie, the Shades seemed to overdose on me.

"The blank stare isn't making your case," Cada said. "You say he's different, but I'm not hearing any reasons."

"Look—I don't know. He's old. Maybe he's easy to manipulate. They tried it on me. First time mostly worked. Second time didn't turn out so well for the Shade. But that guy—" I shot a finger at the doorway off the kitchen— "his strings are being pulled every time."

She looked at the baseball bat I held against my leg. "You just going to pound his brains out then? Or is something pulling your strings?"

Fuck. Talk about being blindsided. She sneaked-up on me, and I had no answer.

"Uh-huh," she said smartly. "Just what I thought." She about-faced, heading through the door.

◆　　◆　　◆

The room was dark, and the air was thick. The two windows were covered with heavy drapes. It felt more like a funeral parlor than someone's bedroom.

"Mr. Hanson?" Cada whispered. She raised the lantern again. Yellow light chased away the shadows.

I heard a raspy wheezing, mostly covered by the snap-snap-snap of gutters overflowing and splashing in a puddle at the corner of the house. Without the heat of the fire, I felt the dampness in the air. No doubt the septic tank would be backing up if the rain continued.

"Can you hear me?" Cada approached the bed.

Metal clanked against metal as the old man shifted, handcuffs sliding against the iron rails. There was a nauseating kinkiness to the scene that sank in my gut. Old men shouldn't be sprawled out, cuffed to a bed.

"Help me," he said. "Please. I'm sorry."

I gripped the bat, moving alongside Cada. The old man's eyes widened, his face wrinkled by age and fear.

"I'm sorry . . ." He shook his head.

"You're safe," Cada replied. She gave me a quick glance. "He's not going to hurt you."

"Their car broke down," he rambled. Hard gasps filled the spaces between his words. "Said it stalled when she tried to drive through the water. I had to let them in. Those girls would catch colds in this weather."

"Shh . . . shh." Cada sat on the bed, resting a hand on the old man's forehead. "It's all right. You were just dreaming."

I should have let Paul tag along. I already saw the ending to this one—unless the old man did lose his mind.

"We're going to bring you with us," Cada continued. She handed the lantern to me. "He's not running a temperature. But being locked-up in here probably confused him."

"No, they came here. The woman and her two little girls," the old man said urgently. He tried to sit up, but with both arms above his head he only wallowed. "That's when the darkness came. It filled my mind, told me what to do. I didn't want to–" His head dropped into the pillow, flipping sideways.

Cada looked at me, her face as hard as granite. I wanted to shrug, but I remembered she still had the Colt.

"Both of them," he spluttered. Now he was whimpering. "I killed both of them with a butcher knife. Dear Lord forgive me . . ."

For several seconds Cada turned back and forth, trading gazes with me and the old man. Then she leaned closer to him. "Maybe you dreamed it. These creatures cause bad dreams."

"No!" he howled. "I pushed the blade into their chests while their mother held them. Killed both. Then they woke up and started feeding on her." Handcuffs clattered as he wiggled and pulled. "Please help me."

"Did you see them?" Cada asked me. "Or was there just a woman up there?"

Bile burned my throat. I gripped and released the bat, fighting back memories of my own. And I knew if I lied, she'd go on a hunt for the girls. At least telling the truth got us out of here faster.

"They were up there," I said, sucking in air to push down the gorge. "Dead . . . Or undead."

Cada pushed to her feet and wandered toward a corner, blanketed by the gloom. I didn't have the words to help her.

"Please," the old man repeated. He angled his head toward the table next to the bed. "Help me. It's been so long since I've seen Emily. She's waiting. I know it."

A bottle of pills rested on top of the table. I shook my head. "The pills might do it, but it won't stop them."

"The drawer," he said. "I'm not leaving here. This is my home. And I won't let the darkness return."

I pulled open the drawer. Inside was a snub-nosed .38 revolver. *Should have searched the place for weapons.* "How many bullets do you have for this?"

"The same six that have been in it for twenty years."

No need to search.

"Let me go to Emily," he said in a sad tone. "Remove these and leave me here."

Some people thought early check-out was for cowards. Sure, cowards did it all the time. Those are the ones who'd rather avoid dealing with the tough stuff. They just wuss-out and surrender to the pain. But sometimes, all of the obstacles have been beaten and a lifetime of pain has been felt, then all that should be left was the easy ride out. The old man had done his time. He wasn't a coward. He didn't want to die, but he knew he had to. He wasn't living if he was like a puppet, dancing to the jerk of strings, playing a part in someone else's play. He just wanted to take control. End it his way.

I approached Cada. "I know you don't trust me," I whispered. "Don't expect you to. But the old man deserves to do what he wants. And I'm not saying that because–"

"I don't care why you're saying it," she interrupted. With quick steps, she returned to the bed. "We can take you with us."

"I can't go," he moaned. "Let me be. Leave me here."

"We can leave Temperance . . ." Cada wiped at her eyes. "It doesn't have to be this way."

The old man offered a faint and tired smile. "I just want to see Emily. Please . . ."

Cada nodded, and pulled the keys from her pocket. Her hands shook as she struggled to unlock the handcuffs. I moved close to help, but she ordered me back.

"I'll be fine," the old man wheezed. Hard eyes settled on me. "When the darkness returns, then I'll give it a real taste of my mind."

"I'm so sorry," Cada said. She cried, brushing away the tears as they flowed from her eyes. "It's not fair."

The old man pushed upright in the bed, neatly folded the blanket over his waist, and then removed the revolver from the drawer. With a quick push he closed it.

"Go," he said. "When you hear this go off, you'll know the darkness is here." He shook his head slowly. "But it won't have me."

CHAPTER

17

I PULLED THE BEDROOM DOOR closed behind me only to meet Cada's haunted expression. I knew she wanted to make sense out of this jumbled mess—but there never was nor would be a way. Her lips quivered in the dingy yellow light. Shoulders slumped, arms wrapped around her frame.

Shifting toward the table, I set down the lantern and bat on the table. My arms barely opened before she jumped forward, burying her face against my shoulder, weeping sorrowfully, fists knotted against my back.

If there were words I needed to speak, they eluded me. I wasn't wired that way. I felt vacant . . . useless. I folded my arms around her. Her body shook with each breath. And I waited for it to pass. Like everything else, misery burned itself out. Sometimes it left a renewed energy behind. Mostly, or so it seemed to me, it produced a void.

Moments passed as she sniffed and gasped. Her body was warm. Her embrace soft. It had been so long, I'd forgotten what it felt like to simply hug.

Memories of my mother shuffled-up. *I'm fine, Randall . . .* . My mother whispered to me after a beating. She clasped me in her arms, rocking my body back and forth. I'd been ten years old the last time

I was hugged. And then my mother was reassuring me about the bruises on her face.

The report of a gun caused Cada to jump. She lifted her face, glassy eyes meeting mine. I wondered about the sound. It seemed distant, muffled. Not right.

There was another shot, and a third. I recognized it. Paul was firing the Desert Eagle outside.

"We got to go," I said. But before I'd finished, Cada had grabbed the lantern and was rushing toward the front door.

With the bat, I followed. Stepping onto the porch, I saw Paul standing on the slope beyond the house, firing at zombies. Nate guided a flashlight from one target to the next.

Rain sizzled on the ground, and coaxed the leaves on the trees into chattering. Even on the porch, the pistol sounded faint—weak.

"What are they doing?" Cada asked.

"Wasting bullets." I walked down the steps, looking over my shoulder as I went. "Close the tailgate on the Traverse. Get it turned around in the driveway. We need to leave fast. I'm going after these two morons."

The grass in the yard was short, and my boots easily pushed into the sodden earth beneath. As I neared the edge of the hill, the grass was tall and slick from the rain. I carefully planted each foot as I moved down the slope.

"Right . . . right!" Paul yelled.

Nate moved the flashlight, the beam passing through the murk, freezing on a zombie.

The pistol boomed. The zombie jerked to the left, momentarily halting. Then slowly, it lifted a foot and dropped it, continuing its upward climb.

Scattered around the bottom of the hill, and closer up the slope were at least fifteen zombies. Waterlogged clothes clung to their forms, hair flat against heads, sometimes covering eyes completely. Every one of them looked grubby . . . and dead.

Eyes rolled back, luminous, they seemingly returned my gaze. The strange colors in the sky painted their flesh in a dusky green hue.

The pistol boomed again. This time it was a headshot. The zombie flew backward, vanishing into the tall grass.

I tromped downward, calling out before I arrived—didn't need to surprise these two.

"Out for some target practice?" I said. "Sure beats shooting at paper, doesn't it?"

The flashlight hit my eyes. A warning flashed through my head. *They might be possessed . . .*

"Get that fucking light away from me," I yelled. "They don't need any help finding me."

"Sorry," Nate replied. The light returned to the starring cast in the field. I loosed my grip on the bat.

"Sending them a message," Paul said truculently. Guess he didn't like my target practice remark.

"Think they got the message a while back," I said. "They're just ignoring it."

"They were getting closer," Nate said. "We weren't just going to sit out here while you and Cada debated about the old man." He quickly scanned the house and driveway. "Where are they anyway?" Then his eyes dropped to the bat in my hand.

"In the car," I said. "Safe. Where all of us should be." I knew what epiphany he'd had when looking at the bat. Trust wasn't easy anymore.

Paul lowered the Desert Eagle, head cocked as though lost in thought. I figured now wasn't the time to ask about a gun shop.

The red glow of taillights appeared in the driveway as Cada backed the SUV out of the umbrella of trees.

"You're right," Paul said. "We should go." He holstered the pistol and hiked up the slope. Not another word escaped his mouth.

Nate snapped off the flashlight and followed, his windbreaker greasy-wet from the downpour. I followed, keeping balance with the bat.

Within a few strides, Paul and I were ahead of Nate. He wore high-tops. Stylish, but useless on slippery grass. With every other step, he slipped, sometimes catching his balance, other times falling to his knees.

I slowed. "Use the flashlight. Follow my path. And push your feet down when you walk."

"Thanks. I already know how to walk." He raised his head high and quickened his pace.

In the murkiness beyond Nate, zombies plodded ahead, gaining ground. *Sorry, man. You don't know how to walk if a zombie beats you in a foot race.*

I looked through the gathering crowd of undead, each clad in suits, dresses, pants, shirts, skirts, uniforms. A true democracy. Walking dead from every strata of life.

Each one mimicked the other with stiff legged steps, arms extended for balance. However, it wasn't their movement that interested me. I was looking for the fast one in the group. Those in plain sight were dead. But how many living ones lurked in the tall grass?

By the time my gaze returned to Nate, he'd vanished. I halted— shot a look over my shoulder. Paul was at the SUV, lights beaming brilliant red. Cada was ready to go.

"Nate," I yelled.

His head popped above the grass. "Don't say it. I slipped." He shuffled about, arms reaching into the grass. "And I lost the flashlight."

"Forget the light. Just get up here."

He prowled through the grass on his hands and knees. Either he didn't hear me or decided to ignore me. All right, he was ignoring me.

I stepped down the hill. "You're being stupid. Get up and move."

He stopped long enough to flip me the finger.

As I moved closer, I noticed a handful of zombies falling, while others remained standing. Then one rose up from the grass, no more than ten feet away from Nate.

"Run!" I yelled.

Taking long strides, I slipped and scrambled toward Nate, planting the baseball bat into the ground here and there like a fence post, keeping myself upright.

Nate looked behind, then clawed at the ground, trying to get speed, and scramble up the hill.

The zombie shambled forward a bit faster than Nate. It fell— landing on him.

I gave up on running. Instead, I jumped toward the two, hoping to tackle the zombie. I missed both, tumbling past, sliding across the watery grass.

As though joining in a chorus, the night filled with voices. Random sounds.

A yelp came from behind. I pushed to my feet. I saw Nate, his stickman frame twisting, trying to crawl away from the zombie. It wasn't speaking. Head raised high, mouth stretched wide, it gurgled in anticipation.

I stuttered upward, keeping hold of the bat.

The zombie reached, seizing Nate's ankle, climbed up his length.

Nate flipped onto his back, and delivered an open-hand punch to the zombie's nose. I recognized the motion. The little geek knew martial arts. He'd been holding out.

The blow snapped back the zombie's head, but it ignored the pain. Quickly, its head dropped, open mouth biting deep into Nate's chest. A tortured cry washed over the hill. Arms and legs flailed. When I reached them, I heard bone crunching.

"Kill it!" Nate pleaded.

Right. It's already dead. But if I miss, you're dead too.

There was little choice. I raised the bat. The zombie shook its head back and forth, flesh dangling from its mouth.

Nate screamed. And then it felt like a hammer hit my gut.

◆   ◆   ◆

The blow bowled me over. As I sailed downward, I kept both hands fixed on the bat. I landed on a shoulder, sinking into the soupy earth.

Hands clawed at my body. One of the living dead had tackled me. Now it scurried upward for a face-to-face. Fingernails scratched at my leather coat. They pressed hard enough to cut through the material.

In the blowing wind and rain I heard Nate screaming.

Blood pounded in my head. Hot mercury boiled inside me. I was always up for a fight—regardless if the other guy was alive or dead.

Shifting my weight, I rolled flat on my back. The zombie huffed with excitement as it crawled closer, searching for a place to bite. I changed my grip on the bat, one hand at both ends. Dropping it beneath the zombie's neck, I pushed upward. It gurgled and hissed.

With a thrust, I pushed it off, flipping it over, pinning it to the ground. The bat pressed against its throat. Claw-like hands pawed at me. Feet kicked the ground. It spat wildly, sickly greenish-white eyes wide.

Putting all of my weight and some muscle into it, I forced the bat downward. It crushed muscle and bone. I continued until the neck snapped. Demonic eyes faded. Human pupils returned.

Curtains of rain washed over me. And the ground trembled from the approaching thunder. I knew what came next.

On my feet, I searched for Nate. The only sound I heard was the disharmonious choir of undead babbling.

"Nate!" I yelled.

Unnatural light smothered the landscape, making it difficult to see any movement in the grass. I took a few steps, still calling his name. *Now* this *is a good time for target practice, Paul. Guess you don't like them this close.*

I spun in a circle, searching the hillside. Then I spotted a huddle of zombies. They formed a circle, all kneeling, viciously digging and pulling at something.

Like a lightning strike, another one popped out of the grass. It stood before me, fingers splayed, arms low and wide. A malevolent grin split its grayish-white face. It wanted to party.

Don't have time right now.

A hand swiped at me. I leaned back, letting it slice the air. For a moment, I wavered, almost falling over. A quick shift of my foot kept me upright. Even in the rain, I felt sweat bead on my forehead.

I double-stepped, moving up the slope. This one was fast—another of the living dead.

I turned, waiting.

It bounded forward, snarling, gleaming eyes vacant. In rapid movements, it clawed at my chest with a mad frenzy, hands moving like a dog digging a hole. Sharp nails caught in my jacket, ripping from the fingers. The zombie continued trying to burrow through my flesh.

With a growl of my own, I knocked away the icy hands, driving a hard fist into its face. The zombie sprawled backward, landing in the grass. While it hurried to its feet, I rushed for the bat. As I raised it to my shoulder, the zombie sprinted toward me.

Blood surged through my body, heating my face and hands. My lungs filled so deeply, it seemed like my chest would burst. I felt alive, posed for a homerun. And in my mind's eye, I saw my mom's face behind the zombie. It was still sorrowful.

If the creature had any instinct to survive, it would have dropped to the ground, sliding beneath my swing. But it didn't. The body was alive, but the brain was running at some insane animal level. It drove straight into my swing. My hands stung from the impact. The zombie's head crushed, jetting gore as it crumpled to the earth.

I didn't wait to make sure it stayed down. *Hang around too long and another pops up.*

Instead, I charged across the hillside, sliding into the gathered zombies. My boots slipped, sending me spinning, tumbling past. I hooked one with an arm as I went, pulling it down.

It quickly scampered back to the others.

I pushed to my knees. Strewn over the muddy earth was Nate's eviscerated remains. The zombies ignored me, and continued groping at fleshy organs and sinewy intestines. Mixed in the carnage were pieces of Nate's windbreaker.

Raw rage became a living thing inside me. My actions were mechanical. In a second I was on my feet, swinging the bat at a zombie's head. Kneeling made it an easy target, and I put every muscle into the swing.

The head shattered, erupting like a rotten melon. Blood and brain splattered across my face and chest. I moved to the next zombie, and took another swing. With each hit, my fury increased. I didn't stop until I stood over all of the unmoving corpses—including Nate's.

CHAPTER

18

GRISLY, MUTILATED BODIES COVERED the earth. The rain continued, showering down undaunted. A deadness filled me. The feeling was an old companion. Armor of my own making.

I looked around, expecting to see other zombies approaching. None moved. Each stood like statues in the field. Waiting.

In the driveway, the red taillights of the Traverse blinked on and off hesitantly. I let the rain splash against me, looking at each of the undead in the field, ready to accept any challenge. Thunder rolled across the heavens.

I turned to see the SUV stutter—roll . . . brake . . . roll . . . brake.

Lightning slashed the sky, followed by a seemingly endless peal of thunder.

What I wanted to do was stay and finish. But I didn't know how. I didn't know what the fuck I was fighting. All I was certain of was that I intended to kill it.

The Traverse rolled down the driveway, gaining speed. A flurry of thoughts scrolled behind my eyes. I didn't know why Cada was leaving, but in the back of my mind, one of the random thoughts buried itself.

I skimmed the malevolent darkness, looking for a shadow that moved among shadows. Only the motionless undead remained, and the windblown grass.

The driveway winded around to Oakwood. If the undead wanted to play statue for now, it was fine by me. Tempting as it was, I didn't go through the field, putting every one of them down. A useless action. No matter how many I killed, my anger wouldn't be quenched. Not yet. Who the fuck was I kidding. I just needed a trigger to set me off. The anger was always there.

I dashed down the hill, cutting through the trees, heading in the direction of Oakwood. *Got to go. Know most of you hated me when you were alive. Don't worry. We'll meet again.*

As I weaved around trees, I considered my options. *Stand in the road? Or just start shooting?*

◆　　◆　　◆

The road was shiny black. The wind blew sheets of rain across the surface. Bloated drops of water exploded, shimmering in the dull glow of the storm.

I stood in the center, both hands holding the Beretta.

My coat snapped with each gusty breeze. Tiny pellets of rain stung my cheeks and forehead. I counted the seconds, waiting for the SUV to crest the hill.

Maybe Cada thought I'd lost it. Hell, if anyone saw me cavorting in the field, they'd think as much. Still, something inside me centered on Paul. The Shade didn't touch me—least I never felt its cold kiss on my neck. Perhaps that was because Paul had its attention.

Beams of light flashed against the trees lining the side of the road. *Guess I'll know soon.*

The SUV roared over the hill, tires spraying long arcs of water. I kept the pistol low, eyes fixed on the blinding headlights.

The engine growled, then groaned as the Traverse slid to a stop a few feet away.

I waited in the rain, keeping the Beretta at my side.

Through the glowering the light, I saw the driver's door swing open.

"Screw you, Paul! How do I know you're not nuts?" It was Cada.

I used the brief diversion to slip into the darkness. I knew Paul would be looking at her, trying to coax her back into the vehicle.

Then Paul's voiced sounded. It was muffled, indiscernible.

Cada kicked closed the door. "Rand!" she called. "Where are you?"

Hunkered in a drainage ditch paralleling the road, I watched as the passenger door of the SUV opened. It hung there for a long moment, no one stepping out.

"Rand? Get out here," Cada screamed. "Prove to this cowboy you're not crazy."

Crazy—not sure about that. Possessed, no.

"All right by me," I answered, yelling loud enough to overcome the rain. "Just looking for a ride."

"Rand, listen to me." It was Paul. "I had no way of knowing. You looked like you'd lost it."

"I did, but not the way you're thinking. Oh, and thanks for the help. Good to know you've got my back."

Paul stepped from the SUV, Desert Eagle in hand. "Come on. I covered you upstairs. This time it looked like the fight was over before it started. I didn't know what the hell was going on."

Cada walked in front of the SUV, her body blocking the headlights as she passed through. "Is Nate with you?"

Even from halfway across the road, I heard the despair in her voice. She already knew the answer.

Anger tried to resurface, I wrestled it down. "I was too late."

Rain and wind hissed for several seconds. I kept my eyes on Paul. He remained motionless, partially hidden behind the SUV door.

"You left him out there!" Cada stabbed at the air. "He didn't even have a gun." She pushed pale hands against her cheeks, wiping away the water, and started walking in a circle. "It's all getting worse. I don't know how much longer I can do this. Everyone I know here is dead or has died in just the last few hours. Even Mr. Hanson, who I didn't know, killed himself. And it's not going to stop. It'll just keep on going. I–I can't take that anymore."

Then it snapped into place. The old man had been waiting in the bedroom for the Shade to return—just as I had been waiting in the field. When it did, it searched him out. Except, the old man had a surprise. That brought everything to a halt. Zombies froze and the Shade never touched me. But for now, I returned my thoughts to Cada. It felt like she was about to crack.

Nate was her new family. And from how close they seemed, so was Dave Greene. Losing both probably connected the dots back to her childhood where her family had tossed her aside.

"There's just no way out of this," Cada screamed. "We're all fucked. So why not get it over?"

"I know this is hard to deal with," I said, climbing onto the road, tucking the Beretta underneath the back of my belt. Paul didn't shoot. *Score a point for me.*

"Okay, scratch that, it's shit, and it keeps coming. Just push it aside, plow through it. I know the memories hurt, and you'll never forget them. But you can handle that. Let them fade into the background noise."

Suddenly, I felt Cada's arms locked around me, hands holding my shoulders. She pressed her face against my chest. Tears mixed with the rain. Her sobs were swallowed by the storm.

I gently gripped her shoulders, pushing her to arm's length. Didn't mention what was on my coat and shirt. She was already on the verge of a breakdown. Then I remembered Nate's body. *Fuck. Screwed that one up, asshole.* His body had been peeled apart, but his head was still attached. Things would be worse for Cada if he returned.

"What do we do?" she asked.

"Leave this place."

"The road out of town is flooded, and I'm not walking through the forest. Zombies are everywhere—"

"There's a State campground up ahead," Paul said, full of ideas now. "Doubt anyone was there before the storm. If so, they probably left. Bound to be as empty. And there are some buildings we can hold-up in."

"What then?" Cada asked. "We just sit there and wait?"

Paul looked at the sky, shielding his eyes from the rain with a hand. "It's got to stop raining sometime. There's only so much precipitation up there. Besides, it'll be daylight soon. Things look different in the sun."

They sure do. Ugly and foul as Hell.

"I don't care where we go," Cada said. Her voice was soft, the words were meant for me. "I want out of the rain, and I as far away from Temperance as I can get."

She wrapped her hands around my wrists, squeezing them gently.

"Good," I said. "That's what we'll do." I aimed her toward the SUV. "Take a break, I'll drive."

"No. I'll drive. You stay in the back and keep an eye on him." She nodded at Paul. "He kept a gun at my head until I agreed to leave you behind."

It didn't surprise me. Paul and I merely tolerated each other—except now I tolerated him less. Gingerly, I guided Cada toward the driver's side of the SUV. Once she was inside, I walked to the other side.

Paul waited at the door, pistol holstered, looking to make peace. "You'd have done the same," he said.

"Yep."

I slammed a fist into his face. His head bounced off the side of the Traverse. Then I locked a hand on his throat, squeezing the soft fleshy part.

Leaning close, I whispered, "That was for Nate."

He gasped, but didn't try to stop me. Must have known I wanted him to fight back.

I squeezed. "And this is for threatening Cada. You ever try that again . . ." I didn't need to finish. He was a cop. Following leads and finding clues, even ones as subtle as mine, were a part of his job.

"Remember what Franklin said at the store?" I asked. "'We're the law now.' You don't need a uniform and badge to be that kind of man."

He struggled, gasping, cranking back his head, pushing onto his toes, trying to suck in air. Blood oozed out of his nose from my punch.

"If it's okay with you, we'll play it that way from now on. No badge needed." I grinned broadly, close to his face. "Enjoy the irony."

Our eyes locked for a moment, then I released him.

He sank down, dropping against the SUV. No doubt he wanted

to shoot me now. But something kept him from doing it. "I didn't know," he said hoarsely. "I didn't know they killed Nate, and I didn't know if you were crazy."

"I'm crazy," I said, opening the back door. "Just not possessed."

I climbed into the SUV, pulled the door shut. The vehicle rocked.

Cada sat in the driver's seat. She looked back, eyes blank.

"He knows the way." I gestured to Paul who was climbing inside. "A dry place sounds good right now."

CHAPTER
19

THE TRAVERSE RUMBLED OUT a rhythm along the road. Normally, it would have been relaxing. Instead, it served as a minor distraction. *Good enough.*

After giving it some thought, I liked the idea of spending time in a State built facility. Knew my way around them. For the most part, they looked the same—cinderblock walls, chipped paint, and tiny windows. Good for keeping the weather off and zombies out.

"How far is this park?" I stretched in the seat behind Paul. He was tall enough to poke above the headrest.

"About ten miles straight, and a couple down a feeder road." He didn't bother turning around.

"Just tell me when to turn," Cada said sullenly.

"Look . . . I know it's not the time," Paul started. He seemed unsteady, head turning toward the passenger-side window, shifting up and down. "We have to know what we're up against. I don't know what it is. Although, I get the feeling the two of you know more about it."

He was right. It wasn't the time, and we did know more about it. A wild call on my part. Still didn't make him wrong. After the storm hit, we'd been playing cat and mouse. It had to end.

"What do you think is happening?" I asked.

"I just told you, I don't know. I've no explanation. No idea. At times I'm not sure what's real and what's in my head."

Not the best confession for a guy toting a gun. However, I let it pass because I had the same problem. The difference was I trusted myself.

I scooted sideways, sliding into Cada's line of sight in the rearview mirror. "Earlier," I said, "Cada thought the storm pulled toxins out of Lake Michigan and rained them down on us. A good idea, but it didn't explain the weird colors in the sky."

Paul cocked his head. "The lake has some pollution, but nowhere near that much."

"What I *said*," Cada interjected, "was that it might be the rain. Other people suggested terrorist attacks and chemical weapons." Her arms remained stiff, fingers knotted around the steering wheel. "If we didn't have Shades jumping around, I'd go with the terrorist explanation."

I grabbed one of the duffle bags in the back seat and tossed it on the floor, trying to get a bit more space. On the seat, beneath the bag was Nate's cell phone. Must have put it in the car to keep it from getting wet.

Then I did exactly what I told Cada not to do. I remembered Nate. Didn't really know him, other than he was Cada's pouter pal. Nonetheless, he had spirit, and the right idea—even if he'd borrowed it from John Lennon. Looking back, I probably would have spent my days playing computer games if I had the chance. Although, my style was more *Grand Theft Auto* than *Rock Band*. But why do it on a computer when you can be out living it? That was my problem. Might have been Nate's problem also.

I stuffed the phone in my coat pocket, and wrestled down the memories.

"Didn't Dave Greene say something about the storm covering North America?" I asked.

Cada fumbled around the dashboard. The SUV swaying along the road. "I'll get them," I said. Knew she was going for the smokes.

Stretching forward, I reached into a slot below the radio. With two fingers I pulled out a crushed pack of Marlboros. As I slipped out a cigarette and lit it, Cada continued.

"He had a shortwave radio. Said there were reports from all over North America about the storm."

"Not sure I believe that," Paul said. "My radio was out the minute the heavy weather hit."

Cada took the cigarette from me. Puffed on it, blowing curls of smoke against the windshield. "Dave wouldn't lie. When he gave me the gun, he said there was something strange about the storm. It was a bunch of technical stuff. Hot spots in the atmosphere or something. Whatever it was gave the radio super range."

Where's a geek when you need one? Nate would have been overflowing with babble about now.

"So what does all of this have to do with zombies and Shades?" I asked. Didn't expect an answer. Mostly I was flushing my mind, and putting the idea out there. Trying to keep Cada's thoughts away from what she'd been through.

"How the fuck should I know?" Cada snapped. She glared at me in the mirror. "Unless everyone's being controlled by some massive burst of radio waves, I don't know. And either way, I don't see a connection." She took a drag, and tossed the question to me. "You have anything to add?"

I leaned back. "Yep. I need a beer."

"Geez, Rand. Can't you be serious? The entire world could be crashing."

From my perspective, things were looking better. My life was already shit. So, if someone hit the reset button, I had nothing to lose.

"All I know is there's a crazy-ass storm brewing. The sky is the wrong fucking color. People, dead and alive are turning into zombies, and there's at least one strange shadow-like creature drifting around." *And I want a beer.*

Cada sat upright as though her spine were an iron rod. She twisted around, looking at me. "That's it! You reminded me of something."

The tires whined on the wet surface as the SUV swerved across the center of the road. Short yellow lines darted past.

Paul grabbed the wheel, angling it.

"Eyes on the road," I said.

Turning back, Cada slapped away Paul's hand. "I got it." She steered to the right lane.

I didn't know what she was talking about, but whatever it was seemed to have whisked away part of her pain. I was glad.

"Anyway, do you remember what Mr. Hanson said?" She waved dismissively at Paul. "You wouldn't, you were out cold. He said something like *humans didn't possess the structure to comprehend this.* Or pretty close."

"I remember," I said, "but figured it was old man talk."

Cada nodded hurriedly as though she were waiting for me to finish so she could get to her point. "It wasn't *old man* talk. But it was the Shade speaking through him, or mixed-up with him. I don't know. Either way, what Mr. Hanson said proves the Shade isn't human."

"Unless there's a way out of this circle we're following, I think we already knew that. I can vouch for the Shade—or whatever it is. Not human."

"Right. But it's like Nate said . . ." Cada's voice thinned and faded. She exhaled a stream of smoke, letting it roil around the windshield before continuing. "The Shade isn't supernatural. There's no such thing."

I swirled a finger in the air, forming an O. "We're back in the circle."

"What if the Shade is an alien?" Cada stated flatly. "And all of this is because of some kind of invasion?"

Paul remained silent. He didn't have to comment. A cop, a Texan, and former military. No room for extraterrestrials in his world.

I dropped against the seat. From terrorists to aliens. Not sure which theory I liked better.

"Yeah, I know it sounds half-baked," Cada said. "But we're running out of options. Either Temperance is being overrun by otherworldly creatures, or somehow . . . some way—" she flipped a hand toward the roof— "this storm is connected with the arrival of aliens."

I had nothing better to offer. And the idea had an upside. Aliens can die. Or so I assumed. Ghosts and shadows seemed more challenging. And in a bizarre way, Cada's theory felt like a better fit with what was happening.

"Our road is coming up," Paul said. "Over there on the left."

The SUV slowed. The *bump . . . bump . . . bump* of the spacers in the road reminded me of an overworked metronome preparing to die.

Cada rolled the steering wheel left, pulling onto a macadam road. Lights flashed past a large, wooden sign welcoming us to Prospect State Park.

I didn't like old roads, and this one would have put a smile on my landlord's face. This road and the old house she rented to hapless people like me belonged in a film about the Civil War.

I was a creature of the city. When proper pavement vanished that meant there were fields between buildings, few corners to hide behind, and rednecks.

"Can't the State afford to cover these roads?" I asked. "I mean with something other than glue and gravel?"

Tires buzzed the rough surface.

"This isn't Detroit," Paul said. "The city and county want people to come here, not run away. Keeping the campground looking natural does that."

"Right. Tourist zombies."

Temperance was as close as I wanted to get to Nature. Honestly, I didn't want that close. But like the man said, when you're tired of sailing, shoulder an oar and walk away from the water until no one knows what you're carrying, and then you've found home. Figured if I wanted to get away from the life I had, I'd follow his advice. Turned out to be bad advice. Obviously, he *did not* have the Internet. I thought I was hiding in a small town. Instead, I was its biggest pastime.

After a few minutes, we hit the first crater. The SUV's frame rocked as a tire dropped into a pot hole.

"We might have to go slower," Paul offered mildly.

He was as subtle as an electric chair.

As though in response, the road presented another hole. Cada hit it dead on. This time I bounced up and down. The hit vibrated my spine.

"Let me guess, these are country speed bumps," I said. "Sure does give it a *natural* feel."

Paul ignored me, turning his head to the dark wall of trees on the right side of the road.

Cada dropped the SUV's speed to tortoise, still swerving to avoid the treasures offered up by the archaic road.

After we passed through the macadam minefield, we glided to a stop at a gatehouse. It was a one-man booth, designed to keep the weather off a person stuck inside. To me it looked more like a target for a crazed camper in an RV.

A CLOSED sign rested against the window facing the road.

"Looks like the Park Rangers cleared out early," I said.

Paul pointed ahead. "Stay to the right. That way brings us to the beach house."

"What beach?" I asked. "Did we just drive around the edge of Temperance to end up at the lake?"

"Yes," Paul said. "But the lake is about a quarter-mile away, down that southern access road." He pointed at the road on the left. "We'll be on high ground."

"Still too close for me," I said.

The wipers swished back and forth, alternating the view between a blurry world and a focused one. I wondered if Paul was stuck in the blurry world.

"I'm all for empty brick buildings, but I'm not so sure about the ones near a lake." I leaned against the door window. My breath fogged the glass. The tree line was still visible. "This isn't quite what I was thinking when you said State Park."

"You don't get out much," Paul said.

"Fucking funny," I replied. "Oddly, *camping* wasn't on the prison venue."

The SUV jostled as it rolled across a washboard road of gravel, causing my head to continuously bump against the roof.

"I'll be happy with a dry building," Cada said.

"The showers and toilets won't work without power," Paul said. "But it will be good shelter."

A shower would have been nice. I'd had my fill of being drowned in the rain. I wanted to wash off the gore, and change clothes. Guess there was enough rain to handle the shower so long as I found soap.

The single laned, gravel road eventually ended at a long rectangular building. Cada cranked the steering wheel hard, making a sharp turn into the parking lot.

Several streaks of lightning came one after another, illuminating the world before us. Past the building was a gridiron of narrow paths, decorated by a scattering of trees—all very natural. Row after row of parking spots flanked the paths. I imagined what the place looked like when it was full. Long columns of cars and RVs covering several acres. A horde of people trying to get in touch with nature, or maybe hiding from their lives. I related to the last part, but this place wasn't where I'd go to do it. Of course, I was wrong. I went to Temperance.

"Should we unpack everything?" Cada asked.

"Let's check it out first," I said. "Other people might have the same idea. I don't want to crash any parties."

"No vehicles in the area," Paul said. His tone was dipped in smugness. "Unless they walked here, I'd say it's empty."

Cops. Always looking for the evidence and conclusions they wanted to find. Sure, the police were always suspicious as hell, but the glare of the badge blinded most of them.

I leaned forward, pulling out the Beretta. "Cada, you stay here. Turn the car around and keep it running. I'll check out the building." I angled my head toward Paul. "You follow me to the door and stay outside, just in case."

Paul slipped the Desert Eagle from its holster, snapping off the safety. "I've done this before."

"So have I."

CHAPTER
20

A N UGLY GREEN COLORED wooden door stood between me and being dry. I slipped across the concrete walkway, pressed against the building. The word MEN hung above the door. Chose that one out of habit, I guessed.

Paul followed me, flashlight and pistol readied.

I studied the door for a moment. It pushed inward. No need to press an ear against it, the splash of the rain and far away grumbling of thunder made hearing anything impossible. My gut told me it was too easy. But I reconsidered it. *Entering a bathroom is too easy? I've reached the summit of Mount Paranoia.*

Quickly, I nodded to Paul. He stepped closer, and I pushed open the door. It was heavy, and didn't want to swing wide. No way to check behind it—not good. To keep it from closing, and losing all surprise, I shouldered it open. Just as I reached the edge, I felt a gun barrel press against the side of my head.

"Don't move, fucker." A voice ordered. "Come on in and drop the gun."

So much for too easy.

I lowered my hands, and casually stepped past the door, letting it swing closed. Hopefully, Paul knew something was up.

A light flicked on, shining in my face. The barrel continued pressing against my temple.

"I'll be damned, Emmitt. It's that convict. You know the one who lives up at Dorothy Ford's place . . ."

"Hush-up, Jimmy. Don't chat it up when you're staring at a killer." This time it was a woman speaking. That's a count of at least three in the *empty* building. Emmitt, Jimmy, and her. Paul had to be proud of his detective work. No wonder he was doing time in Temperance.

"Listen—" I started.

"You just keep your damn mouth shut. Didn't I tell you to drop the gun?" He punctuated the question by slamming the back of my head with the barrel of what I took to be a shotgun. Guess *Emmitt* was tough when he had the drop on someone.

I made a show of dropping the Beretta, letting it land at my feet.

"Tell him to kick it out of the way," the woman said.

I wondered if everyone but Paul watched television cop shows. Those programs were making my life difficult.

"Kick it," Emmitt said.

I kicked it to the left, listening to smack against a wall. At least I had a rough idea of where it was.

The light drew closer. I squinted, turning away slightly.

"Who said you can move?"

Another rap on the head with the shotgun.

I counted the seconds, waiting for Paul to make a move.

"He ain't jackshit when he's outnumbered, is he Emmitt?"

Jimmy had a keen eye for the obvious. I despised his type. Blurting out the obvious, pushing buttons, always looking for a fight—until there was one. Then the pleading started.

"Heard you killed your daddy," Jimmy said.

"Now don't get too close," the woman warned.

"Good Lord, Amanda, do you think I'm an idiot?"

"Let me answer that one." I couldn't resist.

The steel barrel did a repeat act on the back of my head. Warm blood slowly traced a line down the back of my neck.

"This is the police," Paul yelled from outside. "I want everyone to come out, hands on your heads, one at a time."

Brilliant fucking plan. No wonder I hated them. They never worked.

Emmitt jabbed at my head with the shotgun. "You move over there. Jimmy, keep the light on him."

"What about the police?" Amanda asked. "Aren't we going out?"

"Christ-o-mighty," Emmitt growled. "There ain't no such thing as the police anymore."

Precisely the point I made with Paul. Then again, Franklin had tried too. Guess small towns go wild when the system breaks down. At least in big cities, we threw a riot before it all fell apart. Seemed like a thunderstorm was good enough reason in Temperance. And a few zombies.

"I said *move!*"

Emmitt was predictable if anything. But this time, when he hiked back the shotgun to hit me, I spun, clamping a hand around the barrel.

Although I didn't see it, I knew Emmitt's face was clouded in confusion. No worry, things would be clear in a moment.

I shoved the barrel downward and pulled it toward me. Spots danced in the darkness thanks to Jimmy's flashlight. *Just keep your rhythm. You can do this blindfolded.*

With a grunt, Emmitt collided with me. Felt like running into a dump truck. He was a big fellow.

Keeping one hand on the shotgun, I moved sideways and forward, hooking a leg behind Emmitt's. With my free hand I gave a hard shove at his center mass. Or where I figured it to be.

He dropped, letting go of the shotgun as he sailed downward.

The scuffle caught Jimmy's attention, and the flashlight hunted me down. But this time I was holding the shotgun. Ten-gauge, judging from the barrel size.

"Stop," Jimmy ordered. "I'll shoot you."

I never enjoyed gambling, except when it was with my life, or someone else's, and Jimmy offered interesting odds. Admittedly, the flashlight had kept him hidden from sight. That meant he had a handgun at best. I knew he didn't have time to find my Beretta. So maybe he was bluffing. All-in-all, the odds were stacked in my favor because Jimmy was a rotten bluffer.

The shotgun's slide *clacked* as I ejected the shells one at a time. My foot rested against Emmitt's body. He hadn't moved—maybe bounced on his head and was out cold. Good luck for me.

As each shell clattered on the floor, Jimmy blurted out warnings. And behind each of his sentences was Amanda's plea for him to do something.

"Put the gun down now you motherfucker, or I'm going to blow your head off." Jimmy shifted into high gear. Clearly getting worried.

After I'd emptied the ten-gauge, I stretched out my arm and dropped it on the tiled floor. Either Emmitt was an expert at playing opossum, or he was down for the count. Didn't budge at the sound of the gun.

Outside, Paul continued yelling. "I repeat, this is the Temperance City Police. Come out with your hands on your heads . . ."

"Jimmy," I said. "Why don't you show me what you've got? .38? .45?"

The light jumped from me to his hand. He was holding a .357.

Fuck. A crazy redneck with an elephant gun. Got to be losing my edge.

Again, the beam of light stabbed my eyes.

"You are one stupid fucker," Jimmy said. His boots slapped against the tile as he approached.

"Be careful, Jimmy. I think he's gone and killed Emmitt."

"For his sake, he'd better not," Jimmy said. "Or there's a bullet for him. With his name. It's going into his head."

"Need to work on those threats," I said. "Let implication do the work for you."

"Shut-up you sorry motherfucker. Don't tell me how to talk."

I nodded.

"Now put your hands in the air. I want to see them."

I mulled it over. There was a chance Emmitt hit the floor with the back of his head and ended up with an aneurism or something. Or maybe just a severe concussion. Unless there was another person who was mute, it left only two people. Two, not-so-bright people.

"And make yourself useful, Amanda," Jimmy continued as he approached. "Chain up that door so no one else comes in." He stopped before me. Light no more than one foot from my face. "Terrance is going to like you."

Jimmy was full of surprises. Didn't know how to take that last remark. Not really sure I wanted to know.

Chains rattled and a lock snapped.

"Is that a key or a combo lock?" I asked.

The rain simmered on the roof, filling the long pause. It was a tough question.

"Why the fuck do you care?" Jimmy asked.

"Combination locks require one person left who can speak." I knew he didn't understand. "Never mind. Just making plans."

"Don't get so close," Amanda said. "Hurry and put him in with the others."

Jimmy lowered the light. For several moments, my world remained filled with fuzzy circles and tiny glowing sparks.

"He's not like them," Jimmy said. His words were slow, not the usual jumpy tone. It sounded like he was frustrated . . . or maybe confused. "We'll have to tie him up and wait for Dale."

Things were becoming quite elaborate. I had no idea what they were up to, but there was certainly a plan in place. And it sounded like *Terrance* was the mastermind.

"Keep an eye on that cop," Jimmy said, his usual pacing returning. "He's got a surprise coming when the bus returns. And then when you're done, check on Emmitt."

"Shouldn't I check Emmitt first?"

"Do what I tell you the way I tell you."

While my eyes re-adjusted, I tried to make sense out of what was going down. From the sound of their voices, which really wasn't much of a measure, I guessed Jimmy and Amanda to be in their late teens or early twenties. Emmitt, he'd sounded older. No doubt they'd encountered the local zombies, and yet they were working on some scheme.

"Now what am I going to do with you?" Jimmy asked.

"Let me go," I suggested. "It works best for all of us."

It was Jimmy's turn to hit me. Cold steel slammed against my jaw, knocking me back a half-step. Below the white-hot pain was the warmth of an open cut.

I turned back, scanning the room. Most of it was blanketed in thick shadows, but near the top of the walls were squat windows, each glowing with the greenish-blue radiance of the storm. The silhouette of what I took to be Amanda popped up in one of the windows, shifting left and right.

"They're gone. Don't see the car anymore."

"Good." I heard Jimmy smiling behind the word. He was proud of himself. "Now get a light and check Emmitt."

My fists formed hard balls. If Paul forced Cada to leave, he was going to pay. The image of him pointing the Desert Eagle at her flashed before my eyes. Then I remembered Cada had the Colt. Knowing her, it would be pointed at him the moment he opened the door. Maybe they had another plan.

"Looks like your pals left you," Jimmy said. "Bet you think you're hot shit 'cause you come from *Deetroit*? Well, you're wrong."

"Murder City," I said. "We like that name better. After all, we did earn the title."

I heard the *click* of the revolver's hammer, and then felt the barrel press against my forehead. "I'll show you some Murder City, motherfucker. Is that what you do up there, kill your parents and strut around?"

My teeth ground. Electricity vibrated along my nerves. I didn't care enough about their plan to put up with Jimmy much longer. He'd keep going until one of us was dead.

"No smartass remark that time, huh? In case you didn't know, killing your folks doesn't make you mean, it makes you shit."

"Killed my dad," I said, my words measured. "My mom killed herself."

"Holy fuck! Did you hear that, Amanda? Kills his daddy, then makes his mamma kill herself. And the judge lets him walk."

"Leave him alone," Amanda said. "Just tie him up."

Stark light washed across the room as she snapped on an electric lantern. An upside down U-shaped fluorescent light sat inside the red plastic casing. It even tried to resemble the kerosene lantern old man Hanson had.

In unison, we looked at Emmitt. He lay on the floor, arms spread wide like he was making snow angels, and a halo of blood surrounded his head.

CHAPTER
21

SELDOM DOES ANYTHING GO my way. Emmitt proved the rule. It wasn't just the expanding pool of blood. The empty stare didn't bode well for him, or me.

Amanda gasped, hand covering her mouth. She stumbled backward, holding the lamp away from her as if she were afraid of it.

For a moment, Jimmy was speechless. Believing what he saw must have been like trying to fit a square peg into a round hole. I saw him struggling with it, trying to squeeze it in, accept it. But it wasn't going to happen.

I'm not sure why, but Jimmy admired Emmitt. I'd seen it before in followers—guys who tagged after what might be called the *alpha male*. These followers pictured their heroes as bigger than life people. The type who didn't die.

Any second, Jimmy's marbles would drop back into the bag, and he'd be hot to put a slug in my head. Not good for me. So, I seized the moment. I ducked and grabbed Jimmy's hand, hoping that somehow one of my fingers would end up in front of the revolver's cocked hammer.

The revolver fired. The roar bounced off the walls. Amada screamed, and Jimmy tried to yank free. Right behind came the whizz of the slug ricocheting off the cinderblock walls, ending the trip with a hard smack into a wooden crossbeam above.

Jimmy was becoming more trouble than he was worth.

Keeping low, I whirled around, twisting his arm as I went. Then I stood, pulling him up with me. So long as he had a finger on the trigger, I wanted the revolver pointing away from me.

My body buzzed with adrenaline—more from Jimmy's remarks than our tussle. Before he said another word, I used my other hand to wrench free the gun.

The flashlight dropped to the floor. Jimmy stumbled, eyes wide, lips trying to form words.

I leveled the revolver. "We left off with some questions about my past . . ."

He looked like a scarecrow with two broomsticks shoved up his ass, making him a few inches taller than me, and bright-eyed scared. A black baseball cap covered his head with a tangle of brown hair escaping beneath its band. Below that was a moon-face and tiny rodent eyes. He wore a black aviator jacket, black jeans, and finished off the ensemble with a wide belt decorated with black diamond studs.

"Wow," I said. Didn't know what else to say. He looked ridiculous in the getup. "Uhhhh . . . wow." I left it at that.

"Leave her alone, son-of-a-bitch." Jimmy stepped in front of Amanda. Still spooked, but stupid enough to go another round.

It took me a moment, then I understood. He thought I was going for his girl. I was wrong about Jimmy. No eye for the obvious at all. Or maybe seeing Emmitt did cause a few marbles to roll away. In the end, it didn't matter. He was light years from being a genius, and twice as far from being smart.

"Stay put," I said. "She's safe. Wasn't talking about her."

"Fuck you," Jimmy said. "Guess she doesn't look enough like your mamma." He tugged at the bill of his cap, pulling it down and pushing it up.

There was no winning with this guy. And he had some serious mother issues.

"I'll give you the key," Amanda said. "To the lock." She waved the lantern at the chained door. "We won't bother you. Just leave."

She had to be at least ten inches shorter than Jimmy. Otherwise, they seemed like a matched set. A spray of short hair covered her head, starting out brunette, ending blond. She wore a matching jacket and jeans. But her belt had silver diamond studs.

"Let me deal with him," Jimmy said.

"Don't tell me what to do, James. So far you've done nothing but dig a hole—"

"Both of you shut-up, move against the wall and sit on the floor—backs *against* the wall."

They shuffled toward the wall, and then both dropped down. Amanda shot sharp glances at Jimmy. He managed a stony expression.

"Put the lantern on the floor, and give it a push so it's out of reach."

Amanda did as I said. Jimmy looked confused, as though he'd missed an opportunity to use the light as a weapon. I simply didn't want the place going dark again.

I snatched-up the lamp and set it in the center of the rectangular building. Then I grabbed the flashlight Jimmy dropped and the Beretta from the far wall where I'd kicked it. I pocketed the shotgun shells as I went. The shotgun itself was too cumbersome for me to carry, but I didn't need them using it again. Finally, I hunkered down next to Emmitt, placing two fingers on his throat.

No pulse. Or so faint I didn't feel it.

I examined the flashlight. It didn't survive the fall either. This place had some hard fucking floors.

Just to be sure, I checked again for a pulse. Emmitt wasn't more than forty years old. His shaved head told me most of his hair was already gone. And the paunch pushing over his belt matched a middle-age bulge. Looked sturdy enough. But still gone.

"Is he dead?" Jimmy asked. "You'd better hope not."

Yeah, yeah, I got it. You'll throw some words at me and then . . . Then who knows.

"Alive," I said. Stupid and angry were a bad mixture. Jimmy had enough of both. I didn't want to give him reason to act on it. Occasionally, ignorant luck did as well as experience. And next to me, Jimmy was lucky.

I swapped the revolver for the Beretta, doing my best to push the bulky .357 in my pocket. Jimmy didn't strike me as the type of guy who owned revolvers. I imagined him rolling the quaint streets of Temperance in a pick-up with a rack of shotguns and rifles in the cab. No, the .357 was a cop's gun. That bothered me.

I stood, keeping the Beretta pointed at the adorable pair. "One at a time, stand up with your hands high. I'm going to pat you down for weapons."

Jimmy looked at Amanda, then at me, and back. His head bounced back and forth like a tennis ball. "You're not frisking her."

"I'm not frisking anyone. But I do have a gun. So it's your choice. I check you alive or dead. Make the call."

His small eyes burned with anger. He climbed to his feet, striking the scarecrow pose that came naturally to him. "You try anything with her and I'll kill you. I don't care what you did in *Deetroit.*"

"Turn around," I said. *This* would *be easier if he was dead.*

I ran a hand along the length of his body, around his legs, and belt. Found two speed loaders for the revolver, each full.

"Holding out, Jimmy?"

"Must be tough for you. Living out here where you have to work. Not like prison where you got a paid room and board, cable, and nothing to do but sit around."

I shoved the Beretta's barrel deep into the small of his back. He flinched, inching forward on his toes.

"You know what I miss, Jimmy? Rubbing lye soap on the legs of my bed to keep the roaches out of my nose, mouth, and ears while I slept. Sure, they still got into the food. So you either closed your eyes and imagined potato chips, or raked everything you ate with a fork. Keep it up, you'll be living the high life in prison soon."

Can't count how many times I'd heard that bullshit after I was out. Prison was the good life. Inmates had it easy—education, television, nothing but free time and fun. Maybe in the movies. Everything I got, I paid for, before, during, and after. Inmates earned wages and paid for cigarettes, television time, candy bars, postage stamps. Except in there, half of what you got went to the bull or inmate running the block.

I gave the Beretta another press. "Now don't get me wrong. I was doing life for killing an asshole just like you. Probably what you'd call early retirement." I eased up with the pistol and spun him around. "Sit."

He sank to the floor, except now he matched my gaze. A part of me wanted to provoke him. *Not a good idea. Not now. Keep it moving.* But I couldn't.

"What I'm saying, Jimmy, is that I'm the kind of guy who doesn't belong on the streets. Someone crosses me or pisses me off, I kill him." I shrugged. "Probably in my genes."

I stepped toward Amanda. She stood, arms extended. Her face was hard. No doubt it masked fear, but my antagonizing Jimmy had sparked emotion in her.

"Turn around," I said. I repeated the process. Didn't find anything large enough to be a threat.

"You can sit," I said to her.

"Enjoy yourself?" Jimmy asked.

I gave an exasperated sigh. Jimmy was setting a record with me. The longest living asshole. Didn't want to ruin it now. Instead, I focused on the building.

It was rectangular, with urinals on the left side, becoming stalls midway through. Shower heads hung above each. Toilets probably took up the rest of the space inside. Graffiti boasting various creative promises, phone numbers and names covered the ugly green paint. Sinks hung on the both sides in the front.

"Going to need the key," I said to Amanda. If I'd removed it from her front pocket, things with Jimmy would have turned physical.

Fear and anger divided her face. I wanted to keep it that way. If they remained occupied with thoughts of me being a stone cold killer, things would go smoothly. If they kept cooking-up plots to turn the situation around, things would still go smoothly. I just needed time to get away.

Her hand jammed into her jeans.

"Slow it down," I said. "Remove it from your pocket and toss it at my feet."

The key jangled on the floor, bouncing across the tile. With it came the rattle of a stall door.

I shifted, pointing the Beretta so as to cover the line of stalls and the Natural Born Killers against the wall. One of the stall doors rattled again. Then two, or maybe three.

"You don't know how fucked you are," Jimmy said.

"Jesus H. Christ," Amanda whined. "Learn when to shut-up."

I squatted, looking down the length of stalls. In the gap between the floor and the stall walls there was a crowd feet. Some remained motionless, others shuffled about. The movement was easy to recognize. Zombies.

"How'd they get in there?" I asked, rising to my feet.

"We put them there," Jimmy said. He went for self-satisfied and hit dead center in self-doubt. "Emmitt too." He looked at Emmitt. "You going to let us help him? He's bleeding."

Was bleeding. Pretty sure it stopped a few minutes ago.

"One thing at a time," I said. I considered the situation for a moment.

More thuds and knocks came from the stalls. If they'd been asleep before, they were waking now. They must be why the bus was coming. I let the thought rattle around my head for a while. *That's one ride I want to miss.*

"Okay, I give up. What are they doing there?" I knew the answer was going to be like a joke without a punch line. No matter what was said, it just left you hanging.

"Probably not what you'd do with them," Jimmy answered.

Yeah, no punch line there.

"You're right," I said. "I'd kill them."

Gazing down the length of the stalls, I noticed hasps with padlocks on the doors.

In the middle of what was looking like the end of the world, here was a group of small town losers collecting zombies. I mean, I'd done time with some crazy-assed people, but this stuff made them all look . . . normal. Or at least mildly strange. Okay, no it didn't. Most of the guys I did time with were fucked-up. Even so, Jimmy and Amanda were still fucked-up, and now the world was fucked-up, so that left me . . . Guess I didn't have to say it, or think it.

Looking back at my life, I started it running downhill. And with each step the angle grew steeper and steeper. I always wondered when

I'd hit bottom. If the end of the world was bottom, then what's left? *Collecting zombies.*

Even though I was facing Jimmy, I was looking at a distant place. Jimmy didn't realize it. His eyes zipped around, looking everywhere except at me. "I'm not telling you what we're doing," he spontaneously announced. "None of your business."

Don't care. And don't have the time to care.

I went to the entrance. The chain they used to lock the door snaked through the handle and a newly anchored ring in the cinderblock wall. This was organized far beyond the abilities of Jimmy or Emmitt, or even Amanda. And I didn't want to get caught-up in another *plan*. *Last time I go with one of Paul's ideas.*

I tugged up the chain, used the key, and the lock snapped open. As the chain rattled free, a hand grabbed my shoulder. It was a big hand. It didn't belong to Jimmy. I pivoted, pulling free, finding Emmitt swaying before me—eyes empty and glowing.

"Way to go, Emmitt!" Jimmy yelled, jumping to his feet. In the periphery of my vision I saw Jimmy hike-up and plant the baseball cap on his head—anticipating the fun. He didn't know Emmitt was dead. I was so wrong about Jimmy's keen sense for the obvious. A mile wide of the target on that one.

Emmitt's beefy hand reached out. I leaned down, and bull rushed him. The man had gone down easily when he was alive. Being undead had to make him a pushover.

I hit him hard. My shoulder sank into his flesh. If he was breathing, I would have squeezed the air out of his lungs. Guess it didn't matter with a zombie.

He tumbled like a tree, arms flapping, neck stiff. This time I saw him hit the tiled floor. He even bounced. And again the thick sound of his skull crunching followed. Maybe some zombies can get by with less brains than others. It was a question I'd ponder later.

I aimed the Beretta at his head.

"Emmitt!" Amanda cried just as Jimmy charged me.

CHAPTER
22

I WASN'T SURPRISED, AND IN a way, even less disappointed. Like Jimmy, I had some frustrations to purge.

He came at me with a flurry of punches. A couple landed before I was in position. Jimmy wasn't a brawler, but he was fueled by anger. That went a long way in a fight, quite often compensating for size and strength. And his storm of swings slapped the pistol from my hand.

My arms went up blocking his wild swings. He screamed insanely, and ducked, lunging at me. A boney shoulder drove into my gut. Then he was up, hands clamped on my throat.

"Fuck you!" he bellowed. Saliva splashed my face. Fingernails digging into my throat.

I grabbed at his head, catching the baseball cap instead. He squirmed, tightening his grip until my throat clamped shut. Beyond him I glimpsed Amanda running toward the stalls. *She can't be that stupid. Jimmy and a room full of zombies, with Amanda cheering them on. Fuck.*

Thumbs pressed into my larynx, pushing hard. I slipped a hand around one of them, yanked a hand away and shoved Jimmy back with my other hand. He did a pirouette as I cranked back his thumb, lifting his arm with it.

"Shit!" he screamed. "Let go, fucker!"

I kept the pressure on his thumb, causing him to walk in the direction I guided—away from Emmitt's body.

"Fight me like a man, you pussy!" His face was flushed and he danced around trying to escape. I obliged him.

As he rose, I clipped him in the ribs with my elbow. Even through the puffy aviator's jacket, I felt ribs crack. Then I slammed a fist at his nose, driving the other into his throat. He reeled back, rolling across the floor, knocking over the electric lantern as he went.

Shadows loomed. The rattle of latches drifted from the back with Amanda's mutterings. "Open . . . open . . ."

Jimmy groaned, spat, and then said something. The words were too croaky to understand.

"Can't hear you," I said. "You're choking on blood."

Quickly, I pulled the .357 from my pocket and fired a round at the wooden ceiling. Too dark to see anyone else, and a miss meant a wild slug jumping off the walls.

"Stop, Amanda, or the next one goes in Jimmy's head." It was a lie. Wouldn't waste a bullet on him. I'd do it the old fashioned way.

Jimmy spluttered a few words, but was interrupted by Amanda. "Don't! I stopped! I stopped."

"Close any doors you opened." I shifted back a few steps, taking cover in the darkness. Didn't think Jimmy would move away from the lamp anytime soon.

"None are open," Amanda said with frustration. "There all locked."

A heavy sigh slipped from me. *Guess I do have some good luck.*

"Get back to the wall," I said. "Stay away from the stalls."

A ragged cough issued from Jimmy. He flopped on his back, gagging.

Amanda stepped into a slash of light. "Let me help him." She looked at Jimmy sorrowfully.

"He has a broken nose," I said. "He'll live—if he sits up so the blood doesn't drain down his throat."

Amanda flashed a look around the room, searching for me. With the close walls, I sounded like I was coming from every corner.

"Okay, drag him over to the wall with you. Hurry it up. But set the lantern away from him first."

Like a bullet, she was next to Jimmy, holding him, wiping blood from his face.

"The light," I reminded.

She pushed the light away, whispering all the while to Jimmy. He coughed and gasped in response. The gloom receded to the far corners. My eyes locked on Emmitt—not moving.

Time to try this again.

◆　　　◆　　　◆

My luck was holding. It didn't take a slug to the brainpan to keep Emmitt down. Seemed the second visit to the floor did the job. I still kept an eye on him, and still didn't want to waste a round. Didn't plan to hang around much longer.

"After I leave," I said, "count to five hundred, and then you can get up and help Emmitt." They still thought he was alive. I knew they wouldn't count. Jimmy wouldn't. But it was worth trying.

"I ain't counting," Jimmy managed to utter.

"Shush," Amada chided. "Don't go and say that–"

"Why not? What's he going to do?"

I made a show of aiming the Beretta at his head. "Shoot you in the head. So are you counting or not? Because I'm not wasting any more time."

His swollen lower lip rolled up. He looked at Amanda, and then nodded his head.

It was bullshit. He wasn't going to count. Shooting him was easier, but on the chance things did turn back to normal, I wanted to keep my body count as low as possible. Not that it mattered much. A target was already painted on me—had been all my life.

"Start now," I said. I jerked open the door and slipped into the rainy night. The blustery wind was a welcome relief after being in there.

I trotted across the parking lot, hoping to get some distance before Jimmy fired-up his brain and sparked an idea. If Cada did what I'd expected, the SUV would be parked somewhere beyond sight of the building.

My boots splashed across the gravel road as I trailed back to the park's entrance. Rain pelted every exposed bit of flesh as I went. Tree branches whipped with a burst in the wind like demented cheerleaders shaking pompoms.

I crested the first hill, reaching the macadam road. A pair of headlights greeted me. The wall of rain made them dim. And they were too high for an SUV.

Then, I slammed headlong into a wall—or it felt that way. Bands of pain tightened around my head as I hit the ground. The rush of wind and the slap of rain followed me into blackness.

The sound of rain drumming against metal pulled me awake. At first it felt like a dream. I was sitting in a prison bus, facing the back entrance, waiting for the rest of the shackled occupants to be herded into the empty seats. Close.

I was on a bus. But a long way from Jackson State Penitentiary in Michigan. Wind whistled past the open door. My leg was chained to the chair mount of a bus seat, and zombies were being tugged through the rear emergency entrance by some guy I'd never seen before.

My head felt like it had been cracked by a hammer.

"Get him away from me!" The voice was loud, and it made my head thrum with pain. "Get him away!"

Next to me sat a lumpy man. He was middle-aged and balding, with a long face and dark crescents below his eyes. He was round, although a bit rounder at the middle. A ripped and wet gray suit wrapped around his rotund shape to make him look like a walking pair.

"He's not undead," came a reply. "Will be soon." The man speaking chuckled with the last remark.

Bruised brown eyes examined me. "You alive?"

I pressed a hand against my head. The touch caused the left side to sting. I felt the warmth of blood on my fingers.

"I'm alive," I said. "Who are you and what's going on?"

The man dropped into the seat. Relief caused his jowls to drop. "They shot you," he said. "In the head. Not sure how you're living. But zombies don't speak as smoothly as you."

From what I'd heard, zombies didn't speak at all.

"Thanks for putting me at ease," I said. "And they mostly missed my head. But I didn't ask about that."

"Oh . . .. Sorry. I'm Hank." He pushed a hand at me. After I didn't shake, he continued, "We're on a bus headed for downtown." He motioned toward the front. "Those . . . well, I guess you know, are zombies. Terrance Egan's new *gang* is rounding them up."

Second time I'd heard "Terrance" mentioned tonight. Figured they were one and the same. The odds of it not being the case seemed long.

"Who told you to speak?" A tall man with greasy hair strode down the aisle to the threshold of the emergency door. His hands held rails on each side of the opening, back facing outward. "And you—" he looked at me— "Jimmy's going to pay you back."

"So there is a silver lining in this cloud," I said.

He jumped inside. Probably stood six-one, late twenties. He had a mop of brown hair, maybe red, hard to tell because it clung to his head like damp noodles. Not the typical buzz-cut most of the locals had, which must have made him a real rebel. But it wasn't long enough to cover his eyes. A little less rebel. The armless T-shirt, and haggard jeans did a good job of showing off his muscled body. I noticed my Beretta stuffed into his waistband. Next to it was a bulky keychain.

I made a mental list of things I needed.

Then a sharp sound came as he jerked his right hand downward. Glistening in the faint interior light was a retractable baton.

"Now I want one of those," I said. I adjusted my list.

Hard metal collided with my head. Flashes of light and more blood followed.

"I don't take shit from you, got it?" His left hand still gripped one rail. The right hand held the baton high.

If I was smart, I would have taken the opportunity to be quiet. There was the problem. Being in and out of lock-up most of my life had already proved I wasn't smart. Didn't want to ruin my rep now.

"Did you buy that?" I asked. "Thought they were illegal—except for cops. And, it's clear you're not a cop."

He hammered my skull again. This time adding a few follow-up lashes. I felt the welts quickly forming.

"I can do this all day," he said.

"Look, Dale," Hank interrupted. "He's been shot in the head. The man's delirious. Terrance isn't going to like it if you scramble his brains."

The baton sliced through the air, stopping just before it hit Hank's face. "What did I say about talking?"

Hank waved his hands in surrender, remaining silent.

"Good boy," Dale said. "See, you can be trained."

He stepped back, collapsing the baton against his leg. "Now we have some more cattle to load. Once we get downtown, we'll continue this."

The first few swings I'd been off my game. I didn't want Dale to go away without a prize. He was kind enough to leave my hands free, so I wanted to repay the favor.

As he stepped down, I said, "I hate long interludes. Any way we can finish now?"

"What are you doing?" Hank asked. "Just be quiet."

Dale froze halfway in and out of the doorway. He shook his head and flashed a smile. "Jimmy was right about you–"

He was interrupted when the rear door slammed against his head. It hit with a hard *thump*. Dazed, he grabbed the frame for support, and the door closed again and again and again. It continued until he dropped to the ground. Then Cada leaped forward, kicking him in the crotch.

"I'll finish it, asshole!" She stepped back, and like a football player making a punt, she stepped forward and drove a sneakered-foot deep into his groin.

He tried to scream, but nothing came out. His hands went low, blocking any more kicks.

Rain splashed against the jean jacket she wore. Her ponytail had escaped. Without looking inside the bus, she kneeled next to Dale, grabbed a handful of hair, hiked up his head and slammed it against the gravel surface.

"Sorry. My hand slipped." She grabbed the blossoming keychain on his belt, slipped out the Beretta. "Can you hear me?" she asked.

Dale mumbled something.

"Sounds like 'yes.'" She bounced his head another time.

Hank watched wide-eyed. He turned to me to speak, but stopped, returning his gaze to Cada.

She reached into Dale's pockets and pulled out my spare magazine and Nate's cell phone. As the rain fall on everything beneath the heavens, she silently stared at the phone. I knew what came next.

A hand reached beneath her jacket, producing the Colt. She shoved it against Dale's eye.

"Cada!" I yelled. What she wanted to do, I understood all too well. In a broken world the answer came easily. And when it did, it made broken people—ones who can't be repaired. She wasn't that way. I couldn't let her be. "Cada, walk away."

She leaned close, whispering in Dale's ear, the .45 settled against his eye. The rain washed away her voice. Dale didn't move. My heart raced as I awaited the report of the pistol.

Then she stood and faced us, gun at her side, Nate's phone in her other hand. Everything else sat at her feet.

Hank pushed farther into the seat.

"He took the phone from me," I said. "I found it in the car."

Wet hair draped her face. With the pistol and jean jacket, she looked like a haggard cowboy.

"She's with me," I said to Hank.

CHAPTER
23

CADA STOOD AT THE door as I shuffled through the keys, trying the close matches first. Normally I had an eye for locks. This time it was taking longer. Countless red-hot needles pushed out from inside my head. A bullet haircut and a baton lashing had me off my game.

"They're coming," Cada called to me.

"You're not leaving me, are you?" Hank asked.

"Thinking about it." I worked on my lock first. Hank was the runner-up for remaining behind if time ran out. "Unless you can help, then be quiet."

"It's a crowd, Rand. Hurry it up."

There had to be twenty keys on the ring. *What the fuck does he do with all these keys?* Sitting on the floor, I fanned-out each one, examining the edges, skipping past car keys and anything with a cut on only one side. I needed a double-cut key.

"Can't we pull out the seats?" Hank asked. Panic rattled his voice. "Shoot the leg or something."

"Zip it," I growled. "Or you're staying."

"Rand . . ." Cada's voice grew urgent.

I selected the best match and hoped I was lucky.

Not so lucky. I twisted, but the lock didn't give.

Cada's Colt boomed outside. Two shots, then she hopped into the bus. "Geez. Only a couple of them bothered to duck. Talk about macho."

"Most are zombies," Hank said.

I slid the next key into the lock.

Click.

"Got it!" I exhaled, trying to ignore the sharp pain expanding in my skull.

"Are you serious?" Cada asked. "They're working with zombies?"

"Can we get to my lock now?" Hank asked.

I looked at him—purple bruised eyes returned the gaze. My instincts had kept me living for twenty-nine years. And they said to leave Hank. Reaming in my hand were three possible keys.

"Pick a number between one and three," I said to Hank.

"Uh . . . Rand. What are you doing?" Cada asked.

Hank eyeballed me. Either his mind was flooded with thoughts, or it had just flushed.

"Pick!" I shouted.

"T-two . . ." He hiked his foot, dropping it on the seat. "What are you doing?"

"Cada," I started, "empty your pistol at the building." I should have brought the shotgun.

"Are you still with us, Rand?" she countered.

"Yes. It's me. Just fucking shoot!"

"All right." She jumped to her feet, leaned out the door, and blasted away. The .45 kicked. Each shot followed the last, hiking the gun higher and higher into the night sky.

Muzzle flashes danced along the keys in my hand. Casings *pinged* on the floor.

I looked at the three remaining keys. The odds of picking the right one were one-in-three. My guess had been the first key. Hank guessed "two." So I tried "three." Our predicament underscored how much my luck sucked. That meant going with the third key put the odds in our favor. I know, it wasn't logical, but it made sense to me.

The key snapped into place. I turned it, and the lock popped open.

Hank yanked at the chain, unraveling it from his leg.

"I hope you have a plan," I said to Cada. "Otherwise, we're just running through the woods." I nodded at Hank. "And not very fast."

"About time," she said. "This part I have handled."

◆   ◆   ◆

I jumped from the bus into a gathering of zombies. Gray flesh and white teeth swarmed around. Hank hung in the doorway of the bus, and Cada had skipped across the parking lot—hopefully reloading.

Since my luck was running cold, I went for a long shot. Ducking down, I scooted toward Dale's prone form. Above the rain, I heard the zombies mumbling guttural sounds.

I straddled Dale, grabbing at his sides until I felt the cold steel of a baton. Feet shuffled around me, closing in. I tugged the baton free, snapping it to full length with a quick jerk of my arm. Figured I'd start low and work my way up.

Thrashing at the knees of the closest zombie did nothing. They were completely immune to the pain.

"Look out!" Hank yelled.

I tumbled forward with the weight of a zombie on my back. Hands pawed. Teeth chewed on my leather jacket. Then a jagged pain coursed up my leg. I felt the jaws gnawing, tugging at my jeans, tearing the flesh underneath.

Pushing myself up with my left hand, I swung the baton with my right, over my shoulder, striking wildly until it connected with something hard—a head I hoped. It was a bad position, my blows were weak, but it was all I had.

My left arm trembled under the weight of the zombie squirming up my back. I continued swinging, battering its head, hitting harder with each stroke, until I heard bone crack.

The zombie rolled off, body rippling with spasms. Letting my arm collapse, I dropped onto my left shoulder, bending at the waist.

Fire coiled along my leg as the second zombie continued gnawing. More shuffled closer.

I batted with the steel weapon, lashing against its forehead and eyes. While it didn't feel pain, my blows distracted it, drawing its attention. Now luminous eyes held me in their empty stare.

A pistol sounded. The thum of a slug bouncing punching the earth followed. Had to be Cada.

"Don't shoot," I called. The last thing I needed was playing target to a stray bullet. "Get out of here. I'm on my way."

I sat up swiftly, bending my knee and kicking the staring zombie in the face. Blood splattered as its nose crunched. I pumped my booted foot again. This time the head flipped backward. The zombie dropped flat.

I bounced on my rear, looking through a forest of legs. Beyond them a flashlight glided through the rain and darkness.

Hank grunted as he jumped from the bus. The large man landed running, shouldering into the gathering mob of undead. The first one he hit bowled over, face kissing the ground. The next spun aside. I scrambled to my feet. He was bulldozing straight through them, and I was following in his footprints.

"Shoot 'em!" The throaty growl of a shotgun followed. At least two zombies jerked and stumbled.

The wind and rain covered the voice. Even so, I knew it was Jimmy and that fucking ten-gauge.

"You got the lead," I called to Cada.

She stood a few yards away, dancing in place.

"Go! Go!" I said.

I grabbed Hank's shoulders, pointing him toward her. In a few steps we were in the forest.

My head rattled with every step. It felt as though my brain were an overripe grape pressed in a vise. Adding to the misery were bushes and branches, stinging my hands and face.

Not quite the plan I'd been hoping for when Cada said she had it handled. Still, it was better than a bus right to zombietown.

"Where are we going?" I asked.

She led the way, dashing in one direction, then another. Every fifty yards we halted, letting Hank catch-up.

"Don't distract me," she said. "I've got it mapped in my head. I need to count from each landmark."

Mapped? Trees and bushes and grass everywhere. What fucking landmarks? Also, I wanted to ask about Paul—his absence was dazzling. Nestled inside me, in some dark recess was the tiny hope Cada had shot him. I rethought it. Didn't want her following that road. It'd just have to remain a fantasy. I was definitely mis-wired .

"This way," Cada said and sprinted away.

I put a hand on Hank's shoulder, turning him in the right direction. "Keep up with her."

He was huffing like a bull chasing red. Had to admit, he was trying. Not a single complaint. I wondered if our jaunt through the blustery landscape was prepping him for a heart attack. Be a shame to reach the SUV and have him drop dead.

Cada continued following an invisible trail for another five minutes. When we stopped, we were on a ridge, overlooking a partially flooded dirt road. It cut into the earth—man made, mildly graded downward. I realized it was the lake access road Paul had mentioned. Water reached up its length from the east. The Traverse sat just beyond the water's grasp.

"Are . . . we . . . there?" Hank asked. He gasped for air with each word.

"Who are you anyway?" Cada asked.

He was bent over, large hands on his thighs.

"Hank Adams." It took a few breaths to push out the words.

"As in Henry Adams?" Cada asked.

He nodded. The motion was slow. "Same as the famous historian."

Cada and I exchanged bewildered gazes.

"The only Henry Adams I know is the reporter for the *Temperance Herald*," Cada said. "You him?"

"Editor," he said. "Mark Boyd is the senior journalist. Or was. Most of the rest were college students working as interns."

The topic rejuvenated him. He was taking short steps, walking in a shallow circle, head cocked upward. Looked like he wasn't going to die after all.

"Hey . . . look at that," he said. Excitement carried the words. "It's stopped raining."

I looked upward. For most of our trek, trees sheltered us from the rain. Now we stood on an embankment, in the open and no rain fell.

"About time," Cada said. She thrust her arms upward like she was embracing the sky. "Thank you!"

Not only had the rain stopped, the clouds had thinned. Between the scattered gun-metal gray puffs was the backdrop of night. No stars shone or sparkled. Only the churning colored lights were visible. Long streaks of green and blue unrolled, tangled, and pulsated.

"Really something, isn't it?" Hank said. I turned to him as he followed the luminous heavens.

"What is it?" I asked.

He tossed his hands in the air. "Don't know. Well, I have an idea. Or I should say Thomas had an idea. He'd know better than most, I suppose. Said it was the Aurora Borealis."

"Ha!" I leveled my gaze at Cada. "I was right."

"Not really." Her face wrinkled. "You said it looked like an aurora."

"I was closer than you. *Reflected lights.* There's no power. That means no lights. No reflection."

"Still wrong," Cada said.

"Um . . . I hate to bring this up . . ." Hank continued marching in a circle, although each pass increased in size. "I appreciate you two helping me. I really do. But I've no idea who you are and what you're doing."

"We're waiting for Paul," Cada said.

The statement garnered a blank stare from Hank.

I was interested in Paul's whereabouts. I didn't ask while Cada was following the unseen breadcrumb trail back to the Traverse. But now we had the time.

"He's hiding at the park's entrance, waiting for us, and keeping watch for any more *visitors.*"

"I'm sorry," Hank said. "I've no idea who any of you are. So when you say 'Paul' it doesn't mean much."

Cada bumped an open palm against her head. "Right. What am I thinking. I'm Cada Finch." She gestured at me. "This is Rand Clay."

Hank's eye switched in my direction. *Here it comes.*

"Randall Clay?" he asked. "From Michigan?"

"Rand," I said. "And yes, I'm that guy."

"Paul Harris is with us," Cada said. "Or maybe you know him as Officer Harris."

I appreciated Cada's attempt to redirect the attention, and even make me seem legit by tossing in "Officer Harris." Most likely Hank thought I was in Paul's custody. Then again, who hadn't heard of me in Temperance? I was as close to a celebrity as they got.

Hank's eyes remained on me.

"Look," I started, "I've got a Jurassic-sized headache right now, so let's just get to the point. I'm a murderer. I belong in prison, but I had a lucky break, a second chance. Given the way things are going at the moment, I'm the least of your worries, or society's. Or what's left of society."

Cada moved closer, peering at me. "Oh my god, you're a mess. There's a First-Aid kit in the car. Let's get down there."

She grabbed my hand, pulling me along. Her flesh was soft. The touch had already eased some of the pain. As we skirted down the ridge, I searched my memory. It was a strange and welcome sensation, holding hands. Sure, when I was young, my mom would take my hand. But this was a different creature. I'd never done it before.

CHAPTER
24

CADA WRAPPED THE BANDAGE around my head, hooking it in place. The hydrogen peroxide made my cheek and head itch, while the aspirin did nothing. *Not much First-Aid in that kit.*

"Do we have any beer?" I asked.

"No," Cada said. She snugged the bandage in place.

"I can handle it from here," I said, dropping into the passenger seat. Cada leaned on the center arm rest, watching me for a moment.

"Guess your jeans have to come off." She smiled.

"Think of where I've been," I said. "I've no shame."

She grunted, then moved away.

"Paul should be here soon," she said. I heard the doubt in her voice.

Hank sat in the rear, silent since my introduction.

I stashed the Beretta and extra magazines in the glove compartment, and started peeling off my pants. Just needed them to hang at my bent knees. Wish I'd worn my flowered boxers now.

The tear in my flesh looked minor.

"Peroxide," Cada said. I never noticed the sadistic side of her before.

The peroxide foamed and tingled on the bite. Satisfied, I bound it with a gauze bandage. Then I tugged up the soaked jeans, pulled down the sun visor, and examined the bruises and welts on my head. Didn't blame Hank for being quiet. I looked undead.

Cada peered at the rearview mirror. "You said you knew about the lights in the sky."

"I don't," Hank said. "I know what Thomas told me, and he was mostly guessing."

"Thomas?" I asked. "Who's he? And how does he know anything?" The world was full of good guesses. In fact, history was replete with them. Most of the time they were wrong.

"Thomas Meyer," Hank said. "He's a high school physics teacher. He's pretty smart. Pieced a lot of stuff together."

"Where is he?"

"Was locked-up with me. When we escaped it was total confusion. He went one way. I went another. Looks like I went the wrong way."

"Locked-up?" Cada cranked the engine. She snapped off the interior light and the headlights.

Hank shifted about in the rear seat, not answering right away. "Terrance Egan captured us, and a few others who were downtown helping with the sandbags."

He had my attention. The visor snapped upward, and I joined Cada, turning to face Hank. "Can you rewind this story a bit?"

Cada quickly added another question. "Terrance Egan, the Police Chief?"

Hank gave a slight shrug, keeping his gaze on Cada. "Not much to say. I thought you guys knew about Terrance. I mean because of what happened back there and Officer Harris. He was friends with Terrance. Close friends."

Good point. Can't see why Paul didn't mention the Temperance Chief of Police was possessed—the other half of the city's police force.

"I don't think he knows," Cada said.

"Let's not make assumptions," I offered.

"Don't start, Rand. We're not going that way. Yeah, I have issues with Paul, with what he's done. But things are weird right now. People aren't themselves."

"Has he been possessed?" Hank asked.

"Paul? Yeah. One time," Cada said.

"What about *him*?" Hank gestured at me.

"If you have a question for me," I said, "then speak to me." I felt like I was at Murderers Anonymous, every five minutes I was admitting to something. "Yes, I was possessed. Twice. Maybe three times. But I've built-up an immunity. Or something like that. What about you?"

"No. Just a few headaches," Hank said. "I didn't know someone could become immune."

"Then it looks like the high school physics teacher doesn't know everything."

I felt Cada's eyes burning holes into me. It wasn't my fault. I wasn't good at making friends. Most people rubbed me the wrong way. The world was filled with a bunch of moody bastards.

"Okay, I'm lost," Cada said. "Can we go back to the part where you were locked-up?"

"Please do," I said. "I adore prison stories. And direct any questions about me to Cada. I'll just sit here and keep an eye out for Paul—who may or may not be possessed." I held up my palms, surrendering to Cada before she spoke. "Just want to make sure Paul finds us. I'm quiet."

"Ignore him," Cada said. "A few too many bangs on the head."

"That's okay," Hank said. He shifted. The Traverse rocked slightly as he moved. "Terrance Egan is dead . . . .. I think he was possessed just after it all started. There were about twenty of us downtown, stacking sandbags to keep back the water. Terrance didn't look well—now when I look back, I think he might have had a heart attack. We told him to go rest in his car. A little after that we saw the first of *them*. The zombies. They filled the streets. Started mobbing us." He swallowed deeply. "Eating anyone they cornered."

"It must have happened all at once," Cada said. "Early on, the streets were swarming with people."

Hank nodded. "Thomas said it affected all of the city. Or so he figured. But everyone we saw was actually alive, just zombie-like. I suppose most everyone was asleep, and it seems to be easier to control a person who is sleeping. But then we realized some of them were actually dead and still moving. Soon after that Terrance returned."

The man was a reporter, and he was spreading this story across as many pages as possible. So far, he didn't offer anything new, except word about Terrance. I was the cut-to-the-chase kind of guy. Ignoring my vow of silence, I prodded Hank along.

"Can we skip to the *lock-up* part?" I said. "Don't get me wrong, I want to hear the rest. But if the punks we just escaped are working with Terrance, I'd like to know why, only because they didn't look possessed."

"Sure. Sure." He rubbed his eyes. Probably hadn't slept for nearly twenty-four hours.

He started again. "Terrance is organizing gangs to pick-up people . . . zombies." Hank said. "He can talk to them or something. It's like they're all under remote control, and the longer they're that way, the easier it is to manipulate them. Terrance is rounding them up. It's like he's building an army. And even though he's dead, he can talk. Sounds a bit like a loud speaker. You know, like someone else is talking through him. He's slow to respond. But maybe being dead does that. Don't know . . ."

"And you were in lock-up because . . ." I added. Just wanted to keep Hank on target.

"There are a bunch of people who didn't get possessed. Terrance didn't want us wandering around causing problems."

"So far that isn't working-out for him," Cada said.

"Terrance locked you up," I said. I was beginning to miss Paul. And I'd heard enough liars to know when someone was omitting details. Hank was holding out on the whole story. "How many of you were there?"

"Don't know," Hank said. "Ten or twelve, maybe more."

"Tell me about Jimmy, Amanda, Emmitt, and Dale," I said.

"Who the hell are they?" Cada asked.

"I don't know," Hank said. "I mean I've heard their names. They're the ones working with Terrance. Dale is like the ring leader. He captured me just outside of downtown. Brought me here."

A heavy knock sounded. Hank jumped, and Cada jerked forward, slapping the electronic locks. They repeatedly snapped as she jammed down the button.

Loud, heavy handed. It was the knock a cop makes. Although Cada came damn close. She had quite a swing.

"It's Paul," I said. Didn't look. If someone wanted to kill us, they wouldn't be knocking.

A flashlight snapped on at the driver's side window, revealing Paul's face. He gave it a few seconds, then turned it off.

I wondered how close Paul and Terrance were. Dead cops were always bad news. Learning your pal was a zombie wasn't going to help. There was no doubt what Paul's would want to do.

◆　　◆　　◆

"None of you have to go with me," Paul said.

Cada had recounted the short version of Hank's story. Any uncertainty about Paul keeping secrets vanished with the hard lines on his face as he listened. I knew what was zipping around his head. A part of me wanted to go downtown. I didn't have any friends, other than Cada—if that's what we were. Although, for a few hours, Nate came close to being a second. Even if he didn't like me, he deserved payback. So did the old man, the kids, and their mother. The longer I thought about it, the longer the catalog became.

Hank fidgeted, tapping fingers on the window, changing positions in the seat. He wanted to be comfortable, but whatever he was holding back prevented that.

It looked like I was the only one who noticed. Maybe Paul was lost in other thoughts. Don't know. What I did know was there were endless methods of getting the truth out of someone. Years ago, I knew a real hard guy. Luis Sanchez. A hammer was his method. Place a man's hand flat on a table, and smash the tip of one finger. Just the tip. Luis always started small. Then he'd give it some time. Let the nail blacken. The follow-up was an offer to pull the nail off, let the blood drain out. He always said it to the victim like it was a favor. Guess it was, in a way, because what came next was a knuckle. And then the time table kicked-up a notch. Luis worked his way up one finger at a time.

He always said, "You follow a pattern. Keep it simple. And anyone can see the future. One finger at a time. A man can see the direction.

Can think about it. Decide if the secret is worth exchanging for a different future."

I don't think Luis ever had to use his hammer on more than one finger. Give a man a choice, and he'll probably choose the way of less pain. Least that was how Luis explained it to me when it came time to use the hammer on my hand. Didn't like my options. Already saw my future. But Luis was right, in a way. Once I got the hammer away from him, all it took was one finger.

"Hank, we need to talk," I said.

"Hmm? Sure. What about?"

My eyes remained forward, looking through the windshield. I felt the others watching me. Must have been the tone of my voice.

"I don't like hammers, so I'm just go to ask. What are you not telling us?"

"Not telling . . .? What do you mean?"

"I mean Paul wants to head downtown. I understand why. But if you're holding out, and there's a surprise, well . . . Things will turn bad."

"Hammer?" Cada asked. "What are you talking about?"

The SUV jiggled slightly—Hank changing positions again.

"Is there something?" Paul asked solemnly. He was sitting next to Hank. I figured that pushed-up the heat a few degrees. Lying to cops undoubtedly wasn't a part of Hank's daily routine. Having the cops a few feet away, locked in a vehicle, with an ex-con as the only protection was icing on the cake.

"It has nothing to do with you guys," Hank said after a moment.

Cada silently mouthed, "Hammer?" Her face was wrinkled with confusion.

Miming, I answered, "Later." Pretty sure I wasn't going to share that story with her. In some crazy way, criminals were semi-heroes to her. A few of them, at least. Maybe it was because they were outsiders like her. I supposed that was true, except she wasn't like them. No need to bring more darkness to her dreams in the form of a long departed Luis Sanchez. Fuck, someone needed to keep faith in humanity. It wasn't going to be me.

"Before Thomas and I were captured," Hank said, "we were

trying to make it out of Temperance. The newspaper building has four-storeys."

I laughed harshly. "A pun," I explained. Everyone was looking at me. "Newspaper building. Four stories." I shook my head. "Keep up or get left behind."

Cada sighed. "Sorry, Hank. Please go on."

He waited a moment. Probably making sure he didn't make any more unintentional puns. "Anyway, a group of us had been hiding there. The area is flooded. That kept everyone away."

I sighed, waiting for what was coming. Should have asked Hank when we were alone.

"How many people?" Paul asked.

"Yeah. And they're not zombies?" Cada had forgotten about the hammer for the moment.

"They're all normal, like . . . us." Hank had a hard time getting out "us." Guess I was the odd man out.

"Why didn't you stay there until morning?" Paul asked. "Going out at night, in a storm is insane."

I stared at the roof. "Probably not the time for me to point out where we are and what we're doing, is it?"

"They were safe," Paul said curtly.

Hank grabbed my seat, pulling his bulk in some direction—probably facing Paul and Cada. "We didn't know that. Besides, Thomas thought things were going to get worse. I mean, let's face it, something unusual is going on, so the normal rules don't apply."

"Right," Paul said. He was rotten at hiding his frustration. "Whatever. Doesn't matter now. After Terrance found you two, did you tell him about the others?"

"No." Hank answered fast and firmly. *Not hiding anything now.* "No one even asked."

"Then we should go there," Cada said. "Get them or maybe work together."

First the park, and next downtown. I just wanted to leave Temperance.

CHAPTER

25

"I T'S ALL A GREAT idea." I spun toward Cada, between the front seats Paul was visible in the blue-green glow of the new aurora. "Except, why do I give a fuck about these people? All night we've been trying to get out of Temperance, now you want to go downtown."

"We have to help them, Rand." Cada reached out, grabbing my hands. The softness and warmth startled me. "Someone has to."

The touch of her hands was amazing and foreign all at once. I wanted it to continue, but a tempest whirled inside me, and my emotions spun in wild circles. I pulled away.

Someone has to do it. Right. I'm not that fucking someone.

"I have to help?" I asked. "Why? This town is always a little short when it comes to helping me. I mean, I can get behind what Paul wants to do. But going after a bunch of people in a building—people who are probably going to end up dead anyway. Sounds fun, but I'll pass."

"That's what I expected," Paul said sharply. "It's all great now, isn't it? You can stay out there, doing what you want." He squared his shoulders, raising the volume of his voice. "I've seen you in action. No need for you to be possessed. You just lose it naturally. You're a killer, Rand, and the world just opened a buffet. No, I don't expect you to help anyone but yourself."

"Shut the fuck up," Cada screamed.

I popped open the door, locking eyes with Paul. "You're the one hiding. We both know you slipped out of the military on some kind of technicality. Got an Honorable, but only a small town is buying into the bullshit reason for it. You're right. I am a killer. And I can recognize them too." I planted my feet on the ground, gripping the door, ready to swing it closed. "If all this ends, Paul, you'll have to go back to paper targets for weapons practice."

The door shut with a heavy thud.

I'd taken a few steps toward the washing water when Cada was chasing behind me. The good news was I didn't have a limp from the zombie bite.

"What's wrong with you?" she yelled. "And where the fuck do you get off saying that shit?" She marched directly at me, feet slapping against the muddy road.

I was right. She was cute when she was burning mad. I remained silent, knowing if I spoke, I'd utter only sharp words.

"Did you forget who just saved your ass back there?" she said. "You might not like it, but Paul and I did it. Just like Nate and I got you out of the store, only to have Paul save your ass again at the farm house."

She sidestepped, splashing through the water climbing the road, planting herself directly in front of me. "And I've been there since you came to Temperance. Nate would have too if you weren't such a hardass." Her hands locked on her hips, and she shook her head. "You're spooky sometimes, Rand. That keeps people away."

When Cada was pissed, ignoring her was like ignoring a tornado. Just didn't happen. For a few moments, I did my best. I watched the world beyond. The road stretched out of Lake Michigan. Its choppy and never-ending surface mirrored the night sky. Twists of light shone upon the water. Waves rushed back and forth, inching up the road and sliding down.

I thought about Paul's words. I didn't want him to be right. But, what I wanted didn't much matter. Darkness had always shrouded my life and it always would. Selfishness, anger, cruelty, death, those gave me purpose and shape. I'd never cared for anyone else—until now. And it was fucking confusing.

I stepped back, giving Cada the space to move out of the ankle deep water. Sneakers squished as she followed.

"I don't know what to do," I said.

She calmed. A faint smile touched her lips in the wan light. "Just help." She pushed onto her toes, pressing soft lips against mine.

◆　　◆　　◆

The Traverse rolled along Oakwood, in the direction of downtown Temperance. We were loaded with a plan. It still had some wrinkles because of some trust issues.

"It's 4:30," Paul said. "Dawn comes in another hour or so. We have to get this done before daylight hits."

There were no apologies when I returned. No surprised looks either. Not a word was said, except by Cada. She'd made it clear we were all doing this together.

"Just call out the drop-off point," I said. "Then give me twenty minutes and I'll have the town heading toward me."

"A few more miles," Paul answered.

As far as rescue plans went, this one was at the bottom of the heap. Paul and Hank were heading to the *Herald* building to round-up the people there. They were walking, staying on the edge of Temperance to avoid being seen. And according to Paul, everyone would trudge back through the knee-high water to meet-up on Oakwood.

I was heading to the highest point in Temperance to provide a diversion. Cada was chauffeuring me.

Then there were the wrinkles. Paul was the biggest for me. Just strolling in and out, not saying a word to Terrance. It just didn't feel right.

"How long do you need?" I asked Paul.

"Still the same answer. Fifty minutes. Keep asking, and it will be the same."

I caught a sideways glance from Cada. A quiet reprimand. A warning to watch my manners.

"It just seems short," I said. "Moving through darkness, water, streets in twenty-five minutes. Then gathering everyone together and returning in the same amount of time. Maybe an hour and a half is better."

"And you're going to keep the town occupied for that long?" The words had a slight edge to them. "Or are you wanting an excuse to leave?"

"You know," Hank said, "come to think about it, maybe we do need more time."

"If we take more time, then we'll get caught," Paul snarled. "I know Terrance. He's not going to be fooled by this idiot's shenanigans."

"Turn it down," Cada said.

I waited a half-beat, then jumped in with both feet. "Terrance isn't in Kansas anymore. You know that, right? He's somebody or *something* else."

"Fuck you, Clay. I don't need your advice. We're going in and getting out. Just make sure this vehicle is ready to pick us up."

Cada grabbed the Marlboros and tossed them at me. "Get one out and shut-up."

Maybe he didn't want revenge. With the rain vanishing, Paul might believe things would return to normal. In that case, saving a group of people promoted him to hero. It might be enough time to play knight in shining armor.

I fished-out a cigarette. Lit it, and took a long drag.

"It's for me," Cada said. She reached across the armrest, wiggling fingers in the air. "Hand it over."

"Just warming it up," I said.

This was the second time we'd driven the length of Oakwood, and the scenery wasn't changing. Back and forth. That's what we'd been doing, and there was another trip once everyone was together. Except this time we were following my original idea and hiking across the fields to the Interstate. *Nothing like a plan coming together.*

I snapped on the radio. A sharp hiss filled the SUV. Memories of Nate tuning through the stations jumped to mind. I did the same, concentrating on the buzzing and fragments of what might be words. A few times, Cada grabbed my wrist, halting me while she listened. The warmth of her hand held my attention.

"Shouldn't there be an Emergency Broadcast?" she asked. The

question hung in the air. No need for me to answer. Paul was going to snag it no matter what.

To my surprise, Hank fielded it. "There might be one, but the electrical activity could be interfering. Again, Thomas said that. I don't really know. When this started, he said the Earth is like a giant electrical generator, and those lights in the sky are sparks."

"If it's a generator," Cada said, "why's the interference only happening tonight? Why not every day?"

"I'm not the guy–"

"We know . . ." My voice remained level—I was trying. Hank had a habit of burying the lead in his tales. *Very* annoying. "Just tell us what Thomas said."

"Umm. Right. I guess you could say the generator wasn't turned on before. What's happening now is due to some kind of experiment." Some of the worry threading through Hank's voice disappeared. "The government has been researching the Earth's magnetic field for years. That much I do know. Wrote a few articles on it a decade ago when it was controversial."

Grassy hills rolled past the windows as the SUV continued heading toward the center of Temperance. I turned down the radio volume. Hank was becoming more interesting.

Paul refused to enter the conversation. He used a penlight to scrutinize a city map.

Actually, none of us responded. Cada usually had a television archive of knowledge on every subject. She pulled on the cigarette instead. Guess it was my turn at bat.

"So, you're saying some geek did all of this? Someone cranked-up a machine, and boom–" I waved my hands in the air. "The world becomes a jumbo-sized power plant."

Hank cleared his throat. "In a nutshell."

"And that makes it rain?"

"Produces thunderstorms. Yes. I mean, I guess. When I looked into the projects years ago, most of them predicated some influence over the weather. But I can't really answer–"

"I know. I know." Didn't want to get him stuck on Thomas again. And I didn't press about the zombies. That answer was going to take more than Hank and Thomas—if there was an answer.

"We're stopping in five miles," Paul announced. He snapped off the penlight and folded the map. "Can I count on you?"

He met my gaze with no fear in his eyes. It felt like he was taking measure of me, trying to peek at what was hidden inside me. *Good fucking luck. No one looks there.*

"I'll do my part," I said.

The SUV hummed down the lonely road.

CHAPTER
26

THEY CLIMBED OUT OF the Traverse next to a fire trail. It carved through the trees on the northern edge of the city, or so Paul and his map said. Worst case, they make a wrong turn and end up at Prospect State Park. Then again, that might be worse.

As Cada guided the SUV onto the road, I watched Hank and Paul shuffle into the shadows.

"We're on the clock now," Cada said. The SUV whined as she pressed down the accelerator. "I can get us to Greene's Store in another fifteen minutes."

"Not going to the store." I looked at her. "Little change of plans."

"Don't do this, Rand. You just promised them–"

"We'll be there to pick them up." She calmed a bit after hearing that. "Thought it was best not to mention too much. I don't know if those Shades can read minds or not." I knew they sensed emotion. Bet there was one fucker still rocking back and forth in whatever it called home after the trip it took with me. "This way we don't run into any surprises."

"Where to, then?"

"Same direction. Cut onto Height, and then move halfway to Main Street with the headlights off. From there, we'll go on foot to the gas station."

"Good. I need another pack of Marlboros."

The needle on the accelerometer dangled around eighty. Cada concentrated on the slippery blacktop, pushing the SUV's speed.

"We can slow down," I said. "Got plenty of time. Although, I'm not so sure Paul and his gang can make it back as quickly."

The engine exhaled as Cada eased back on the pedal. She bunched her shoulders, then relaxed. In the dull light, fences, mailboxes, and road signs blurred past. I wondered if those things would matter tomorrow. I'd spent less than ten months of this new century as a free man. Entered prison at the end of the last century, and got out in time for everything to crumble.

Cada must have sensed my mood. She fired a question that was dead center. "Think things will ever return to normal?"

"You're asking the wrong guy about normal," I said. "Bet Nate would say that things are normal now, and before all of this we were just riding a merry-go-round. Running in circles, doing things, but not living."

A mixture of happiness and sorrow crossed her face. "Sounds like him."

I nodded. Didn't know Nate long enough to quote him. Borrowing from John Lennon worked just as well.

"There was a guy I knew in prison who was the size of Buddha and loved to babble about life. Everyone called him Stubbs. Not sure if that was his name, or someone pinned it to him because he was short." I shrugged. "Either way, he always said 'happiness is imaginary and pain is real.'"

"What did he do?" Cada asked.

"Mostly nothing, except spout that line every day."

"No. I mean, why was he in there?"

"Murder, probably. Think about his philosophy. Anyway, at first I thought it was the usual prison manure. Everyone inside can tell you how to live, but none of them are ever going to practice it. Meanwhile, I'm ramming heads with everyone who looks at me sideways. Stubbs gives me a few months, then has some of his goons haul me into his cell. They knock me to my knees, and anchor my head over the toilet.

"Stubbs puts his slab-of-beef hand on my shoulder and with the other, flushes the toilet. He says, 'What do you see?'"

Cada giggled. It was a pleasant sound. "I know you. How many times did he slam your head against the toilet before you answered?"

"That's the thing. I wanted to be a smartass. Throw something out there, even though I knew pain would be my reward. But my mind went blank. Just me there, watching water swirl around the drain. Then I blurted, 'The world.' He nodded, pulled me to my feet and patted my back. Said I was a wise man."

"Yeah. Sounds wise to me," Cada said. "And it doesn't make sense."

"It did to me," I said. "What Stubbs-the-Buddha taught me was everything is going down the drain in time. Right now, we're all just swirling around the edge. Inside prison or outside. All we can do is enjoy the ride. Got me through almost ten years in there."

"Then you believe this is the end," Cada said sadly.

"I think we're still spinning around the drain, and there's no need looking down the dark tunnel on the horizon."

"Geez . . . Don't ever write inspirational greeting cards."

It took a special perspective to appreciate jailhouse philosophy, I supposed. Looking at bars and gray walls everyday fooled me into believing there was nothing to miss. I leaned back, stretched my legs, clasped my hands behind my head, making a show of how enlightening my story was.

The right side of my head stung. The bandage was still wrapped around my skull. *Totally does not help my image right now.* I snagged the hooks, and started unwrapping it. *Has to come off anyway. No need to spotlight my wounds.*

Cada rolled back into the seat, arms taut, form stiff. She looked like a diver preparing to jump into icy water. "Rand, you know I've never asked—never even looked it up on the Internet. And maybe now isn't when I should . . ."

"Wait," I interrupted. "Wait until we're done here." I already knew the question. She didn't deserve a short answer. I owed her that much. She'd never asked. Many times, I'd wondered why. Guess I'd always hoped she wanted to know me. Not sure that was a good idea, though.

"Sure," she said, nodding quickly. "If you don't want to tell, no problem."

"I want to tell you." *I'm afraid of telling you.* "You're the only one who deserves to hear it from me."

The remaining miles passed without either of us speaking.

◆　　◆　　◆

There was no sign of anyone at Greene's Store. Cada parked about fifty yards away, and we trotted from car to car and shadow to shadow. Crouching behind a silver Ion, I scanned the gas station.

I slipped the Beretta from my belt. Cada already gripped her pistol.

"We're going to cut across the street," I whispered. "Then head down Main to the Gas and Go." I nodded toward Cada's hands. "Use your left hand to hold your right wrist when you shoot. Fire twice, level the barrel, then fire twice again. Just keep doing that."

She inhaled deeply through her nose. "Got it."

I led the way. We threaded around the Ion, staying clear the nearby buildings. Didn't need a zombie jumping out.

We hit Main Street at a fast pace. Cada's soggy sneakers slapping the pavement behind me. When we reached the gas station, I cut right, darting behind a rusty pickup truck.

The station sat on a ridgeline—just a bit lower than Greene's store. It overlooked downtown, which was painted in solid blackness. Not even the neon sky penetrated the gloom.

Staggering in circles at the far corner of the gas station were two zombies. Each seemed to be following the other, going no place quickly.

"What are they doing?" Cada asked.

"No idea. Looks like they're lost."

The taller of the two wore a water-weary sports coat, grimy white shirt, and a tie. His hair, once a comb-over, flopped on his head with a life of its own. The other zombie appeared to be ready for work.

A dark jersey hung over him, the kind of attire worn in hardware stores. He also sported a pair of fashionably distressed jeans. In the unearthly frost of light, his hair was dark, pasted around his skull with long spiky strands. It was what I'd heard called an "Emo-do."

The wind puffed at us as we watched. The thought of sitting on my couch, watching videos with Cada floated up. Battling over fistfuls of popcorn and dubbing in our own dialog to the bad movies was a part of that. A long way from spying on the undead.

I motioned for Cada to stay put. Taking small steps, I tip-toed near the rear of the pickup. The tailgate was open. In the bed were tool kits, an old tire, chains, jumper cables, a gas can, and a jump-start rig.

Trying to be stealthy, I half-stood and prowled through the truck's bed until I found my prize. A siphon hose. I grabbed it and the gas can, returning to Cada.

The zombies stopped walking, and appeared to be looking at the ground.

The gas can was a rusty, a red ten gallon rectangle. Given the amount of driving we'd been doing, the Traverse was going to need gas at some point. If we followed through with our plan, we had enough. However, if the plan went astray, we'd have some extra fuel. And getting it kept Cada busy.

"Now what are they doing?" Cada whispered.

I followed her gaze to the zombies. They were huddled together, tugging on what looked like a carpet.

"Earlier, it looked like they were trying to walk," I said. "Right now, I've no idea."

I twisted the cap off the can and unrolled the hose.

Snarls of wind blew past us. I peeked at the zombies. They'd dropped to their knees and were still playing tug-of-war with a black rug.

Cada suddenly lowered to the knees, hand over her mouth.

"What?"

"They're eating a dog," she gasped. "A dead dog."

A second look confirmed it. The rug was actually a husky-sized canine, black and bushy. It was long dead, judging from its rigid body. It wasn't a zombie dog. Just a dead one. And now a meal.

It hit me then. Throughout the night, I'd been trying to blindfold

Cada to the horrors taking place. She'd been in the store, but most of what happened was covered by shadows. At the Hanson farm, Nate and me were distant figures hidden behind curtains of rain. Paul had been the closer threat. Cada had been through a firestorm in the last few hours, enough to set anyone on edge, or push her over it. But she hadn't seen the worst. Glimpsing the two zombies feeding carried her closer to the border of a new dark land. A world I couldn't hold back any longer because we were heading headlong into it.

Then I remembered, not for the first time, how my mom reacted to the horror uncovered inside me. Reducing my dad into a broken, bloodied heap was too much. Her grief still felt fresh, and painful. I'd seen it in her eyes that afternoon. And she understood I wasn't different from the man who brutalized her, cut her, and delighted in her misery. When I was released, the courts called my action "justifiable homicide." She saw it as something else. After the court's ruling, she put a bullet in her head.

I gazed at Cada forlornly. Like I said, I bring my own darkness with me. Fear stirred within me. I wondered if Cada saw me separate from the blackness surrounding us. *Not so sure there is a difference.*

"You doing something with that hose?" Cada said, knocking me out of my revere.

"Nope. You are." I handed it to her. "Need you to siphon the gas out of this truck. Fill the can."

"Why don't we just set the truck on fire? That will attract attention."

I smiled, and silently moved the gas can next to her. "We'd need a bigger fire. Besides, this gas we can use. While you're doing that, I'll work on getting the town up here."

She examined one end of the hose. "This is disgusting. I'm not sure I can–"

"There are worse things," I said. "Just fill the can and put it in the back of the Traverse. Wait there for me. We'll need to fly out of here."

Cada gave the hose a second look, then offered it to me. "How about you put your mouth on that and I'll summon the undead."

"No way in Hell." I shook my head. "Let's go."

CHAPTER

27

AS I'D EXPECTED, THE Gas and Go had a propane generator behind the building. During the summer tourist season, when the weather was at its worst, risking no electricity and no sales to the invading host of visitors was suicide for a business.

The generator sat there, silently, with a tall hurricane fence surrounding it. Scaling fences was old news. In Detroit, private homes sometimes erected ten-foot, barb-wired crested barriers. After mastering those, this one gave me no trouble.

I went through the motions—opening valves, checking gauges, and lastly punching the starter. It sputtered, then thundered to life. The station must have had an auto-connect because corner lights on the building flashed bright circles.

In moments, I was around the building. Cada still sat behind the pickup, one end of the hose in its tank, the other in the gas can. A hint of happy surprise shone on her face. Guess she thought power had returned to the town. The two zombies on the edge of the station perked-up as well.

"I did that," I said to Cada. "There is a generator around back."

"It's just good to see lights."

I nodded. I thought back to the countless days I'd spent in solitary.

The compact room had lights, but the guards always turned them off. Kept them off day and night. But there were still gaps around the doors. I'd spend hours admiring the door's halo, dreaming of sitting against a shade tree in a green field on a hot summer's day. Didn't see much green in Detroit.

"Keep behind the truck," I said. "I'm firing the Beretta, and I don't want any ricochet shots finding you." Mostly true. Doubted I'd miss. Mainly didn't want her to see it.

"Few more minutes and I'll have the Traverse started," Cada said.

With the lights as a spectacle, the pair of zombies had given up on the dog and were bumbling toward me. I stood in front of the station, allowing the interior fluorescents to backlight me.

They weren't fast, or at least not in a hurry. Each step was painfully slow to watch. When they hit five yards or so, I leveled the 9mm at the taller one—the one wearing the haggard suit. As I aimed, I noticed his doughy flesh. My eyes dropped to a dark stain in the center of his chest. He *was* dead. Someone had put a hole in him, center mass.

When things went down the drain, people changed. I knew a few cons who were ideal inmates—which meant they did everything they were told and kissed ass. Always calm, avoided eye contact, never spoke back. Then when a brawl broke-out, they'd go feral. It was like they suddenly exploded. They were living fireworks with everything packed and compressed inside them, waiting for the fuse to be lit.

I didn't see what was happening now as being much different. Maybe the lights go out, the dead start walking, and that boss everyone hated gets one right in the chest.

I squeezed the trigger. The zombie's head snapped back violently, then it fell over. *Where's everyone during proud moments like this? One shot, one zombie.*

Completely ignorant of its fallen comrade, and of my impressive marksmanship, the second zombie stumbled closer. If someone had shot his boss, I'd pick this one for the shooter. Pale skin and dark eyes gave the jersey-clad zombie a look of half-dead and half-alive. The Emo haircut pushed the scale in favor of alive. Probably wanted to be a vampire before the storm. *What rotten luck.*

I grinned at my pun, took aim, and fired. This time I was off the mark. The slug grazed the zombie's head, spinning him about. I fired a second time and it was a head shot. And the kid was alive. As the zombie sailed downward, spurting gouts of blood drew a line in the air. Its head thumped against the hard surface. Blood quickly gushed from the open wound, pooling around the body. As I watched, the zombie continued to kick. Feet kicking, once . . . twice.

An icy weight sank in my gut. Don't know why. Maybe guilt was waking inside me. Or maybe I was thinking too much about what the zombies did in life. Who they were, where they worked. *Need to keep a distance from it. There's going to be too much killing. This is a war. Just shoot and move.*

I pressed a hand against my pocket, making sure the second magazine was still there. Keeping in the light, I walked to the edge of the lot, and looked down the hill at the center of Temperance. From this angle, I saw through the sickly gloom. And I saw them. There had to be hundreds, bumping shoulders, funneling between the old brick buildings, spilling onto Main Street. All coming here. Probably attracted by the lights.

Turning around, I spotted Cada. She stood at the front of the rusty Ford F100. The red gas can rested on the ground next to her. A blend of horror and shock covered her face. Arms hung listless at her sides as she looked at the zombie bleeding out in the stark glow of the lights.

"You have to leave," I said hotly. "They're coming."

"I knew him," she said. "Mike Mayhouse."

"Don't look." I was angry with myself for not checking on her first. *Too excited about killing.*

I moved to her. Hands on her shoulders, I turned her about. "It wasn't him anymore. Don't think of it that way."

Glassy eyes looked at me. "Is that how it's going to be? We just stop thinking of everyone as being human. What if it's a sickness and there's a cure? Then what? We keep shooting them, and not worry about who they *were* before?"

"Please, grab the can and leave," I said. "All I'm saying is don't think about it right now."

She brushed my hands away. "You were almost like them. More than once. Did you stop being who you were?"

"That was different," I said. "But I almost did become like them. And then it wouldn't have been me."

"I can't do that." She pointed at the zombies. "Killing is easy for you."

A searing knife sliced through my heart. My pulse thrummed at my temples. There was nothing I could say. She was right.

"I don't know what to do," she continued. "We don't know enough about what's happening." Tears rolled down her cheeks. With a quick movement, she rubbed at them. "If I turn into one of them, are you going to kill me?"

I stepped back. Now the light was too bright. I didn't want her to see me. "No," I said heavily. "No, I wouldn't. I couldn't. And I can't tell you what the right answer is. I don't know either. I've never known the right answer. That's the joke of life. Some of us pretend to know. The rest of us are lost, looking for a way to make sense out of all this shit." My throat felt tight, choked as though invisible hands were squeezing it. As I spoke, my voice grew gravelly. "I want you to go back to the Traverse. Someone like me should do this. Someone like you should never have to see this stuff. But because the world is fucked-up, you do."

Shame burned my flesh, washing over me. I was a wretched thing, and I didn't belong in a world with people who were kind and gentle like Cada. After I was released from prison, I'd convinced myself there was a way to start over. *Lies.* Lies I told myself to hide from the truth. Everyone around me saw it. I was the only one who was blind.

"Go," I said sharply. "Take the gas and get away."

She looked at me as though I were a stranger. Her narrow lips trembled. She continued crying.

I faced the front of the station, trying to not look at her—to see the fear and horror I'd inspired. Her expression resembled my mom's so long ago. Cada saw the darkness in me. It was a gaze I couldn't endure again.

"Get the fuck out of here now," I yelled. In a few steps, I pushed through the doors of the Gas and Go.

CHAPTER

28

THE PLATE GLASS WINDOWS of the Gas and Go door were missing. Didn't take long for people to start pillaging. The interior looked like an army had passed through. Everything was pulled from the shelves. Crunched boxes, glass shards from broken bottles, paper cups, plastic forks and knives, and most everything else that didn't belong on the floor now covered it.

I stomped over the debris. A bitterness spread through me like an oily poison. "Fuck!" I screamed, stopping at the glass doors of the refrigerators. Most everything had been taken. A few scattered cans of Budweiser remained. "It is the end of the fucking world when the only beer remaining is this." I jerked open a door, grabbed a warm can, and popped it.

At least it was beer—or so the label promised. I gulped down the can, took another, and went outside. Along the way, I grabbed a stray pack of Marlboros from the counter. Figured Cada needed to quit, so one was all she got. If she ever looked at me again. *Might not even be waiting for you.*

The thoughts stirring in me didn't help. Ignoring them, I followed the plan. But first I guzzled the second can of beer.

With the generator still running, the gasoline pumps worked. I grabbed the handle of the one nearest to the road. A cable attached to the hose pulled back, trying to retract. One pass with the pocket knife ended the debate, and in seconds I had the hose stretched to full length, nozzle aimed at the downward slant of Main Street. I locked the handle into place, then returned to the pump, jabbing at the type of gas I wanted. *Highest priced works for me.*

Thankfully, like most of Temperance, the gas pumps belonged in another age. No need for a trip inside. They activated them outside, without a credit card. Just select fuel and let it flow. And that's what I did.

Gasoline streamed from the nozzle, gushing around the parking lot, spilling onto Main Street. The downward angle carried it onward. The hardtop was still dark from the rain, so the flammable liquid moved over the road invisibly.

I strolled to the far corner, overlooking downtown. Twenty-five, maybe thirty zombies had already climbed halfway up Main Street. More stepped behind them. *All in a zombie-rush, dying to get to me.*

Neon colors crawled across the sky, brightening as the night passed. Everything below took on a sea green hue. Beyond, bordered blackness—there, figures darted through patches of light, quickly appearing and vanishing in the murk. They were faster, seemingly smarter. Those were the ones I'd taken to calling the living dead. Alive and possessed, like I had been.

I remembered Hank saying he didn't know if someone could become immune. *How many were? Maybe it faded in time.*

The number of zombies increased as the main body inched up Main Street like mercury rising in a thermometer. In a grisly way, it was fascinating to watch. A few zombies heading one way, attracting others, and those attracted more. Eventually, they transformed into a massive horde, bouncing back and forth, struggling to get to their goal. Me.

I unfurled the wrapper from the Marlboros. Stuffed the pack in my pocket and removed the lighter. The top opened against the leg of my jeans. I waved the blue flame across the end of the cigarette in my mouth.

The *Zippo* went back into my pocket as I puffed on the filtered

Marlboro. *I hate filtered cigarettes. Bud and filters. It had to be the summer tourist trade.*

Blowing small clouds of smoke, I wondered how Paul was doing. There was no debating it now. I was playing the villain to his hero. If things did return to normal, I'd have a long stretch of hard time ahead of me because I was upgrading—mass murderer.

I drew another lungful of smoke. A hard hit in my gut forced it out. I flew sideways, landing on the hard parking lot surface. A zombie blindsided me. In its hurry to attack, it rammed me, sending the zombie sprawling as well.

Once I understood what happened, I jumped to my feet. It crawled toward me, face flush, teeth dark and shiny. A shredded flannel shirt and torn jeans hung from its body.

Frenzied eyes held me in their gaze as the zombie pumped its hands and knees, getting closer. Besides the speed, the color of its flesh told me this was one of the living dead. It scrambled in, pushing to its feet.

It howled, spraying the gruesome contents of its mouth. I hesitated. And in that short time, I fancied trying to reason with it. See if it might return to what it was. I'd tried communicating with them before, when they'd formed a line in the road. In the end, a lug wrench was the only reasoning they understood.

As quickly as the idea entered my mind, it shot away. In my life, I'd learned to respond to violence with violence, to threats with threats. But maybe the zombies deserved a second chance. But it wasn't coming from me.

The zombie lurched, wrapping arms around my body, biting at my shoulders. I fell back, sprawling on the hardtop. The reek of its breath filled my nostrils, along with the sharp scent of gas. Then I realized I had no idea where my cigarette was.

With one hand, I gripped below the zombie's chin, pushing its head upward. Teeth gnashed at the air. My muscles burned at the effort.

A hard jab to the solar plexus knocked the zombie upward. It wheezed, gasping for air, but otherwise didn't respond to the pain. In an instant, talon-like fingers clawed at my throat. Fingernails made tiny incisions in my flesh.

I hammered a fist into its gut. A hacking sound followed, then it vomited up a repulsive mess of meat and blood. I heard it coming, and quickly pushed the zombie away, rolling in the opposite direction.

It tried to stand. Instead it staggered, convulsed, and continued puking. I wondered if I'd ruptured an organ with my blow.

The zombie wriggled about, swiping at the air, spewing a vile liquid from its mouth. It continued for several seconds, until it collapsed.

Now, in the distance, hundreds of voices drifted up from downtown. Gibbering and howling, seemingly spurring each other to louder cries.

I slipped the Beretta free. I half expected the station to go up in flames. Any other time, a cigarette falling to the ground would burn out. Given the way things had been going, I imagined this one bursting into an enormous fireball, sparking a greater conflagration—one with an equal only found in the bowels of Hell.

From around the side of the gas station, another zombie appeared. He shambled toward me, moaning weakly. I refocused my aim and fired three times in rapid succession.

Two rounds hit. The zombie jerked with each, then spun around, flopping on the ground.

Seconds passed. My heart sank back down into my chest. I searched the area. In the sparse light from the gas station's corner lamps, the missing cigarette was invisible. Finally, I decided if I wasn't already burning, things had gone my way this time.

A fast glance down Main Street revealed a multitude of zombies approaching. Men and women, teens, and children, boys and girls all tromped along the pavement. Although it was hard to tell, from what I saw, most of them were re-awakened dead. The living ones were probably lurking on the sidelines.

A spreading stream of gas washed downhill. The air was heavy with the odor. If any of the zombies had memories or could think, they'd certainly know what they were walking through. And walking into.

I dug the lighter from my pocket. Its silver surface glistened in the eerie light crisscrossing above. Nearly ten years ago, I was handed a life sentence for the murder of one man. Arvin Hames was bland in appearance, and soulless. He did whatever he fancied. Killing was mainly what he fancied. Most people don't think about it, but there comes an time when gangs lose their appeal. In Detroit, this led to the creation of gentlemen's clubs. Arvin easily stepped from gangs into this new world because he was a natural fit. A lifetime member of the most depraved club in the Murder City.

Strip joints or archaic secret societies were what most people thought about at the mention of a gentlemen's club. In my world, designer drugs, teenage prostitutes, human trafficking, and killing formed the foundation of these private enterprises. When it came to those things, the Diamond Club was a gem. And it didn't take Arvin long to climb its ranks.

Like I said, I don't make friends easily. That always placed me in the empty spaces between gangs and clubs. It also meant I was the 'go to guy' when one of the girls ran away from the Diamond Club. Didn't mind it, much. Most everyone left me alone. Might say I lacked a certain charm which kept everyone at arm's length.

One night, a girl named Alexandra showed up at my place. Fourteen, maybe fifteen years old. Hard to tell because of the way she was dressed. One look, and you knew what she was. She was waiting in my doorway, bouncing like a nervous rubber ball, asking to be let in. I already knew what it was about. She wanted to leave town. Get away from the *Gents.* The funny thing was no one really cared if she lived or died. No, the men who believed they owned her only cared if she was working. Replacing a dead whore was easy. But a living whore, hiding, was another deal. An insult. That's when Arvin handled things.

I let Alexandra into my place. Told her the ground rules. Needed some of her clothes and some blood. Always needed blood stains to convince cops quickly that someone's been killed. Get the detectives thinking along those lines, and word would quickly pass to the Diamond Club. Soon everyone forgets about a missing girl. Sure, the city had some rotten cops who'd take money for information. Good thing was it worked both ways.

That was my MO. I fixed it so the girls looked like a john killed them, and then the girl disappeared into a new life. But Alexandra had a different story. It was an outing for her. She had five friends who'd split at the same party. All of them wanted to skip town. Since she spoke the best English, they sent her to visit me. The rest hid in an abandoned house on the west side of the city. Empty houses grew like weeds in Detroit. Never hard to find one.

My gut told me to walk away. Too much trouble, too much work. In the Motor City, one death doesn't attract attention. Six deaths, on the other hand, brought out the local news crews. Cameras, lights, interviews. Everyone had something to say then. Not that it did much. I always found print reporters to be the real risk takers. Explained why they were a dying breed. Either way, with a half-dozen dead girls, things would turn upside-down in the city, the police would be forced to investigate.

To me, the job looked lopsided, leaning heavy on the "lose" side. Of course, I wasn't known for making wise calls. I never let good sense stop me from doing something. And there was a plus to the situation. I'd piss off everyone at the Diamond Club, and maybe get some heat on them as well.

Someone else might have looked at Alexandra's sad and forlorn face and decided to help. That didn't persuade me. I did it because I wanted to tighten the screws on a glorified gang. To send a message. I didn't know they'd send a message of their own.

The next day, I went to the address Alexandra had given me. Simple plan. Pick up the girls, drive them out of town. From there, they were on their own. When I returned, I'd rig the house, creatively drop some evidence, then burn the place down.

Except, it didn't go down that way. One of the six girls got spooked. Traded the truth for protection—or so she'd thought. Instead, she earned a bullet in the head. The rest were tied up, butchered, and left to bleed out. As I took in the sickening scene, I understood Arvin's message. Maybe it wasn't the one he was trying to convey, but that was his problem. Arvin was telling me he wanted to play.

Sick fucks have always polluted the world. There's too many of them. One less wouldn't make a difference in the big picture. Didn't matter. I wasn't trying to make a difference. Just wanted to put Arvin down.

Everyone knew his handiwork. He liked blades and carving-up

people. No one had to tell me that Arvin had had some fun before he'd left. All of the girls were face town, clothes ripped from their bodies. He'd taken his time. Enjoyed himself in a few ways. Then he probably listened to them plead as he worked the blades.

Later, during my trial, I discovered he'd taken photos. Hung them on the walls at the Club. Arvin's message to future runaways: *Don't fuck with me.*

Arvin never had a chance to rebuke the accusations. Or to recount what I'd said to him before I started breaking bones with a baseball bat. After that, he was through making public appearances. Closed casket all the way.

And here I was in Temperance, about to up my score. I wondered how many of the living dead who'd been possessed would run away if given the chance. Guess it didn't matter.

The zombies staggered closer, hands clasping at the air, eyes wide, glowing with a greenish hue.

I moved back a few yards. Just enough to clear the gas covered ground. When the flames started running, they'd race back to the pumps. And all of Temperance would hear my message.

I thumbed the wheel on the lighter. Hated to lose it. But I wasn't going to waste time rigging-up a wick of some sort.

"Help! Please help!" a voice called from my left.

CHAPTER

29

"WE'RE NOT LIKE THEM." It was a woman. A man clung to her shoulder, hobbling with her.

"Please help us," she said.

Fuck.

Do I look like the kind of guy you ask for help? Throw the lighter and leave. You know how this will end. Not your problem.

"We've been hiding, but they're going to find us now." The woman slowed her pace, allowing the man to gain his balance. "The entire town is heading this way."

I sighed. "Don't come to me. Head over there." I pointed to Greene's Store. "Go that way and you'll find an SUV. Mention *Rand* sent you."

The woman pivoted, and the two hobbled toward the store. They moved irritatingly slow.

"Speed it up," I called. "The fireworks for the parade on Main Street are about to start."

If they said anything else, I didn't hear it because the howling from the zombies flooded the world. The cries weren't in unison. One overlapped another, creating an endless wave of shrieks.

If you're mad now, just wait until you get up here.

I divided my attention between the limping couple and the crest of Main Street. Now I had to buy a few more minutes until the man and woman were clear.

I shifted backward until I stood a few feet away from a pool of gas. I decided against tossing the lighter. Didn't want to risk throwing it only to watch the flame disappear before the fuel ignited. And I got to keep my lighter.

Heads popped above the horizon. First a few, then they appeared in groups. All of their unearthly eyes gazed forward, at me, or so it felt. Shoes and bare feet shuffled across the street as more and more zombies swarmed into the Gas and Go.

I glanced over my shoulder to find no one there. *Good.* Then, I skimmed the growing crowd for anything moving quickly or darting behind other zombies. Getting tackled again was not on my agenda. As insurance, I pulled the Beretta, holding it in my left hand. Probably couldn't hit anything more than a few feet away. Good enough.

When the zombies were a few yards from the pumps, I kneeled down, stretched my right hand toward the puddle of gas. I thumbed the wheel of the lighter and let the wiggling flame kiss the ground.

Yellow flames jumped upward. The heat pushed me back. I clambered to my feet, trotting away.

Like fiery dominoes, the flames split, tracing circles around the ground. One burned toward Main Street, setting ablaze everything in its path. The other rolled straight for the spurting gas pump nozzle.

Before the pumps exploded, the wailing swelled until it was deafening. Like a prelude to a symphony of destruction, I heard the pop and sizzle of human flesh before the whoosh and boom of the gas tank below ground. A second explosion followed fast. By this time I was at a full run, but the blast still bowled me over. Pungent, hot breath blew across my body as the Gas and Go lit-up the night sky. Red and yellow tongues licked at the heavens. And beyond the nearly blinding fire, more zombies strolled into the hellish flames.

Others stumbled away, burning like human torches. Aimlessly, they walked, grabbing at empty air. The sight was astounding, un-believable. It resembled a crushed anthill. Zombies charging in every direction, blazing and setting others afire. Some collided with buildings, igniting the structures.

The roar of the explosion rang in my ears, and the putrid stench of burning flesh twisted my stomach. Dazedly I watched. Icy hands climbed up my spine as I realized Arvin would blush at what I had just done.

◆　　◆　　◆

"This is Brianna and Zev Hably," Cada said as the Traverse rumbled toward the pickup point. "They're married."

They cannot be from around here. Not with names like that.

"And you two have met Rand already," Cada continued. Her voice was thick and hard. No doubt our previous conversation still weighed heavily on her mind. If she could see what I'd just done, the struggle with her conscience would abruptly end.

"Thank you for not leaving us," Brianna said. "Everyone else did."

"Uh-huh," Zev added.

I waited a few seconds after they'd heard my name, and then watched them in the mirror. No reaction. No questions. They had to be from outside Temperance, else it seemed they'd already be asking about me—*that guy from Detroit.*

"Not from Temperance?" I asked. Might as well set things in motion. The red glow from the burning gas station glowered above the trees behind us.

"Chicago. Just vacationing here," Brianna said. Then they murmured to each other. In the car for a few minutes and they already had secrets.

"Are you all right?" Cada asked me. She kept her eyes trained on the road.

I rubbed a hand against my throat, feeling the small cuts. My head ached, my leg was sore, and I reeked of gas, smoke, and burnt flesh. "Doing okay," I said. "Ah. Almost forgot." I produced the pack of Marlboros, pushing them into a slot on the dashboard.

Cada stared at them for a moment. Eyes jumping from the road to the cigarettes and back.

The new arrivals jostled around in the back.

"Ouch," Zev muttered to Brianna. "Don't worry about it."

Naturally, I worried about it.

"Where you two staying?" I asked. "Or were staying." I leaned around to get a better look.

"Every summer we rent a cottage on Pine Street. We take the month off to unwind." Brianna didn't look at me. She moved her hand along Zev's thigh. He saw me watching and pushed her hand away.

"Not much of a vacation this year," he said.

Zev had short, mousey hair. It was perfectly groomed. The kind of hair cut that was repeated every two weeks. His face was long and gaunt, and he wore a blue Polo shirt with what I guessed to be khaki chinos. Looked like he exercised, but probably more tennis than boxing.

"I know what you mean," I said. "Ended my vacation, too."

"Rand lives here," Cada said. "He's not on vacation. At least not the sort you guys are on."

"Oh," Brianna stuttered. "I–I see. I guess. In any case, we do appreciate you letting us thumb a ride."

"What part of Chicago?" I asked. I had to work on my segues.

Brianna gazed at me dumbfounded for a moment. "The north side," she managed after a pause.

"Been a while since I was in Chicago. You live near anything in particular? Other than the north side." It had been over ten years since I'd been to Chicago. Didn't know the area well. Thought I'd try it out. But it just didn't have the feel of Detroit. Too clean.

"North Shore," Zev said. Now he was rubbing his leg.

"Wow. Gold Coast area," Cada said excitedly. "I worked at a restaurant there for a few weeks. Great neighborhood. Tough managers, and the customers–" she caught herself. "They really tipped well."

"It is nice, I suppose," Brianna said.

She also had perfect hair, taking the weather and zombies into account. Blond and fluffy, about shoulder length. Most of it was pinned behind her ears. A burgundy, long sleeved shirt with "Harvard" painted on it. The shirttail stylishly hung over the top of her creased-legged jeans.

"Might be less nice after tonight," I said.

Brianna and Zev stared at me blankly.

"Keep an eye out," Cada said, punching me on the shoulder. "Paul might have moved them closer to town."

The former Gas and Go had passed beyond sight. The fulsome shine of the night sky and the headlights were the only illumination. Not even the moon lurked above.

I took a last look at Zev's leg. The chinos were stained in places as though he'd been in a scuffle. But the spot the two of them were focused on had darker stains.

"It's not an infection," I said, watching the shoulder for more people to rescue.

"I'm sorry," Brianna said. "I don't understand."

"The zombies don't pass it along by biting. So you can stop worrying about Zev's leg, and not bother hiding it from us. In fact, there's a First-Aid kit back there if you want to clean the wound. Although, it seems more like a box of stings and strange bandages. Worth a try either way."

"Something bit you?" Cada asked.

"No," Brianna answered quickly. "Well . . ."

They went back to muttering.

"Rand's telling the truth," Cada said. "It's not a virus or bacteria as far as we can tell."

More muttering.

"Oh God, that's such a relief," Brianna finally proclaimed. "We've been so worried. Oh, not that he was acting like a zombie or anything. I was afraid you'd not take us along if you knew."

Lucky Zev. Money must come from her side of the family.

Cada shook her head. "We wouldn't do that."

I continued to scan the gloom, looking for flashlights, reflectors, or just someone standing in the dark.

"Zev," I said over my shoulder, "after you were bitten, did you get any headaches?"

"I've had one all night," he said. "I'm prone to migraines. Thought it might be one starting. Why? That got something to do with the bite?"

From the corner of my eye, I saw Cada look at me.

"Just wondering," I said. "I've been having them too. How about you, Brianna?"

"Zev is headache enough for me," she said with a little laugh.

I inhaled through my nose trying to keep the bile down.

The bite might not cause Zev to become a zombie, but the headache could be a symptom. I didn't think they were hiding anything else. These two were as transparent and deep as a sheet of plastic wrap.

"There's aspirin in the kit," Cada said. "Let me know if the headache gets worse. I might have something stronger."

"Oh, Zev doesn't take aspirin," Brianna said. "It disrupts the body. Takes away from the overall health, you know."

Cada nodded as though she understood. I had no idea what Brianna meant. What I did know was there was enough whine in her voice to annoy me. Had a feeling it would happen with anything she said.

We rolled along for several minutes with Brianna and Zev speaking in hushed tones, and Cada quiet. Figured she was battling with a moral dilemma. One without an answer from my view. Life had short-changed her, and I imagined she was looking for the fairness in it all. She was a wanderer. I was a murderer. One of those was already too much of a burden for her. The best I could do was carry the rest of the weight.

"How much longer before we're out of this wretched little city?" Brianna asked.

"We have a ways to go," I said.

"You must be joking. It's not that big. You can drive from one end to the other in less than an hour."

"Maybe you didn't hear me when you first came," Cada snapped. "I told you we were picking up other people. Then we were leaving."

"Oh, I understand," Brianna said. "I just thought they'd be . . . closer." She said the last word quickly.

Cada grabbed the Marlboros and shuffled out a cigarette. I went through the routine without saying a word. Once the flame from my lighter appeared, Brianna started muttering to Zev again.

A stream of smoke escaped Cada's mouth as she glanced in the mirror at a chattering Brianna. Reading Cada's mood was as easy as reading a road sign. She was in countdown mode to being pissed. Oddly, I was tolerating the new company better than she. Seems like there was therapeutic value in burning a horde of zombies and a few buildings.

As much as I didn't want to hear Brianna speak, I thought I'd defuse the situation. "Were you two staying at the cottage with anyone else?" Once the words were out, I realized what a minefield I'd created. *Say 'no,' and go back to whispering.*

"Nooo." Brianna stretched the word. "We don't share the house."

"I boarded up the windows early on," Zev said. "Used the winter window fillers. I didn't know what else to do. Our Volvo was stolen. The phones didn't work. Thought it was one of those small town riots."

Brianna chimed. "I told you, those happen in college towns. Not places like this. And they're not *riots*. Protests."

"This looked like a riot. That's until we saw people biting each other. Half the street was running around doing it."

"Zev tried to help Mr. Carper next door," Brianna added. "I told him not to. He never listens."

"Carper was trying to get his car out of the driveway," Zev continued. "I was going to ask him for a ride."

"That's when they bit him," Brianna said. "What animals. They jumped on Zev and were nipping at his legs." She shuddered after the last statement.

"See any Shades?" I asked while Brianna was taking time to breathe.

Silence was the answer. For a moment, I thought about leaving it there. But I needed to know. "Shadow men, or dark shapes moving like they were alive."

"Is that a joke?" Brianna said slowly. "If so, it's not funny. Things are weird enough already."

I counted that as a "no."

Cada remained silent—water nearing a boil.

CHAPTER
30

T HE HABLYS CONTINUED THEIR tag team telling of what happened to them. It stretched on for what seemed like an eternity. Nothing new came out of the story. Cada managed to remain quiet the entire time, studying the odometer intently.

"Finally, we were hiding in the attic," Brianna said. "There's a pretty good view up there. And it's not really an attic. We had it remodeled. It's more of a small study. In July we watch the lakefront fireworks from up there."

"I'm certain they're not interested in that," Zev said.

He was rewarded with a piercing gaze from Brianna.

"There's one of those old, wind-up radios up there," Brianna continued. "That's where we heard the Emergency Broadcast—"

"Slow it down," I interrupted. "You heard an Emergency Broadcast? What did it say?"

Cada looked at me, then in the mirror. I suspected this was pure rapture for them. People waiting to hear their next words.

"*Buzzz . . . buzz . . . buzz . . .*" Brianna sounded the alert tone. "Oh, that's so annoying."

"It said there was a global weather alert. With ionic disturbances—" Zev seemed lost amid his memories. He looked to Brianna for help. She screwed her face tight as though she'd just tasted a fresh lemon.

"Ionosphere?" Cada offered. "Ionospheric disturbances?"

Zev snapped his fingers. "Yes. That's it. Or close enogh. The message said to stay indoors until Civil Authorities arrived in the area."

Brianna took it from there. "Like that's going to happen around here. When I saw all those crazy people coming up Main Street, I told Zev we had to leave."

The Traverse slowed. Cada guided it to the shoulder.

"Oh, are we there?" Brianna pressed her face against the window. "Doesn't really look like we're anywhere."

The drop-off point was on the far side of the road. I searched the sparse trail for movement. It wasn't anything more than two ruts and a hump of grass in the center. The trees on both sides reached across the top, nearly touching. Doubt it was much of a fire trail anymore. With branches holding hands, flames could easily jump to the other side. Then I thought about the fire at the Gas and Go. Wondered how much of the town was gone, and going. *Might be testing this trail soon.*

"See anyone?" Cada asked, ignoring Brianna.

"Not from here. Let me go check." I opened the door. "Keep the engine running in case they arrive with someone on their heels."

"What do you mean?" Brianna asked.

I pushed closed the door, and strolled across the glistening blacktop to the fire trail. The wind slipping through the leaves was the only sound. I walked farther down the trail, looking at the mushy ground for footprints or some hint as to where Paul and the others might be.

The concrete jungle was my environment. Brick walls, narrow walkways, tall buildings, burned-out houses were the elements of my world. Grass and trees and open spaces seemed primal. Unnatural.

Hoping to push away the vulnerable feeling, I ditched into the tree line, moving from tree to tree. They were tall, but as skinny as runway models.

Figured I'd go in about thirty or forty yards, then head back to the SUV. They might have someone who's slower than Hank. Or they might be locked-up in Terrance's jail.

"You don't have a feel for the woods," a voice whispered in my ear. "Can't hear behind you."

Street lights. I added lights to the list of things I'd missed. Forests were filled with solid blackness.

"Can only hear around corners," I said. "When there are corners."

The voice belonged to Paul. Warmth touched my cheeks, knowing he'd sneaked-up behind me. No weapon against my back, though. Good news there.

Paul made a half-snorting sound, and moved to face me.

"Where's the others?" I asked.

"Still back here." The shadows obscured most of his face. "One of them was hurt. Might be a broken leg. I don't know. They were pretty hush-hush. I explained the plan. They voted, and decided to stay."

"That's what democracy gets you," I said. "Crazy ideas."

It looked like he shrugged. "They know more than we do about what's going on."

"Don't quote Thomas," I said. "Make it sound like you already knew the stuff." Don't need two Hanks in one night. Then I thought about the surprise waiting in the SUV. He'd get along with Brianna like paper did with scissors.

"Thomas is missing," Paul said. "Probably held at the police station, if the others haven't killed him already. And no, the info came from a radio broadcast. Looks like this thing isn't isolated. Pretty much worldwide."

"Disturbances in the ionosphere," I added.

He remained silent for a moment. Guess he was eyeing me, trying to figure-out how I knew that.

"I ran into some tourists," I said. "They heard an Emergency Broadcast. They're long on chat, but short on information. Just told you all I know."

"Must be getting crowded for you," Paul said, not so nicely.

"I'm used to crowds. Takes them a while to adjust to me, however."

"Right. Here's the thing. I don't see any point in leaving Temperance right now. From what Hank's people said, the government is pushing out the National Guard. That means major cities first. And this place, maybe never."

He sidled toward the trail. The vault above made him visible again. Originally, I'd thought Marines. Now I wondered if he'd done some Special Forces work. He was good at lurking about. Meant he was good in a tussle.

"All of this . . ." He pointed at the lines of light scribbled across the top of the world. "It's caused by some experiment in Alaska. The official take is it was research into enhancing communication signals for the military."

I followed him, keeping a bit more distance between us than we'd shared in the trees. "Did someone's calculator go crazy? Cause it's not helping any broadcasts."

"Like I said, that's the stance now. Probably change when things settle." He lowered his gaze, eyes drifting through the darkness. "If things settle."

"So no communications around the world," I said. "Wonder if that goes for radar and whatever else they use to start wars."

"I think it's screwed-up everything that broadcasts, and offlined most every power station on the planet. The sky's filled with energy right now and it's zapping large power sites on the ground. Like a world-sized short circuit."

It took a moment for the concept to settle in my mind. Then I realized Hank and Thomas were correct about an experiment causing it. Had to admit, it galled me to know Thomas was right again. He'd already sounded like a know it all. Maybe his being missing was good. Then the reptilian part of me stirred in anger. *Wonder what's the sentence for murdering a world? Ten years at least. Maybe five with parole for ass kissing.*

"Does it go away like a thunder storm?" I asked.

Paul tilted his head and straightened his shoulders. "Don't know."

"Did the broadcast mention a reason for the zombies and Shades?"

He grunted. "The story on that is the high energy in the atmosphere *might* affect people causing aberrant behavior."

"They nailed that one."

"Here's the deal, Rand." Paul faced me. "I'm staying in town with them. When dawn comes, I'm going to get some Intel on Terrance and what he's doing. If he's the leader . . ." Paul folded his arms and gazed at the ground. "Well, if you cut off the head of a snake . . ."

Intel. Cops don't use that word. Never heard it tossed around in prison either— "Man, get me some Intel on the food situation. Need a sit-rep pronto." Really only heard it in the movies. Paul was going military. *Old habits.*

"They might even leave at daylight," he added. "Or sometime after that. Can't imagine Terrance—or whatever he is now—wants an army to become King of Temperance. In any case, this looks like the best spot to be until someone gets a handle on the situation."

This was the point where I think I was supposed to say I'd miss him. It was good while it lasted, and all the bullshit attached with it. Of course, I didn't say it. If he wanted to stay in Temperance and play solider while a group of people hiding in a building dabbled in altruism, it was good with me.

Unprovoked thoughts leapt to the forefront of my head. I imagined a huddle of girls hiding in a house, hoping to escape a monster. *No use. The monsters always find you.*

I pushed a thin smile on my face, trying to hide my real emotions. "Mind if four more tag along?"

CHAPTER

31

BRIANNA STARED AT ME, stunned. "It sounds absolutely insane."

"You're right." I grinned. "I'm full of crazy ideas. But this one was his." I pointed at Paul.

I urged Paul to recount what he'd told me. He did, except this time he skipped through it a bit faster.

"And you want to go with him?" Cada asked, standing at the rear of the SUV puffing on another Marlboro. "Don't know. Heading away from here feels like a better idea."

I wondered if it was Temperance Cada wanted to get away from, or the memories of it. Staying here didn't sound like a good plan. But if the entire world was trashed, then Temperance was chump change. No one ever goes for the small stuff when there is a big prize for the taking. It was something I'd heard in prison. Two life sentences were no longer than one. Make it a blood bath instead of a murder. *Arvin Hames did just that. Sometimes you turn out to be the big prize.* Don't think there were any prizes in Temperance.

Everyone else gathered in a tight circle, wind pulling at us. Paul was at the edge of the group. He'd decided and didn't need to hear any more arguments.

"It can't be more than an hour away from daylight." I fixed my eyes on Paul. It took him a moment, but he understood.

"It's . . ." He looked at his wristwatch. "Ten after five. Sunrise in another thirty minutes."

"Then let's just stay here," Cada said. "We can pour the extra gas in the car, and keep the engine running. Then we hoof it to the Interstate."

"I'd much prefer that," Brianna said.

"As long as we leave this place, I'm content." Zev wrapped an arm around his wife, rubbing her shoulder for warmth.

"Already told you my choice," Paul said. "You got to decide fast if you're coming with me. I don't want to head through downtown with the sun in the sky."

"Maybe they'll hide when the sun's out," Brianna added hopefully.

"I'd rather find out from a safe location," Paul said.

Cada inhaled deeply on the cigarette, then tossed the butt on ground and crushed it with her shoe. She gazed at me with what I took for a blend of bitterness and confusion.

She was probably wondering if I'd go with her to the Interstate. Figured I'd put her through enough already. Tagging along didn't seem like a good idea. Staying in a building with a bunch of people wasn't a great notion either. Could always split on them. Just needed some time to get an idea on what was going down.

"You don't think there will be any help out there?" Cada asked Paul.

"Not in a few hours. I suspect all resources are being flowed into Chicago."

Brianna's face brightened. "Uh, that's where we want to go." She gestured between Zev and herself.

"It's a ways from here," Paul said. "A lot of towns in between. That means thousands of zombies. And who knows what else."

Cada turned back to me. "So you're going with him."

"Don't think there's a choice."

She had a predicament. Trust the cop who held a gun to her head, or trust the murderer, who she suspected would hold a gun to anyone's head. I'd been there when Nate died. Put the bullet in Mike's head. Saw no reason for her to believe in me.

"You should come with us," I added.

Brianna's visage soured at my words.

"So burning down the gas station was pointless," Cada said to no one in particular.

I'd thought the same thing before I did it. Now I was certain. I left the remark for Paul.

"There was no way to know," Paul finally spoke. "The people at the *Herald* building voted not to leave after Hank and I got there. When I heard what they already knew, it seemed like a better plan."

The problem with plans was there was *always* a better one. I'd never put stock in long term schemes and machinations. They never worked out for me, the last few hours proved. Blunt bullheadedness was my style.

Cada sighed heavily. "Looks like we're wasting time here." She walked to the SUV, and popped open the back door. "Take what you want."

Her decision was spectacularly obscure, so I applied some bluntness. "You heading downtown or not?"

"Going with you."

Brianna's face deflated. "What are we supposed to do?"

"Take the car, if you want," Cada said, reaching for a duffle bag. "Or come along."

"Oh, Zev," Brianna whined. She was in top gear now. I had a feeling it would take her a while to spin down. "Tell them not to go."

Zev held up his hands. "I can't tell them what to do, Bri. Maybe we should do what they say. Sounds like Chicago might be messy."

I slipped around to the right side of the SUV, opening the door. Checked my duffle. A retractable baton, the third magazine for the Beretta, and a half empty box of cartridges. If I had any reservations before, Paul's news clarified the matter. I'd need more weapons and ammunition. I suspected Terrance's gang was well armed. Like a bullet, the image of Jimmy rushed to the front of my thoughts. He was stalking around with that revolver or shotgun, maybe both. Talk about a guy who was quickly climbing up my list of regrets.

Cada stepped beside me as I zipped the bag.

"I'm sorry, Rand."

I nodded. Didn't know what to say. She needed to be any other place than with me. On the other hand, I didn't want her being anywhere but near me.

"Not a problem," I said. I stepped back, pushing the bag over my shoulder. "You're right. Take a look at the Gas and Go. I'm used to killing."

She huffed. "Don't make this difficult. I was angry—and worn out. I didn't mean it that way. We're not so different–"

"Yep. We are. The world shines brightly for you. You see hope in people. I don't. I look at folks in a different way. Trust me. Yours is better."

"And look where that's gotten me."

I shrugged. "A better place than me."

Her eyes widened. "Look around lately? We're in the same place. Except I was trying to protect the monsters that are trying to kill us. Talk about screwed-up."

She was probably a fistful of years younger than I, and even after being dealt several bad hands in life, she'd moved along. The way I see it, in this world some people start with a losing hand. Others just make all the wrong choices. Then there are the ones like Cada. They play the game well, but always lose to an inside straight. It wasn't fair. But that's the way the game was played. And it sucked.

"I came here," she continued, "so everyone else couldn't screw with my life. And even though this is a shitty little town, I liked it. I had friends here. Then some jerk finds a way to mess it all up with the flip of a switch. He puts the world on wash instead of spin dry." She flapped her arms. Her eyes welled with tears. "I don't even know what that means."

I wasn't sure, either. But I caught the spirit. So I nodded. "Yep. When everything's going smoothly, along comes an asshole who fucks it up."

"Right." She placed a hand on my arm. "Are we okay?"

A few thousand answers jumped to mind. Zombies, shades, storms, everything was falling apart, and we were still a long way from knowing why. But, I knew she meant things between us. Cada was the champion of lost causes, and she wasn't giving up on me. I knew it'd be better for her if she did. Although, she'd never hear me speak those words until she was safe.

"Always," I said.

Before I added more, she jumped forward, arms around my neck, kissing me. This was the second time. A record for me.

Most people viewed me as the kind of guy who doesn't kiss. Mainly, I'd never felt the need. Usually you can't even pay extra for a prostitute to kiss you. Never understood why anyone would. In fact, it was the first warning out of a hooker's mouth. *No kissing.*

Yet, now I understood the attraction. Seemed like it only worked if someone wanted to kiss, which meant they cared enough for you to do it. Sure, moms kiss their kids all of the time. Mine did. They were hollow little things. This one was different. When she'd finished, I wanted to smile and start over.

"Does this mean you're joining us?" Paul asked.

Cada didn't flinch or jump away. Her arms remained wrapped around my neck. "Yes."

"So are *they*." Paul tilted at head toward Brianna and Zev. "Must be losing your edge, Rand. I had to tell them if they didn't keep quiet you'd kill them."

I arched an eyebrow. "Out-of-towners," I said. "My celebrity is lost on them."

"They still closed their traps. Either way, it works for me." He turned, and walked around the Traverse. "We don't have much time," he called out. "Have to hustle, people."

Cada slipped away from me, grabbing her bag from the ground. She pushed a free hand in her jacket. "Smokes and gun," she said. "And what's up with the filters?"

"That's all they had. Don't ask about the beer."

CHAPTER

32

"PUT ANYTHING THE WATER will damage in your bag, or hold it over your head," Paul said.

"We are wading through *that*?" Brianna sounded horrified. "Look at it. Who knows what's in it. No wonder everyone in this town is crazy."

From the peak of a small hill, I saw the dark water swishing back and forth. Plastic cups, plates, cans, clothing and debris I had no name for floated on the surface.

"Think of it as a moat," Paul said. He was standing at the water's edge.

"I am," Brianna said. "People died in those."

"It offers us protection," Cada said. "The zombies probably won't walk through it."

"Then they're smarter than us."

Didn't want to admit it, but Brianna made a good point. Except when a Shade was nearby, the zombies weren't much for thinking on their own. Perhaps their instincts warned them away from water—which made Temperance Hell for them. If not, then there was nothing to keep them from meandering down the flooded streets. Sounded more like a human fear.

Paul gave me an exasperated look. The odd couple were slow walkers, and endlessly whispered among themselves. If I had it right, Paul was asking me to shoot them. *Not a good idea. Make too much noise.*

"Aberrant behavior," I quoted the Emergency Broadcast. "Need to get used to it."

I approached Brianna and Zev, planting my hands on their shoulders. One big group hug. "You can stay here and die. Or you can wade through the water and die later. It's up to you."

They looked at each other, stunned. I walked down the hill, jumping into the water. It was waist high, and I'd landed on concrete. I decided there must be a barrier wall between the street and the tree line. The nearest street sign read "Lakeside." *Fucking clever.*

Paul and Cada followed. Brianna and Zev seemed to be at odds. Then Zev took her arm and led her toward us. As her feet entered the water, she gasped, face rigid.

"It's freezing," he said.

"Helps kill the bacteria," I replied. Cada elbowed me.

Paul swished ahead. "This way."

Downtown Temperance matched Dorothy Ford's house. I'd only ventured in the area a few times over the last few months. The place didn't have anything I really needed, except food. It was a backward city, and because of that the grocery store delivered food like it always had. I'd marveled at the idea when I heard it. Pizza delivery in Detroit was like entering a combat zone. Grocery delivery was suicide.

A part of me delighted in reciting a shopping list over the telephone, having a group of people gather up the stuff, and then bring it to my door. I wondered if they drew straws to see who made the delivery run to the murderer's house.

"Stop smiling," Cada said, pulling me back to the moment. "You spook people when you do that."

"So I've heard," I said.

We splashed between mostly two-story buildings. A few three and four floor structures dotted the area. Guess they didn't build tall in the 1800s.

Like rats in a watery maze, we zigzagged down the streets. Going was slow with our hands over our heads—Cada and me holding duffels, and I had no idea what Brianna was holding. Zev kept his hands around her.

Paul halted when we turned the corner of Dunkirk. A string of bodies floated in the water. All face down, arms spread at their sides. Twenty or more washed along the street.

"I am not walking through *that*," Brianna said. Her voice quavered, either from the cold water or the dead people.

"They're dead," Paul said.

"So I see," Brianna replied.

"Dead as in not zombies. That's what I meant."

Brianna shook her head. "I don't care. It's disgusting."

From where I stood, Lake Michigan stretched to the horizon. A ruby-red glow shone on the distant sky. The strings of light above vanished as they neared it. The sun was climbing upward, but it didn't look like any sunrise I'd seen before.

Paul continued down the street—end of conversation. I followed.

"We're almost there," Cada said, trying to coax Brianna into moving. "You can't stay here."

I glanced over my shoulder to make sure Cada was following. Zev and Brianna bickered for a moment, then with Zev cradling her in his arms, they trailed behind Cada.

Aberrant Behavior, I thought again. Must be true. A few hours ago I'd been itching to shoot those two. The storm must have mellowed me.

Cada hurried next to me. "What if the dead zombies don't breathe?" Cada said in a hushed tone. "They can be hiding underwater."

Now she was ruining my mellow. "Don't let Brianna hear you."

My inventory of fears was small. Least ways the fears I knew about. Who knew what monsters lurked in the recesses of my mind. I didn't. Maybe I just lacked imagination, because I would have walked the entire stretch to the destination never worrying about zombies prowling beneath the water. Would have.

"You think too much," I said.

"Funny. Everyone always says the opposite."

"They've never done this with you."

Paul rushed to the corner of a building. Its red bricks took on the color of blood in the sunrise. He waved urgently for us to follow.

Hurrying down a flooded street, wondering if you were about to step on a lurking zombie, wasn't easy. It was even more difficult for the rest because they were pushing through chest high water. This kept me busy stopping, giving a "hurry-up" expression.

"The building is about two blocks east," Paul whispered.

I stayed behind him, glancing at the rest of the gang. They trudged along slowly.

"Thought I saw flashlights down the street," Paul continued. "Has to be Terrance's crew."

I warmed at the notion. "Not a problem for me."

Paul looked at me. "Get a firefight going and they'll search every building looking for us."

I sighed. "What's the plan then?"

"Don't tell me there's another plan?" Brianna moaned. She and Zev brought up the rear.

"Quiet," Paul snapped.

Thought about repeating his advice to him. Didn't see it helping the problem.

He peeked around the corner again. Bodies drifted past, one after another in a straight line. Some were half eaten, flesh black and shredded. I turned to warn the rest, suspecting the sight might startle them. Instead, I tossed a right hook at Brianna. It was a solid punch, connecting with her jaw.

She collapsed into Zev's arms.

CHAPTER
33

"**W**HAT THE FUCK?" CADA spat.

"Keep it down," Paul said. When he turned, he saw Brianna unconscious in Zev's arms. He glanced at me, nodded, then went back to keeping watch.

"Bri-Bri, are you all right?" Zev held her in both arms, keeping her limp form above the water. He glared at me. "You'll pay for this."

"There's a charge? How much? I might have enough for a second."

"What's wrong with you?" Cada asked. "Are you possessed?"

I nodded toward the disembodied head floating behind Zev and Brianna. "One look, and she'd have screamed. Couldn't take the chance."

Cada's body stiffened when she spotted the head. She gasped, then coughed, struggling to muffle the sound. The head floated like a pineapple on the dark surface, bobbing up and down. The skin was purple, eyes bulging. Only part of the ragged flesh of the neck was visible.

"Don't," I warned Zev as he started to look. "If you look, the both of you will go under. Eyes on Bri-Bri."

"Don't call her that," Zev growled. Or what played as a growl in his case. Without the power of attorneys, or a legal system, neither of which he could rely upon presently, he was short on threats. Even the cop didn't give it a second glance. No question, Zev was in a hard place.

Cada swished in the water doing an about face. "Don't look, Zev. Just hold Brianna."

"Splash some cold water on her face," I said. "She'll wake-up."

"You are a degenerate," Zev announced.

"Only in the D's," I said. "It's a long alphabet, *Zev*, and there's at least one word describing me for each letter along the way."

"Shush," Cada said to me.

"Yes, please," Paul said truculently. "We're trying to avoid being spotted."

I edged forward, ducking below Paul, peeking around the corner.

Two men waded down the middle of the street, parallel with each other. Both played a flashlight across the building façades, one on the left, the other on the right, focusing on street level windows. My jaw clenched when I recognized Jimmy. Still wearing the aviator jacket and cap.

In the distance, on the top of a rise overlooking the city, a fire raged. Smoke belched from what used to be the Gas and Go. Yellow flames spread outward like gigantic arms reaching around Temperance. Even in the dampness, heat was igniting other buildings.

I returned my attention to the closer problem. The two men moved past a bank. Jimmy pushed closer to it, stopping next to one of the brick columns at the entrance, gazing through the broken plate glass door. The other man angled his light upward, examining second story windows. Both ignored the dead bodies floating around them. They blithely bumped them aside when in the way.

"They looking for your friends?" I asked Paul in a whisper.

"Don't know. Might be if they captured one and he talked."

Not a good sign either way. Snooping in the flooded warrens of a dead city wasn't good.

"I know one of them—the one on the right—is toting a .357."

"The one who's eating?" Paul asked.

I took a second look. He *was* eating. Looked like a sandwich.

A feeling stirred inside me. It was revulsion. It didn't twist my gut much. Nonetheless, it was there.

"That's him."

The man on the left called to Jimmy. "We're wasting our time." In the dim light, it was difficult to see much of him. Looked like he wore a leather coat with a fur-lined collar. He stood as tall as Jimmy, and had a stubbly beard.

"Been telling you that," Jimmy said, between chomps on his sandwich.

"You are going to make yourself sick eating out here. You know what's in the lake. And the lake plus some is in here now."

Jimmy made a show of pushing the last bite of the sandwich into his mouth. "Got a cast iron stomach. Ain't nothing touching me."

The feeling persisted, crawling up my spine with tiny hands. I connected it with Jimmy, but I didn't know why. Something just wasn't right.

"Paul." I nudged him. "How you feeling?"

He gazed at me with hard eyes. Before he moved, I already knew the answer.

"Cada, get out of here."

I dropped the duffle and seized Paul by the shoulders, spinning him about and shoving him beneath the filthy water.

"What are you doing?" Cada asked.

"He's insane," Zev muttered. "Completely insane."

Two hands splashed out, reaching for my throat.

"Possessed," I managed while wrestling with Paul. "Get—"

Paul was a bulky man. He was the type who'd workout even if he weren't a cop. But he was a cop, and probably ex-Special Ops. Talk about a handful. If he poked his head out of the surface, I knew there'd be a howl. Then Jimmy and his pal would come running.

I pushed my full weight on his body, sending him deeper. His hands locked on my throat—only as a point of reference. I knew my eyes were their final destination. There was still enough of Paul inside to know how to fight.

I slid my hands to his throat.

Strangling an experienced fighter was pointless. While your hands were wrapped around his throat, his hands were free to kill you. The only reason my hands were clamped around Paul's throat was to keep him silent and from gulping in the water and drowning himself—maybe more of one than the other. Regardless, the situation was fucked. The ex-con who tried not to kill the cop. Didn't think it would work out.

As I whooshed below the water, I saw Cada ushering Zev away. He was dragging Brianna along with him.

My ears rumbled with the turbulent current. Paul's hands crept up my face, fingers searching like a spider walking. I knew when he was close enough, I'd have to let go and try something else.

The both of us were sprawled-out in the water, bouncing up and down, not cresting the surface. I shifted my weight until my heels bounced on concrete. The maneuver spun Paul with me.

My options were limited. Killing him was pointless. He was going to fight dead or alive. The only hope was he'd ditch the Shade before things went too far. Not likely.

Fingers pressed against my cheeks. Then his hands shifted to the side of my head, thumbs over my eyes. I kicked, slamming my boots against the street, carrying Paul with me. He was light until we breached the surface.

I let my momentum push me forward. Once I was up, I heaved him against the corner of the building. His head bounced off the wall, snapping forward. He fell headlong into the water.

If he'd knocked his head hard enough, there was a chance the real Paul would pop-up with the possessing Shade gone. Knowing it wouldn't play-out like that, I sidestepped, pulling the baton from my pocket. I jerked it. With a *snap*, the steel rod extended.

By the time I'd hiked the weapon above my shoulder, Paul lurched upward grabbing at air—not finding me. I thought about hesitating, giving him a moment to see if the Shade was gone. But if I did everything I thought, my life would be far worse. Instead, I cracked him on the head. A solid hit. He sank beneath the sullied water.

CHAPTER

34

DON'T KNOW HOW LONG I searched. The top of the sun was climbing over Lake Michigan before I found the *Herald* building. I didn't stay, making sure Paul was dead. Didn't much matter. Letting Cada know the building wasn't safe pushed me forward. My duffle wasn't floating on the water, and I didn't waste time skimming for it.

Just as Hank said, the building was four-storeys. Being one of the few skyscrapers in Temperance along with floating newspapers helped me discover it. *Pick the tallest fucking building in the city to hide. Pure genius at work.*

I entered through the missing double doors. Inside the lobby, it looked like a naval battle took place. To one side was an area cordoned by tall glass walls. Looked like a small dining space—probably what passed for a cafeteria in Temperance. The water had pulled everything from the shelves. Paper cups and plastic stir-sticks lazily drifted about. A wooden desk bobbed along the murky surface, along with seat cushions. No sign of the chairs. And of course, long spreads of newspaper looked like liquid tile on the water. *Might be a comeback for print media. At least it floats better than a television.*

Toward the rear, in the center of the lobby stood a narrow alcove.

I saw elevators there, surrounded by marble walls. I aimed for the elevators, passing beneath a glass chandelier in the center of the ceiling. Beyond the marble walls was a sign hanging above an open doorway. It was too dark to read, but I guessed it said STAIRS.

Once I angled past the alcove's entrance, I saw two doors on the opposite side with the shapes of a man and a woman, each above a closed door. The stairwell door was missing. In its place was a large metal desk.

I halted. The gray metal monstrosity was wedged in the walkway. There were dark lines on the pale walls, leading me to think the desk had been pushed from a higher floor. Beyond the desk was a clutter of office chairs, piled in a jumbled heap. *The office professional's version of a fence and barbed wire.*

If adrenaline wasn't burning through my body, I suspected fatigue might have caused me to turn away from the makeshift blockade. I climbed over the desk, across the chairs, avoiding the upturned legs, and slowly lowered myself into the water on the other side. I didn't jump. No telling what was waiting beneath the water. Staplers, thumb tacks, bent paperclips. A killing field of office supplies.

Gingerly, or as gingerly as a soggy booted man in hip high water can move, I stepped forward. A metal frame stairwell reached upward, turning at a landing, repeating the act all of the way up.

My boots felt like weights as I topped the first flight. I removed the baton from my pocket, gently extending it with my other hand. How the Shades communicated was beyond me. Telepathy was what I'd call it. Piss poor telepathy. But I knew they could direct both the living and dead to specific areas, and even cause them to speak.

Then I thought about it. That behavior had decreased after the storm passed. So did the appearance of the Shades. Maybe there was something to the increased communication abilities story Paul had mentioned. Except the geeks who dreamed-up this disaster picked the wrong fucking species to help communicate.

Images scattered across my mind. I pictured an endless line of zombies plodding straight for the *Herald* building, with Paul in the lead. I quickened my pace, taking the stairs two at a time. Boots clanked against metal. Figured I'd head to the top floor first. If they were on a lower floor, someone would hear me on the way up.

◆　　◆　　◆

A bright light greeted me as I cornered the final landing.

"Stop there," a voice ordered. "I'll shoot."

It was male. And it sounded doubtful about the "shoot" part. The first half it had down well.

"You have to be expecting me," I said, raising a hand to block the light. *Must have a million watt bulb in that thing.*

I heard someone else speaking. Too faint to understand.

"Who are you?"

"Rand Clay," I said. "But I don't have the fucking password. Check the guest list. Got to be on it."

"Let him in!" Cada sounded from the background. "He's okay."

The light persisted. "What's in your hand?"

"Something to bash out your brains if you don't turn off the light."

"He's here to help," Cada said, sounding closer this time.

I collapsed the baton against my leg, and dropped it in my pocket. "We're all safe now," I said. "I'm no longer armed and dangerous."

The handle of the baton still poked out of my pocket. Hard to find a good concealed weapon nowadays.

"Put it on the landing and you can come up," the man said.

"Geez, you guys need to run a prison," Cada said. She was up there now. And wrong. If they were prison guards, they'd shackle me before letting me inside.

"Not a problem." I grabbed the baton and dropped it on the floor.

"I said put it down, not drop it."

"What's the difference?" Cada asked hotly.

"It bounced out of sight."

"So?"

I exhaled in exasperation. "Look. We don't have time for this. Half the city, or maybe all of it, might be heading here now."

"What do you mean?" Cada asked. Then she spoke to someone else. "Let me through."

She saved them from prolonging the interrogation, marching down the stairs. As she neared, I saw her glistening cheeks, wide eyes, and heard the squelch of her wet shoes.

At the landing, she stopped, briefly examining her noisy shoes, then jumped toward me.

"I was worried," she whispered in my ear, hugging me tightly.

"A waste of time on me," I said. "I'm always fine."

"Might want to rethink that."

During the last few hours, our relationship had changed dramatically. I wondered if Cada was in shock, and misplacing her emotions. Then again, I wondered if I were in shock. Never been the cuddling type.

The voices behind the light debated something. Then another man spoke. "What are you two saying?" That one sounded like Hank.

I looked Cada in the eyes. "I'm going to go up there and kick someone's ass." Made sure they heard that.

"Rand. Don't." She slipped free. "They know a lot about what's going on."

"Why do you think someone is coming here?" the man asked.

"Not someone," I said. "Most everyone. Paul Harris was possessed on the way here. I left him unconscious—or maybe dead. Either way, he'll let the others know where you are."

"Doesn't work that way."

"Tell me that's not Thomas," I said to Cada.

"No."

Then it was Hank.

I wondered why I was debating with them. Cada was next to me, all I had to do was leave. While every zombie in Temperance was converging on the *Herald*, we'd be moving in a different direction.

"Get your things, and we'll just leave." I looked at Cada, watching her face muddled with confusion.

"I have your duffle bag here. I took it when–"

"Even better," I interrupted. "I'll stay here. You can get the stuff–"

This time she interrupted me, placing a warm finger on my lips. "They already know about Paul. It's not a problem. They said he can't tell the rest about us."

Clearly I was spinning my wheels. Not surprisingly, I was in the dark. If Cada believed them, I was willing to play along. Mostly.

"All right," I said. "We'll stay." Then I stared directly into the light. "I'm going to count. When I'm done, that fucking light better be out, and the both of us up there. Otherwise . . ." I let their imaginations do the rest of the work.

CHAPTER
35

"YOU SEE, THEIR MINDS are not linked like computers in a network," Orton Watts said dryly. "We are utterly alien to them, as they are to us." His face wrinkled. A hand pulled at his shaggy goatee. "Or better put, our physiology is alien to them." Then he chuckled lightly. "Well, that's because they *are* aliens."

I looked at Cada. "Does he know who I am?"

"Indeed," Orton answered instead. "You're the felon living in Temperance. Convicted of murder, I believe. Sometime I'd like to discuss morality with you. Your insights, I suspect, would be intriguing."

Cada shrugged. "They all know who you are."

The red glow of the sun poked between gaps in the newspapers covering the windows. The world outside looked Hellish. A reddish-orange color I'd never seen before.

The man lecturing me was on the far side of fifty, with salt and pepper hair, weary eyes, and a sagging smile. He was the person the group offered up to answer my questions—or rebut my argument.

My arrival bumped the number of people on the fourth-floor of the *Herald* building to twelve—including Zev and Brianna.

There were only support columns in the area. Otherwise, short cubicle walls were shuffled about to re-organize the space, offering privacy when needed. I wondered if they'd purchased *Freedom Furniture*. During my time in prison, I'd made a few hundred cheap-ass walls just like the ones being used here.

While I caught Orton's name and hand upon meeting him, I had no idea what he was talking about, or even why I should listen.

"I've always been quite interested in the *aesthetics* of morality," Orton continued. "Those of us who slay fellow humans, I've always suspected, have distinct and differing views from the majority. But it's the structure behind those views which most fascinates me."

Talking to Brianna seemed better.

"Another time, perhaps. There are other pressing matters." Orton waved a hand as though to erase everything he'd just said. "Do you understand the fundamental premise for this unfortunate disaster?"

I inhaled deeply. "Have any beer?"

Orton's eyes narrowed. "None." Then he smiled. "I do have stronger beverages."

"He doesn't need anything to drink," Cada said to Orton. "And you'll have to start from the beginning like you did with me."

"So there is a beginning to all of this?" I asked.

"Quite so." Orton tapped my arm, pointing to five chairs at a long conference table. "Let's sit down, and I'll start fresh."

"How delightful," I quipped, settling into one of the chairs.

"It is, very much." Orton sat opposite me. Cada moved into a spot at my side.

I raised a hand. "Wait." To Cada I said, "Why's he telling me this? How does he know it?"

"A question better directed at me," Orton said. "I'm a retired professor of Philosophy. I *professed* at the University of Chicago." He beamed as though he'd just told a joke. "My area of study was—is actually—Science. While I'm clearly not a scientist, I do have a firm grasp of the subject."

Guess he answered my question. I pressed into the cushioned chair, letting my aching muscles relax for a moment. Figured this was going to be like a first shot of whiskey. Hard to swallow.

"Works for me," I said. "Please *profess.*"

Orton laughed, his thin shoulders bouncing. "Well said."

Right. Armageddon on the way, and I'm telling jokes I don't fucking understand.

"You see, from what I've, or we—" he gestured broadly— "have been able to reconstruct is a high energy, atmospheric research project went afoul. Henry believes it was dubbed the High Frequency Active Auroral Research Program. Or HAARP. The government, particularly the military, loves its acronyms and initialisms. Anyway, back in the nineties, Henry said there was quite an uproar about this program. I recalled a few uninteresting books written on the topic, but didn't give it much credence myself."

Score one for Hank and the reporters. Always liked print better.

"There was quite a bit of speculation as to what this program actually did. Some argued it was a military operation, a means of disrupting the weather, or even turning weather into a weapon." He scooted closer, planting his elbows on the table. "There was also conjecture about possible super-powered plasma weapons, hot spots in the ionosphere–"

I waved a hand above my head.

Orton's forehead wrinkled. "I don't understand that gesture."

Cada came to my rescue. "He doesn't know what you're saying. And to be honest, he's not into lengthy stories."

"Oh, I see." Judging from his expression, Orton's ego was bruised. "I will make it concise as I can."

The more I watched him, the farther he looked on the side of fifty. Maybe mid-eighties. Didn't want the old guy wasting what few hours he had left chronicling histories I didn't care about. The time was better used getting into "the stronger stuff."

"Regardless of the controversy and intentions, what the scientists managed to do is penetrate a barrier between our universe and another. Of course, to do this they required an immense amount of energy–"

"And HAARP turned the Earth into a planet-sized generator," I said, repeating what Hank had told me.

"Astounding!" Orton announced. "I'm sorry, I didn't ask, what level of education do you possess? Being a felon, I assumed–"

If anything, Orton would get accustomed to my interruptions. "One might say, 'Street level.'"

"Intuition suffices for education," Orton offered. "Your conclusion is absolutely correct. The Earth was transformed into a tremendous dynamo. The energy was essentially stored in the ionosphere, and when it was to be discharged, it ripped a gap in the membrane separating our universe from another."

It felt like I needed to start waving my hand above my head again. I didn't. There was enough for me to fill in the gaps. Or picture what he'd said in a way I thought I understood.

"A doorway. Portal. Opening," Orton spoke emphatically. He leaned forward with each word as though pushing them out.

I raised a finger. My index finger, although the one next to it desperately wanted to pinch hit. "I got that part."

"Then you mostly have it all." Orton slapped his hands against the table. "Once the door was open, visitors arrived. Aliens. It appears they are creatures of energy rather flesh and bone. In their home, they exist without any difficulty. But here, things are slightly different. They were attracted to the most complex organism on the planet. I suspect it's because they needed a suitable place to reside."

"They started possessing humans," Cada said. It appeared she'd even reached her limit.

"Yes–yes." Orton said. "Dead or living humans became their vessels. I believe they prefer the dead because there was less resistance to their assuming control. Obviously, occupying a dead body has its limitations. But you might call them new drivers, and the dead allowed them a means of understanding our universe—through our senses."

I pushed up from the chair. It was too comfortable, and if I remained there I knew my muscles would hurt all the more.

"All of this is great," I said. "But how the fuck do you know it? I don't want to be sitting here, listening to theories when hundreds of zombies are searching the town for us."

"You are quite safe here," Orton said. "And your quarrel with my explanation is understandable." Slowly he climbed out of his chair. A tawny sweater hung over his shoulders as though it were on a wire hanger. "I should have started another way. You see, we have one of the aliens here."

CHAPTER

36

IF I DIDN'T HAVE reason to dislike Thomas beforehand, there was certainly cause now. "So there's a Shade inside him?"

Orton, Cada, and Hank stood around a cot where Thomas lay. His hands and legs were bound with white nylon rope, and an intravenous line fed into his arm from two different bags dangling on a T stand. He was gaunt. With his sallow cheeks and closed eyes, he looked dead.

"He's sedated," Hank said sadly. "While I was gone, Ryan and Andrew found him wandering near the hospital—they were gathering medical supplies."

We stood in a compact area, boxed in by the rear building wall and three partitions. Felt like a cell.

"So he's a full-on zombie," I said.

Cada touched my arm, wrapping her fingers around it gently.

"He's living, if that's what you mean. But what was once Thomas has been obliterated," Orton said. "An alien consciousness now occupies his mind. Rather poorly, it seems."

There was too much fuel to ignite my anger. My heart hammered in my chest and ears. Cada sensed it, squeezing my arm. I took a deep breath and looked for a starting place.

"All of your information comes from Thomas?" I focused on Orton. Hank did his best to fade into the shadows. The rising sun didn't help him.

"Some." Orton's lips narrowed. He licked them, preparing to answer. I saw he didn't like being challenged on his own turf. "The bulk of it comes from our gathered knowledge." He gestured at Hank. "Henry did research in the area. The radio provided some information, and I've been able to assemble much of it through reason."

I pointed at Thomas. "And he's a zombie."

Orton sighed. "If you prefer that moniker, then yes."

"Possessed by a Shade—" I caught myself, and emphasized my correction— "alien. Possessed by an alien."

"Occupied seems more accurate, but you have the gist. The longer the alien remains, the greater the damage to the host. Eventually the body will die. However, it is still possible for the alien to occupy it in that state. Quite amazing, actually."

"Not how I'd describe it," Cada said softly.

If I were betting on the next question, I'd go all in—everything on the answer. "Do you know why they occupy some people and not others?"

Orton and Hank exchanged glances. Then Orton took point. "Not precisely. There seems to be some element, for lack of a better term, which stands out to the aliens. They are drawn to it. We've surmised that much from a number of answers provided by Thomas."

"And you believe Thomas?"

Wasn't sure why we kept using his name when *it* was now something else.

Hank inched forward slightly. "Thomas is heavily sedated. Ryan Farland is an EMT, served two tours as a medic in Iraq. He's been giving Thomas Sodium Pentothal and morphine. While it's possible for Thomas to lie, we've not seen him attempt it. And we've given him plenty of opportunities."

"True," Orton said, spicing his tone with a bit of *sage*. "Deception might be more of a human creation. It's quite possible the concept doesn't exist in the alien's awareness."

I wasn't going for it. Maybe Thomas wasn't lying, but *it* understood deceit. "When they are in shadow form, they hide from us. They tangle-up our minds so we can't see them. Then they stampede through our brains taking control." I grunted. "I'd call that deceit."

"Insightful," Orton said. Then speaking to no one in particular, he added, "In that case, it isn't a construct of the mind. Deception is an element of their existence. At least in our universe. Although, camouflage might be a more analogous function. If so, then I don't think we'd call a chameleon a liar, in which case the alien in its energy state—shadow as you call it—is simply trying to hide. Protection, you might say."

I'd felt the touch of these creatures, and I knew what they were attracted to in my mind. I'd seen the results of their actions. They were far more than deceitful. No, they were monsters, inside and out.

Now Orton turned the question on me. "Do you have any theories about their propensity toward particular humans? Given your experience with them, and your keen perspicacity, you are unique."

All along, I'd suspected the Shades were drawn to humans who were in some way loathsome. Only in the case of living humans. The dead seemed fair game to all. Saying as much didn't seem smart. Besides, if we were rating human vileness, I'd peg the scale. Unless, I was right and the Shades could only endure so much darkness. Then I became a poison. Either way, it didn't say much for humanity, or Thomas.

"Emotions," Cada said. "Rand thought the Shades might key off emotions."

"Indeed. Again, our felon proves his acumen." Orton smiled broadly. "I was thinking along those very lines–"

Hank tapped Orton on the shoulder with one finger. A gentle tap. "His name is Rand. 'The felon' sounds a bit . . ." He gave up as Orton nodded vigorously.

"Derogatory," Orton said. "Not my intent, *Rand*. My words come from years of defining variables, nothing else."

I smiled at Hank—mainly because Cada said it spooked people. "Doesn't bother me. I'm that and much more."

"True. Like you, I've committed my share of infractions. I'll save those tales for another time, though." He cleared his throat, tuning his voice for a lecture. "From what I understand of the aliens, while in their 'Shade' form, as you put it, they sense strong emotions in humans. Naturally, memories trigger these emotions, so living humans, while more difficult to *operate*—" he used his fingers to make quotation marks in the air— "are much more appealing. It is a new experience for them. I infer the process is very stimulating."

"You mean they get-off on our emotions?" Cada asked. "Sick."

"That is one way of putting it. And I suppose it is detestable within the confines of most human moral codes. But they are not from our universe. They are not human. The human physical form is entirely unique to them. And I do not believe they can sustain their energy state for prolonged periods in our world. Therefore, it is natural they'd gravitate to the most exhilarating hosts. Sadly, while they retain a higher complexity of mind, they are limited to the basest human instincts."

My mind was a whirlwind of bizarre thoughts. It seemed as though Orton was justifying why these zombies craved flesh—dead or alive. My mind snapped back to the mother who'd been devoured by her children. Whatever controlled them wasn't learning how to drive—it was enjoying itself, mindless or not.

Orton fell silent, his eyes darting between Cada and myself. "From your expressions, I gather you find this behavior appalling."

"You mean eating humans?" She pulled her hand free of my arm. Cada was locked, loaded, and ready to go off on Orton. He didn't know about Nate, and the others she'd lost. "They are killing people, for christsake. How can you stand there and act like they're drinking the wrong wine with a meal? Is there any humanity left in that shell you live in? Don't you care about anything? You call them aliens, but they're monsters!"

Hank moved to Cada, waving his hands, coaxing her to lower her voice. "I know Orton. He sounds insensitive, but he's not."

I could've calmed her. But she'd been through what had to be the worst day of her life, and she needed to burn off anger. Besides, it was a good lesson in Social Studies for the professor.

"You two are no better than the morons who caused this problem. Maybe worse," Cada snarled. "They screwed up the world, but you're up here experimenting on a zombie."

"Shhh," Hank pleaded. It sounded like he sprung a leak. "No need to raise your voice."

Contrary to Orton's blustering about me, I'm not the fastest car in the race. It took me a while, but after seeing the growing panic in Hank's face, I realized some of the others here didn't know about Thomas, or the Doctor Frankenstein experiment taking place.

"I apologize earnestly," Orton said to Cada. "My words are cold, but my heart isn't."

Good luck with that line. Next time don't say it next to the tied-up zombie who used to be your friend.

"You told us someone in here was ill, and couldn't be moved." Apparently Cada caught on as well. She plowed ahead. "I was told everyone voted to stay. Did they know it was a zombie who couldn't be moved?"

On cue, a kid darted around the corner of the cubicle. His eyes had dark half-circles. A black sweatshirt and black jeans made him look like he'd already died. He looked alarmed by the outburst, one hand brushing through his stubby blond hair nervously.

"What's the deal?" he asked. His voice electrified from probably too much caffeine. He set off all of the alarms.

"She giving you trouble?" The kid shot Cada a hard-guy look.

"Nothing, Joey," Orton said. "Just another one of my blunders. I've upset the young lady."

Now Joey shifted gears, eyeing Cada up and down. Must have been the first time he'd seen her. If he continued eyeing her, it'd be the last time as well.

"People are dying out there," Cada said, her voice shaking. "And you're in here, all in one big circle jerk."

Joey's body stiffened. His fists balled at his sides, and his eyes narrowed. He was way too edgy for this group. Definitely needed a time-out chair.

I slapped a hand on his shoulder. "Relax," I said. "*Now.* Don't think. Don't talk. Go back to wherever you came from. This will settle itself."

He glared at my hand, then fixed me with a stare. From his size, I figured he'd done some high school wrestling. Pumped some iron.

Won a few fights. Overinflated his ego. Joey wasn't used to being ordered around.

"Get your greasy hand off me," he barked. "Don't tell me what to do."

"Fair enough," I said. My hand clenched his sweatshirt. I knotted the cloth, and yanked him close. "Where do you want to take this, Joey? Look around. There's no one here to back you." I pulled him closer until I knew he smelled my breath. "Go away. Understand?" *Simple concept. Easy directions. No need for us to start dancing.*

"Everyone," Orton howled. I suspected he was using his professor-take-charge-of-the-class voice. "Please settle down. We can come to an understanding without raising our voices or scuffling."

For whatever reason, it seemed to work. I felt Joey relax, and Cada raised her hands. "You're right. I'm too upset to deal with this right now."

I winked at Joey, released his sweatshirt, and rubbed the stubble on his head. "Guess we're all friends now."

He didn't like me. Not a problem. Didn't like him.

"Good," Orton said. "Let's try this again. But maybe at another venue." When he turned, the exit was filled with faces gazing at him. Looked like the entire crew was here.

CHAPTER

37

EVERYONE GATHERED AROUND THE long conference table. Quick introductions were passed around. The new faces belonged to Ryan, Andrew, and Natalie. Other than names, and what I'd heard about Ryan, I knew nothing about them. Of course, I'd already encountered Joey.

Orton stood at the head of the table, behind him the sun blazed in the sky. It was the color of a prison orange—rotten.

"It is time I announced this," Orton said. "All of you know Thomas. I'm afraid that he is no longer with us. Actually, he hasn't been with us since Ryan and Andrew retrieved him from the hospital."

"When did he die?" Andrew asked in a deep voice.

He was a giant. Stood well over six-five, and easily three-fifty. The man seemed completely out of place here. I figured he was quickly approaching forty from the traces of silver in his hair. Clean shaven, buzzed cut, and clad in a leather vest, T-shirt, jeans, and heavy boots. Had BIKER written all over him. Didn't think Temperance had bikers, and it didn't seem the type of town they visited.

Orton leaned one hand on the table. "He was dead when you brought him back."

"No," Andrew said. "He was whacked, but not dead, not a zombie." I recognized his voice as the one behind the light in the stairwell. Given his size, I was glad we didn't tangle.

"He was occupied," Orton offered. When blank stares greeted him from most everyone, he tried another angle. "Thomas is now what you'd call a zombie, to put it baldly."

The group started chattering, with Brianna leading the way. "What's he doing here? I mean you knew this and you still brought him back?" Her eyes scanned the people around the table. She was looking for more zombies.

"There is no threat," Orton assured her. "Henry and I thought we might be able to help him—at first. When we realized it was too late, it seemed prudent to gather as much information as possible from his condition."

"I'm telling you, he wasn't a zombie when I carried him up here." Andrew shifted his bulk from one foot to another.

"Sorry, Andy," Ryan said. "After Hank said we should bring him here, I gave some heavy tranks. He was pretty toasted when we brought him in."

"Fuck me." Andrew looked at his arms. "You let me carry him. What if I'm infected now?" He stepped away from the table.

"It's not like that," Brianna jumped in, walking on Orton's words. "You can't get infected."

Zev leaned close, whispering in her ear. He probably didn't want to share his secret with everyone.

"She is quite right," Orton said. "There is no biological vector, or disease. Occupation—" he caught himself— "possession occurs through some means of energy transfer that we don't understand yet. Being in proximity to them does not trigger it. However, I think it's safe to say that if you have not already become a . . . zombie, then you won't."

I figured it differently. The aliens started with the easy ones, and the attractive ones—maybe they were one in the same, maybe they had no choice, I didn't know. But I imagined once those bodies stopped working, the alien would jump to a new one. This time they'd have a bit more experience. That meant everyone was still on the menu.

"I'm really sorry," Ryan said to Andrew. He was half the big man's weight. Even so, I'd bet he was just as rugged after doing time in Iraq. Think I liked my prison better.

"Orton explained it to me," he went on. "If I thought you'd get infected, I'd never have done it."

"Please, everyone, let's remain focused for the present." Orton sighed. He was losing control of his class. "Allow me to explain, and I think we'll all understand the situation clearly."

And that's just what Orton did. Judging from the movement of the sun in the sky, I'd guess it took him a little over an hour to explain about the aliens, Thomas, and why everyone was safe. I watched Cada tap her foot from time to time. Probably the night replaying itself in her mind, as I imagined it would again and again for years to come. Knew what that was like. And some memories were never vanquished.

CHAPTER
38

FROM WHAT I UNDERSTOOD, bits and pieces of Orton's knowledge had already been scattered among the group. They knew the zombies became mindless creatures, incapable of coherent communication, or performing anything but basic actions—such as groaning and eating. Most everyone knew they were aliens from another place, and a research project in Alaska had started the entire mess. A few empty spots, but they were ahead of me.

As the meeting broke-up, a revelation struck me like a bolt of lightning. Cada and me, both newcomers, knew secrets the rest didn't—secrets it took Cada's outrage to bring to light. Given the number of knocks on my skull in the last five or so hours, troubling my brain with thought caused it to thrum. As though in one last gasp, it rolled out one more idea, or insight as Orton would say.

I'd been told about Thomas because they needed me. Certainly, if Hank remembered my mention of immunity to possession, then I'd be useful. No doubt Hank was clever enough to know it was easier to negotiate with Cada than me. Or for that matter, keep me calm. As usual in Temperance, my reputation had far preceded my arrival.

A rumble of voices followed as the others cleared out.

Hank approached Cada. "Let me show you your room. And Rand's. I'm sorry we don't have more space. But it does offer some privacy, and there are two foam pads." The last part he said as though it were a bonus feature. Probably was. Didn't think I was ready to move too quickly with Cada.

She looked at me.

"I'll catch up," I said. "Have some questions for the professor."

Eyebrows inched up her brow. "I'll remember this day forever. You hanging after class."

"It happened often," I said. "Just for different reasons than you think."

Hank paused for a moment, switching his head between Orton and myself. He looked like he wanted to stay.

Cada saw it too. She gave me a quick nod. "Hank, will you help me carry the stuff I brought?"

He agreed, and they were off. He looked over his shoulder while following Cada.

"How can I assist you?" Orton said, lowering his wiry form into a chair.

I remained standing, arms folded across my chest. "You want to know why I'm immune."

His green eyes were large behind the narrow glasses perched on his sharp nose. For a few seconds, it looked like he'd fallen asleep. His lids lowered, eyes fixed on me.

"That is correct," he said at last. "These aliens have attempted to gain control of your mind several times. Each time you've managed to stave them off. I think it's important we understand how you did this. It might be able to inoculate others, so to speak."

I shrugged, keeping my arms crossed. "I don't know why they couldn't. I have a few guesses."

"Good. Good," he said, slowly climbing to his feet. "But for now, you need rest. If I'm correct, you've had little sleep in the last twenty-four hours. A clear mind is the best weapon."

Without saying as much, Orton had confirmed my belief. I was his new experiment.

◆　　　◆　　　◆

"It's not really a room," Cada said. "But right now it feels like a suite at the best hotel in town."

"That's not saying much." I knew what she meant. We were sprawled on foam pads, inside what used to be someone's cubicle space. A fishing line was strung across the opening, with a checkered red and green table cloth folded over it, acting as a door. So long as no one peeked above the five feet high fabric walls, there was privacy.

Before we settled in, Cada and me took turns changing. Felt good to get out of the filthy clothes and into the extra set in my duffle. All the while, she scolded me until I cleaned the wound on my leg with peroxide.

Now, with the sun heating the entire floor, we lay on our backs, gazing at the ceiling.

"Did Orton give you any answers?" Cada asked. She hadn't known what I wanted to question him about, but she did catch my intention.

"Yep. I wanted to know why he shared their secret with us before the others. They're interested in my immunity."

"Think you are immune?"

"Can't be sure of anything. Although after what happened at the Hanson farm, I've had the feeling I was off limits. I don't know how to put it into words, but the alien there seem afraid. Or maybe overwhelmed."

In my periphery, I saw Cada roll on her side, head propped on an elbow. "When they told me, I asked about Mr. Hanson. He spoke when possessed. Sorta like the way Hank described Terrance."

I turned my head, looking at her. Heavy, blue eyes greeted me. She was tired. So was I. The embrace of the warm air made it easy to sleep. Still, both of us struggled against it.

She smiled wearily. "Orton suspects some, maybe only a few aliens, are more gifted than others. Like some humans are geniuses."

"I'm certain he put himself in that group," I said.

"Yeah. I'm sure he does. He thought those aliens might have been among the first to possess humans. Maybe the first to enter our world. But most of the zombies Orton said are common, and more or less imprisoned in human bodies. Probably never be more than what they are now."

Imprisoned. I thought about that. If this was global, then there were penitentiaries filled with zombies behind bars. Not sure who I sympathized with—the inmates or the zombies.

"Orton has a way of making it sound like a battle of wits," I said. "Superior aliens and common ones. How many times have I heard that without zombies."

Cada nodded. "It's all too much. I'm still getting used to calling them *aliens.*"

"Let's stop talking about this," I said.

If Orton was right, and we were safe, it seemed best to get some sleep. Wasn't sure how long before things started jumping again. I knew they would.

Cada pushed an arm into her duffle. "I have something for you." She removed Nate's cell phone, and handed it to me.

I stared at it for a moment. "You should keep that."

"No. You're more like Nate than you realize."

"Don't you think he'd want you to have it?" Pain lurked in her eyes. My not accepting the phone was prolonging it. "You're right." I took it from her hand, and placed it in my duffle.

"He'd like that," she said.

"You need some sleep," I said.

When I removed my hand from the duffle, the Beretta came with it. I slipped it underneath my pillow. Cada watched me. Her gaze looked a million miles away. I knew what worried her.

"You won't dream about it," I said. It was a flat lie. "Or, if you do, you won't remember. It's too early for nightmares."

"I'm living in a nightmare," she said.

"Then you're trading a real one for an imaginary one. Win all the way."

She exhaled a puff of air. It seemed no matter how I tried, I couldn't sweeten this one.

"Get some rest," I tried again. "I think we have a few hours before dinner."

She lowered her head on the pillow, eyes meeting mine. "Want me to come over there?"

I didn't have an answer. Okay, I did, but it didn't feel right. She was different. The women in my past had been sailing through, or doing their job. I was lost with Cada.

"Sleep on it," she said. "You might need the extra energy."

In the gauzy warmth, I watched her eyes close, head resting on the pillow. In seconds, she was sleeping. For the first time since I was a kid, I thought about praying. Asking whatever power there be to keep the bad dreams away. Knew it was pointless. If there was a God, it wouldn't like what else I had to say.

CHAPTER

39

SHOUTS PULLED ME FROM a dark sleep. I opened my eyes, purging the image of my dad's dead body, head a pulpy mass. I crouched, Beretta in my hand.

"They've trapped Andy," someone yelled. I took it to be Natalie.

She was the quiet type. Tall, with raven hair draping her angular face. During the few hours I'd been here, I'd only heard her utter a sparse number of words.

Cada sat upright as though a spring had launched her. Eyes blinked as she tried to clear the fog of sleep.

I motioned. "Stay here until I know what's going on."

The sun had dropped below the paper-shaded windows, painting long shadows across the fourth-floor. I kept the Beretta at my side, and moved toward the conference table where I saw everyone gathering.

It turned out to be Joey screaming. "Two guys cornered us. I split out the back of the store, but Andrew was too slow."

Enough said. What they say about bad pennies was true. And mine was named Jimmy. "Was one wearing a baseball cap?"

Joey searched his memory. "One of them. Kind of a weird looking guy."

Jimmy.

The rest of the crew stumbled up. I turned to see Cada peeking over the cubicle walls. Figured she had the Colt in her hand. I nodded, letting her know we were safe.

Orton tugged at his sweater. Looked like he'd been napping as well. Hank fidgeted, rubbing his beefy hands together, wringing them in knots.

"They're going to kill him," Joey said frantically. "We got to go help him."

"What were you doing?" I asked.

Joey hushed long enough to give me a steely gaze. Guess it was none of my business

"It's all right, Joey," Hank said, then turned to me. "Gathering supplies. Food, batteries, whatever we need."

"You think these guys are looking for Thomas?" I asked. *One fucking zombie. Talk about persistent.* I was questioning the can't communicate theory already.

"We got to go," Joey repeated. He jumped about like he was trying to kick start us.

Cada approached, stopping behind Ryan and Natalie. Brianna and Zev stood farther away, clearly doing their best not to be seen. Didn't matter. They were the last two I wanted on the street.

"I'm not sure if going there is advisable," Orton said thoughtfully. "They might assume two people are transient. But if a group returns . . ."

Then they come looking for us. I knew everyone finished Orton's sentence. He was good at leading people to conclusions. And other than Joey, no one else moved.

"What do you mean?" Joey spun on Orton. "We can't just leave him there."

The kid had a lot to learn about life. Especially when it threatened someone else's life. What we were capable of was surprising.

"I'll go," Cada spoke.

Joey looked at her in disbelief. He shuffled through the others. "What about the rest of you?" He stabbed the air, pointing at Cada. "She's useless. Might as well go myself." He looked at Ryan, then at me. "What about you spineless assholes?"

"Calm yourself," Orton said.

"It isn't right," Natalie finally said. "He's helped us. We have to help him."

"I'll do it." Ryan stepped forward.

The entire time, I'd spied everyone's quick glances at me. I fancied the question their minds was, "What about him?"

I raised the Beretta. Popped the magazine, made sure it was full, then slipped it back. "I'll go, but the kid stays here."

"Fuck you," Joey said. "I'll do what I want."

"There's a difference between being tough and being stupid," I said calmly. "You need to work on the 'tough' part. The rest comes naturally."

Kids. When I was his age, it was unheard of to mouth off to a murderer. You gave them space, or they plugged you in the head.

I looked to Hank. "Say the word. I'll do my best to make sure no one gets back to tell Terrance."

Everyone stared dumfounded—including Joey. For a moment, he actually stood still.

"You can't go by yourself," Cada said. She slipped around the group, approaching me.

Normally, I wouldn't go at all. But I had a score to settle with Jimmy. He had a mouth on him as well. And Andrew was the type of muscle this group couldn't afford to lose. I certainly didn't plan on hanging around forever.

"I've dealt with one of these guys before," I said. "I know what to expect." With Jimmy it wasn't possible to know.

"We can't ask you to do this," Hank said. "And if they see you, they'll know there are others. Remember Cada and you helped me escape them."

"Time's short," I said. "I'm going."

I'm not sure how I ended up on what I normally thought was the wrong side of the argument. *Leave it alone. Not your problem. Suddenly you're a hero.* Maybe I'd been fooling myself all these years. Told myself I always walked away, but I didn't. When my dad was on a streak, I should've hit the street like Cada did. When those girls needed help, I couldn't refuse. And I knew if I did it, Arvin Hames would show up. In the end, it wasn't me trying to help people. It was me looking for excuses to kill.

I looked at Hank. "The kid's stupid, but he's right. Not many of us left. Someone has to draw a line."

"Morality is a slippery slope," Orton said. "It doesn't have parameters or boundaries. It is a continuum, ever changing with society."

Didn't know what the fuck he said. I wondered if anyone else did. But I took it and ran. "In case any of you didn't notice, society has changed. No one's here to stop the bad guys anymore."

"That's not quite what I meant," Orton started.

"Hash it out. I've got to move."

While Joey was quiet, I spoke to him. "Tell me where he's at?"

Still dazed, the kid answered mechanically. "On Birch Street, inside the Dollar Store."

Who the fuck loots a Dollar Store?

"Draw me a map." I pointed to a fold of newspaper sitting on the table. He quickly sketched some lines with an X marking start and another for the destination. Could tell he wanted to do more, but I didn't let him. I snatched the paper before he spoke. "All I need."

I trotted to the cubicle, and grabbed my leather coat. Cada was fast on my heels.

"Are you trying to get killed? Because it looks like it from here."

"Maybe later," I said, stepping to the side.

She shifted with me, blocking my passage. "You even going after this guy? Or is it an excuse to skip town?"

The words stung. I didn't know why. It's what I always told myself and everyone else. Guess I didn't expect her to buy into it.

"I'm not leaving yet," I said. "I'm just doing what you'd do."

"Yeah. But we're two different people."

"I want to change that."

She looked dumbfounded. I *was* dumbfounded. Not sure why I said it. Just shot out. One of those thoughts hidden away in your head waiting to leap to your mouth. And it felt good. An invisible weight lifted. Looked like I wanted that second chance after all.

"I'm coming with you," Cada said. Her fingers wrapped around mine.

Enough time had been wasted. There was nothing I could say to keep Cada here, so I decided to go with it. Once we were outside, I'd send her someplace safe to keep watch. Besides, it might be good having her back me. She's saved my hide at least once. Maybe more.

"Get a coat, and keep close to me," I said. "You have to do what I say."

She was in and out of the cubicle in seconds, marching behind me as I passed everyone at the table. Joey eyed me, and then started to follow.

"Nope," I said. "Stay here."

Hank grabbed his arm. I heard Joey's protests as Cada and I trotted down the stairwell.

CHAPTER
40

FINALLY HAD A CHANCE to change my clothes, and I was back in the water. Passing through the ramshackle maze of chairs and tables didn't take long. In minutes, we were trudging down the center of the street in hip deep water—or chest deep for Cada.

The setting sun shone from the opposite of Temperance. Some of the ugly red color had faded. Above, the faint lines of light were returning. They looked like scratches against a glass sky.

I kept a fast pace. Cada was bounding through the water, barely keeping up. At the first corner, I stopped, scanned the area, then continued. Five, no six bodies bobbed against building, pushed there by the internal current of the flooded city.

The first corner turned us west. Then I saw the bellowing black smoke on the ridge. The Gas and Go was doing a slow burn. On both flanks of the gas station, fires raged. Tall flames burned downhill, reaching higher toward the heavens as they descended. I suspected gusts of wind from the lake were pushing it along. Unless the fires stopped, Temperance wouldn't last more than a few days.

Cada bumped into me. "Move," she said. "Don't stop for me. I can keep up."

I didn't tell her why I had stopped.

Unprovoked thoughts tumbled around my brain. The line of zombies parading up Main Street toward the gas station resurfaced. So many faces, young and old. I hoped Orton was right. If so, then they were already dead when I burned them.

The reek of burning flesh returned to me. Then I realized it was the twang of fire in the air.

I pushed headlong toward Birch Street—it was in sight now. In my right hand, I held the Berretta over my head. One magazine was all I brought. More was a waste of time.

I waved for Cada to move against the wall. Only two bodies tumbled on the greasy water near the building. I inched to the corner and leaned my head around. The Dollar Store was right where Johnny had placed the X. A wan glow came from its interior. Not a good sign. I suspected they had Andrew, and knowing Jimmy, he was going through his interrogation routine.

Cada moved close to me. I felt her body trembling. My left arm folded around her, holding her close. "You don't have to do this," I whispered.

"No, I do."

I pressed my face to her head. The action felt so natural and yet so unfamiliar. "I need you to watch this corner. It looks like they have Andrew. My guess is they're asking questions. Probably trying to find others."

Cada nodded. She held a flashlight in one hand. "Waterproof," she said.

"Only use it if you need to. Otherwise, make sure no one else comes down the street."

"What if they do? How do I let you know?"

I slid my hand behind her head, angling until I met her gaze. "Call out, and then head straight back to base. Don't try anything else. I can take care of myself. Your yelling will cause them to react. So don't waste any time. Get back and tell the others. I'll be right behind."

She looked at me. Doubt creased her face, but she didn't say anything.

This time I was the one who pulled her lips close. We kissed for a moment—long enough for me to change my mind. I had to will myself away from her.

"I'll bring Andrew back," I said.

The approaching night brought a profound coldness with it. Loping from one corner to another, nearing the store from the back, I felt the chill leach into my bones.

CHAPTER

41

LIKE EVERYTHING ELSE IN this town, the back of the Dollar Store was brick. I wondered how anything was burning with so many stonework structures.

High, to the west of the city, the fire loomed. Yellow tendrils waved back and forth like they were calling each other. If the water wasn't a problem before, the fire certainly was now. It had spread across Main Street, and reached down both sides of the slope. The only exit from the city was through a tunnel of flames.

Can't do anything about it now. Stay focused.

I slowed my pace as I reached the rear entrance. It was a broad loading dock, with the door lifted open. The entire back portion of the building was about three feet higher than the street. Judging from the shape, the front was closer to street level. I crawled onto a ledge next to the loading dock, completely exiting the water.

Staying against the wall, I walked the concrete lip leading to the ramp. It delved downward, allowing trailers to back in at a door level for easy unloading.

Harsh, electric light radiated past the threshold of the door. Figures moving inside cast large shadows on the walls.

I sidled along slowly, hearing voices. There was no mistaking

Jimmy. Didn't know what he was saying, but it was his usual raving.

I ducked low, and stole a look around the corner. Wooden pallets were stacked throughout the back of the store. Some were twice my height. Beyond them were three electric lanterns perched on different columns of pallets. They surrounded a large man in a chair. Andrew.

Snippets of Jimmy's words echoed off the hard walls. He'd reached his peak. I knew his type. First get worked up, and then do something rash.

I sneaked around the corner, hiding behind the nearest group of pallets. Then I dashed to the left, winding my way between other stacks until I was no more than twenty feet away from Jimmy.

Just as Joey had said, there were two men, Jimmy and the man I'd seen him with before. Jimmy paced in front of Andrew like a riled animal. The other man stood behind Andrew. Given their captive's bulk, both men had to be sporting guns. Otherwise, the giant would have snapped them like twigs.

"Do you think I'm stupid?" Jimmy screamed. His moon-shaped face was red in the bleak glow of the lamps. "If you lie again, I'm going to break something." Jimmy leered at Andrew, seemingly reconsidering his words. "Something on you, motherfucker."

I wondered if Andrew was restrained. If Jimmy came that close to me, he'd be dead. Could be Andrew was a gentle giant? *Bad news for him.*

"Here's your last chance." Jimmy hoisted the .357 high, pressing it against Andrew's forehead. The big man didn't move. Didn't flinch. Just sat there as if nothing more than fly had landed on his head. "Where's your buddy hiding?"

Jimmy cocked the hammer on the revolver.

"Think about it, fucker. It's a pretty big bullet for a pinhead like yours."

He hadn't lost his charm.

I considered the circumstances, all the while waiting for the revolver to boom. Snap decisions usually worked better than plans for me. *Go with your gut.*

My choices were limited. If I startled Jimmy, he'd likely squeeze the trigger. Waiting wasn't an option. Jimmy looked like he was at the end of his rope. The other man stood silently, hands clasped in front of him.

Following my usual strategy, I went with my instincts. "Your answers are over here, Jimmy."

He jumped. The revolver went up in the air with him. But it didn't fire.

The man playing statue spun in my direction, hand digging in his coat pocket. I fired three fast rounds at him. At least one hit. He twirled, then his arms whirled as he dropped.

The glow of the lanterns blinded Jimmy—I enjoyed the irony. He pointed the revolver in my direction, waving it from side to side. Then it growled.

The sound washed over me, leaving a high pitched ringing in my ears. I hunkered down, hugging the floor. Wooden pallets made the worst cover. Thin wood with big gaps.

Just to keep Jimmy busy, I squeezed two rounds in his direction.

He scrambled toward the front of the store, blasting wildly behind him. Slugs whizzed and whistled, glancing off the floors and walls. He kept at it until the last chamber was empty. I stayed flat on the cold concrete.

Hadn't I counted, I'd never know the revolver was empty. My ears rang. All I heard was the rumbling blood pushing through my body.

After the sixth shot, I was on my feet, charging toward Andrew. Figured Jimmy would move slow in the water, and with the broken ribs I'd left him with the last time we were together. Once Andrew was freed, we'd probably be racing to see who got to the asshole first.

I was wrong.

Andrew's chair had tipped over. Looked like he'd busted his noggin. The blood wasn't coming from his head, though. It oozed from a gash in his chest. One of Jimmy's stray slugs found a target.

A void expanding inside. Everything I did went afoul. Except killing.

Without thinking, I was chasing Jimmy. When I hit the front of the Dollar Store, I didn't wade down the stairs. The Beretta went over my shoulder, and I jumped in the black water.

The remaining sunlight sent rays through the front windows, silhouetting Jimmy as he frantically splashed about. I leaped, and swam, pushing off metal shelves, speeding down the aisle behind him.

The mistake he made was looking back. *Just run, Jimmy. Never look back.*

My lungs ached. I huffed in air, pumping my legs until I was within a few feet.

I lunged forward, nabbing his jacket. *That fucking aviator jacket.*

A hard yank pulled him down. He swished beneath the water. My other hand balled into a tight fist, driving into the water after him. Jimmy must have been coming up for air because I thumped him hard.

Arms waggled above the surface. I punched again, still holding his coat. This time I felt his body jerk, then relax.

Keeping his head above the water, I played tugboat, hauling him to the back of the store. In the water he was light as a feather. Figured he was just as light out of the water.

His limp form flopped up the stairs, feet dragging across the concrete, leaving twin wet lines behind. I pulled him into the center of his interrogation area, just like he'd done with Andrew. Then I played basketball with his skull until his eyes opened.

He blinked repeatedly. Knew it'd take a while to catch-up with the latest events. I stepped back, making sure he'd have a good view of me.

"What you doing out here, Jimmy?"

"Huh? Who are you? What the fuck did you do?" He climbed onto an elbow. Looked like he thought about sitting up, then rethought it and remained propped on one arm.

"I'm an old friend," I said. "Don't remember me?" I wondered if the Dollar Store had any baseball bats.

He wiped his eyes, feeling for his cap—which was gone.

"You don't know who you're fucking with."

While his brain tried to make sense out of the world, I strolled to where I'd dropped the Beretta. Picked it up, and came back.

"Can you see me yet?"

Jimmy pushed up on both hands, sitting on the floor, head cocked.

"No fucking way. You son-of-a-bitch, motherfucker. I'm going to beat your sorry fucking ass."

I was astounded by his tenacity. He was like a bulldog, except less dangerous, and missing teeth when he didn't have a gun.

"Your brains are scrambled." I rapped the pistol against his head. "You just had a beating, and things look dire for you unless you start talking."

It was bad for him either way. No need to douse his spirits from the start.

"You just don't get it. This is my town. Not some fucker who gets off on killing his momma."

He knew how to push my buttons. A flash of rage rolled through me. I kicked him. My boot slammed against his cheek, sending him down.

"Killed my dad," I said. "If you only get one thing right, make it that." Then I grabbed his jacket and pulled him to his ass. "Where is Terrance?"

"Fuck you."

Another boot to the head. He went back down. Again, I pulled him up.

"A few more times, and the only thing you'll be able to say is your name."

He spat blood. His lips were red, and it looked like a front tooth was missing. "Terrance is gone. This is my town now."

At first hearing, it sounded like good news. "Where did Terrance go?"

"I don't fucking know, and I don't fucking care. I call the shots now."

"Good. You're doing well. Now tell me who you were looking for."

"You're going to be so fucking sorry when I'm done with you," he said.

Back to that routine.

I shoved the Beretta beneath my belt, and grabbed Jimmy with both hands, lifting him off the ground. He was so tall his feet still dragged on the floor.

My lungs churned like a machine. My head pounded. It felt like the pain would push my eyes out of their sockets. But I held Jimmy in front of me, and spoke slowly. "One last time."

"For fuck's sake, you crazy asshole. Thomas, some zombie named Thomas. Terrance wanted him, so I wanted him."

"What do you know about Thomas?"

"I know enough. You're interested in him, so the fucker dies when I find him."

I chuckled. "Think he's already dead, Jimmy."

"No, he's a zombie. He's not dead until I smash his head."

I dropped him. He hit the floor hard. "Ouch." One hand went to his ribs.

"You still rounding up zombies?"

He was silent a moment, and then softly said, "Yeah."

A boldfaced lie, and a poor one. "Can't control them, huh? Things are getting out of hand, maybe?"

Jimmy sneered at me. "My boys are going to find you, and I'm going to have them work you over. You'll wish you're back in *Deetroit* fucking your momma."

We'd hit the end of the line. Now it was a waste of time. All it achieved was pissing me off.

I kicked Jimmy to the floor. He groaned, calling me names, holding his ribs.

I planted a boot on his chest, pinning him down.

"Listen, fucker," Jimmy said. "You better stop this shit right now."

I pressed the Beretta against his forehead. Gave him a moment to remember how many times he'd done it to others. Then I single-tapped two rounds in his skull.

CHAPTER

42

I WASN'T LEAVING ANY WEAPONS behind this time. Too late for Jimmy's revolver. It was lost under the water in the front of the store, but his chum had a Glock, and four magazines.

I emptied their pockets. No wallets, no IDs—not much need for them now. One speed loader was in a pocket of Jimmy's jacket. Took it just in case.

Knowing Cada was probably freezing, I hurriedly prepped the two men, leaving Andrew for last. Near the back of the storage area was a stack of cinderblocks. Looked like they were used to keep the sliding door open a few feet. The Dollar Store must have been hot when things were selling.

I wrapped Jimmy's belt through the gap of a block, and tied the rest around his hands until he was embracing the weight. Did the same for his friend. Both bubbled to the bottom of the loading dock ramp. If Jimmy was telling the truth, then dunking their bodies didn't matter.

I contemplated Andrew. He was tied to the chair. Since no extra weapons turned up on Jimmy and friend, I assumed Andrew relied on muscle. I stood there a moment, wondering if he'd surrendered to them. Didn't look like he'd put up a fight. By the time I arrived, he seemed placid. Maybe he'd just given up.

It was a challenge, but I managed to haul Andrew and his chair to a far corner. The ropes were a tangled nightmare, and I didn't have my knife with me. *Sorry, pal. The chair stays.*

Like the others, I put a slug in Andrew's head. Couldn't risk a giant zombie running around.

Wooden pallets were all I had to cover him with. I hurriedly stacked them around him, creating a small wall, hopefully blocking view of his body. Then I placed four over him. It'd have to do until someone else came to collect him. Joey seemed like a candidate, regardless if he was told to do it or not.

And with one booming explosion, all of my efforts were rendered moot.

It was a distant, low rumble. I dashed to the rear door. Night settled over the world, bringing to life the new aurora. On the west side of town, a fireball unfurled. The flames from the Gas and Go had stalked there. I imagined they'd either encountered a car or a propane tank. *Not good. This isn't stopping. Soon it'll rain fire.*

The explosion opened skyward like a flower spewing black smoke. Then, in the simpering light, I saw movement. Not one person passing through the murk. Hundreds. Shoulder to shoulder, they weaved forward.

The fire was driving the zombies into the heart of Temperance.

Every other thought flushed away. I edged along the wall until I was clear of the ramp—now the grave for Jimmy and his friend. Not hesitating, I stepped into the water. Its chill bit my legs. I pushed ahead. The deepening night would make it difficult for Cada to see the zombies until they were a block or so away. I had to get her, and leave Temperance.

As I waded across Birch Street, another explosion sounded. This one was closer. Maybe six blocks away. Only its flickering red glow was visible in the gloom. Enough for me to see Cada.

She stared toward the direction of the blast. I knew the fire couldn't have moved downtown that quickly, jumping blocks at a time. Something else was happening. Unbidden came the scenes of burning zombies running in every direction.

Cada watched the distance so intently, she didn't see me approaching. I was no more than ten yards away. Each step was an eternity. Long lopes, as though I was on the moon.

Just as I started to call out, she leaned closer to the wall, craning her neck as though straining to see something. In an instant, she jumped back, using her hands as a makeshift megaphone. Then she spotted me and jumped with surprise.

"Geez, you scared the shit out of me," she said. The flashlight hung from her shoulder on a string. Probably drifted near her and she put it to use.

"Hurry," she exclaimed. "I don't know what's happening, but zombies are pouring into the streets like rats."

I looked down the length of Birch Street. It overflowed with zombies. My gut told me they were all moving away from the fire, spreading-out like a tsunami. And they'd keep going, pushing across the north side of town, into the forest and beyond.

"Go ahead. I'm right behind you," I said. "We need to warn the others."

She headed away with me decreasing the distance. Both of us bounced down the street, springing in the water toward the *Herald* building.

Every street we crossed was choked with zombies. They streamed into every building, quickly overflowing them. Zombies walked out second-story windows, others meandered on rooftops. They mindlessly headed in every direction, except toward the fire.

When we arrived at the *Herald*, Joey stood beyond the entrance, waiting.

"Where's Andy?"

"Have you looked outside?" I asked. I brushed by him, heading toward the stairwell. Cada kept pace.

Joey stared at me, jaw gaping. "You were supposed to get him. What, you chicken-out?"

I grabbed Cada's waist and boosted her over the metal desk. My temper was still brewing from Jimmy, and from the disaster I'd created. *Hold on to it. Going to need it later.*

"They killed him," I said. And before the kid responded, I added, "Take a look outside, and then get your ass upstairs."

Once on the stairs, we quickly reached the top. Another greeting party waited there.

Several electric lanterns splashed rings of light around the fourth-floor. Cada entered first. She marched past Hank and Natalie, heading to the cubicles.

"What happened?" Hank asked. "You cause those explosions?"

"No. The fire did. And I think a few flaming zombies."

He looked mystified. Natalie shared the expression.

"Can either of you use a gun?" I asked.

Hank mumbled faintly while deciding. Natalie shot back a reply. "I'm a realtor–"

I wondered why everyone told me their occupation when I asked if they could do something. When I was asked a question, I didn't do that. *Can you drive a stick shift? I'm a criminal.*

"Great," I said to Natalie. "I'm looking for an apartment in a different city. Can you help with that?"

Amazement welled inside when she started to answer.

"Can you use a fucking gun?" I roared.

She jumped in surprise. "I've never used one. So no."

"I'm not a good shot," Hank finally said. "But I guess I can."

"Great," I handed him the Glock and magazines. "It's a little wet, so get a handkerchief or something and dry it."

"What is all the fuss about?" Orton asked. He'd crept from one of the cubicles. Behind him came the rest.

"It looks like every zombie in the city is headed our way," I said. "Not sure, but probably the fire is pushing them north. Regardless of why, they're coming."

"I seriously doubt they'll climb four flights of stairs to get up here," Orton said.

"They're walking on rooftops south of here. If there's a path, they'll follow it. Add to that a building full of fresh meat, and they'll be fighting to get in here."

"Can't we just shut the doors?" Brianna asked.

Actually, it was the brightest thing I'd heard her say. I searched my memory. I hadn't seen doors on any of the stairwell entrances. Good idea or not, it was useless without doors.

"Where are the doors?" I asked, already knowing the question was pointless.

"We removed them for safety reasons," Orton said.

Brilliant. Remove the barrier separating you from man-eating monsters.

"We were afraid—"

I cut off his words. "Save it. We're need guns for anyone who can use them."

They looked baffled, turning their gaze from one person to the next. Cada returned holding up her Colt.

"I've got one," she said. "Only five bullets, though."

Hank stammered. "I don't think we have any guns. Other than this one." He held-up the Glock.

From the stairwell, Joey screamed. His feet slapped against the steps as he approached "They're coming! We can't stay here!"

I tagged his shirt as he ran past. He jerked back violently, stumbling to keep balance.

"Let me go!"

"There's nowhere to go," I said. "We can head north, but the zombies will follow. Besides, I don't know how many are waiting in the woods."

"We can't just stay here," Joey countered.

"Then you can leave. Everyone else needs to grab some alcohol and start filling bottles." I looked at Natalie. "Realtors can do that, right?"

"Give me the alcohol," she said smartly, pushing a strand of blue-black hair behind an ear.

"We have a few pints from the hospital," Ryan said.

I spun toward Orton. "Time to break out the strong stuff."

Figured he had three or four bottles at least. We only needed enough to start fires and make half-full Molotov cocktails.

Orton seemed to consider the proposal when Hank spoke up. "Orton, we need it all." He looked at me. "We'll have to cut-up the tablecloths for fuses, if I'm right."

"Very insightful," I said. "We also need some desks and chairs moved to each floor."

Joey stood motionless, dumbfounded or dazed. I snapped my fingers before his eyes. "Need you to be our runner. You up for it?"

He blinked, focused on me. "Sure." The word was faint. Probably shock setting in.

"Get to the roof and watch the zombies," I said "When they're about a block away, let us know. After that, you'll have to hustle up and down the stairs as we fall back."

"You can't actually think we're staying here," Brianna said. "Isn't there a yacht at the docks we can use? That has to be better than all of this craziness." She turned to Zev and muttered something, nudging his arm.

"I don't think there are any yachts in Temperance," Zev said after five or six prods. "Start cutting the tablecloths."

Once again, Brianna had a good idea. Hitting the water never occurred to me. Now we were close enough to try. Even so, it didn't smell right. Seemed too risky with zombies moving about. *Looks like you're back at the Alamo.*

CHAPTER
43

HANK, ZEV, AND RYAN hauled large metal desks to the second and third floor stairs. They also stacked chairs at the choke points, both metal and wooden. Perching the desks on the stairwell railing went faster than I'd expected. My thought was to push them over, followed by a rain of chairs and burning cocktails. If the zombies persisted, repeat the process on the next floor. Blocked passages alone wouldn't stop them.

Cada worked with Orton, stretching his ten bottles of Jack Daniel's into more than forty Molotov cocktails. He grumbled the entire time.

Because Brianna refused to stay in one place, I had her hauling bags to the roof, setting them next to a rusting fire escape. Zev did the same since he continually followed her like a puppy-dog.

If the building started burning, we'd need a way out. The dilapidated fire escape seemed the only route.

Throughout this, I nagged myself, wondering what I was doing. Last stands weren't my gig. Suicidal fights weren't either. This promised to be both.

Slipping away and staying clear of the zombies seemed the best thing for me. Babysitting was dangerous. And probably pointless.

The only answer I had was Cada—doing it for her. I just wasn't sure I believed it. There was no way I could leave her behind now. Like Alexandra from the Diamond Club, turning away wasn't possible. Cada always championed lost causes. It was time someone returned the favor.

"Guys, a bunch of them are heading this way." Joey stampeded down from the rooftop. "I think they see the lights."

All eyes fixed on me. *Fuck. Might as well put a neon sign with the word EATS.* Might as well keep them burning now. There was no way we'd pull this off in the dark.

All of this depended upon Orton being right. If the zombies worked on primal instincts, maybe our fires would overpower the desire to eat.

"There's too many," Joey said. "They're going to overrun us." He bolted toward me, halting, eyes wide with terror. In that moment, I pictured his future. Knew too many kids like him. They didn't think. Just got themselves killed. Joey would too.

"Take a breath," I said. "Can't leave now, so just hit the second floor with Ryan and Natalie." I handed him my lighter—probably the last I'd see of it. "Light the bottles for her and help throw the furniture. We just need to scare the zombies away."

He nodded frenetically. Reminded me of a guy I knew in prison. White collar type. He'd scammed the IRS, and was sentenced to five years. Huron Clinton Valley Correctional Facility, a real minimum security place. Easy ride. Guess he didn't think so. He went with another plan. Shot his wife and daughter. Tried to shoot himself. Fucked that up. In the end, he swapped his original five for a life sentence, and was invited to a hardcore prison. Every day he hunched in a corner, bobbing his head up and down. The guy handled prison pretty well. The memories were another story.

Joey grabbed the lighter and was running down the stairs.

"Hank and I can take the third floor," Cada volunteered.

I looked around. "Where's the odd couple? And where's Orton?" *What the fuck? Is there a secret exit I don't know about?*

Hank walked toward the back. "Orton was with Thomas."

Cada looked at me as though recounting memories. "Come to think of it, I haven't seen Zev or Brianna for a little while."

A cry from Hank grabbed my attention. I ran, yanking the Beretta from my belt—ready to put down Thomas. Didn't have to.

When I reached the cot, Hank kneeled next to Orton. The professor was curled on the floor, hands folded beneath his head. A syringe lay near him.

"Morphine," Hank said.

Thomas had looked nearly dead the first time I saw him. Now he looked completely dead. Waxen flesh, chest motionless.

From behind me, Cada gave a sad moan.

"He do the same with Thomas?" I asked Hank.

"Looks like it." Hank checked for a pulse. A forlorn expression hung on his face. I remembered he and Thomas had been friends. "Not alive."

Cada turned away. Her voice cracked as she spoke. "Why go through all this just to kill yourself?"

I wanted to tell her Orton was old. His world was passing, and like the dinosaurs, there was no place for him in the new one. It belonged to people with a continuum of morality—or whatever the fuck he'd said.

What made me different from the sheep wasn't my being a wolf. I was something far worse. Born and steeped in darkness. In the never-ending night, I saw clearly. While they mourned, I chambered a round.

"What are you doing?" Cada asked excitedly. "Don't."

Her eyes told me she thought I was planning on following Orton. No way. I hadn't earned it. At least not yet.

"It's not that," I said. "But I have to be certain."

Hank caught on. "There's no way, not with that much morphine."

I stepped next to the cot. "Do you want to risk it? See him come back?"

"No." Hank's eyes dropped to Thomas. "He was a good friend. It seems I owe him better."

"Then don't stay," I said. Bending, I pulled the pillow from beneath Thomas, placing it over his face to limit the splatter and the sound.

"Come on," Cada said, grabbing Hank's arm. She guided him away.

The Beretta pressed into the pillow. The next one was for Orton.

CHAPTER

44

A HYSTERICAL CRY PIERCED THE air, leaving iciness in its wake. My first thought was of Cada. I ran through the maze of partitions, find she and Hank gazing numbly at the stairwell leading to the roof. Even that door had been removed, and the tablecloth once hanging in its place was now stuffed into bottles or sitting in shreds on the conference table.

"It came from up there," Cada said.

I dashed up the stairs, into the demonic glare of the night. Another scream. This time repeating, "Zev . . . Zev . . ."

On the eastern side of the roof was a gathering of bags and boxes. Among them was my duffel. Cada's sat next to it. They were waiting patiently for our escape. As I approached, I heard the insane ramblings, hundreds of voices. Hacking, coughing, and spitting out unintelligible sounds. Like a wave, it washed over me.

I stopped at the retaining wall. Before it was an ancient looking set of iron cast stairs and rails, mounted on the rear exterior of the building. A rusted grating led to weary stairs, which fed downward to another gridiron platform, and more stairs. They crisscrossed all the way to the second floor. That's where Brianna stood, waving frantically, calling to Zev. He was on the ground, running in circles with a zombie pursuing.

I tromped down the iron stairs, halting at the drop ladder. I pushed on it with my boot. It didn't move. Didn't give any indication of ever moving. Time and rust had set it in place.

"Jump up here," Brianna screamed. "We'll catch you."

Not happening. No way I'm hanging from the ladder like a monkey with one hand on a rung and the other grabbing Zev.

My foot hammered against the stubborn ladder. The platform shook. Brianna gasped, grabbing the railing. The ladder remained stuck.

"Try for the bottom rung," I called to Zev.

He glanced at me hurriedly. Just then the zombie seized him. It buried teeth into his throat and shook its head. A great spout of blood shot through the air. Brianna shrieked.

I still had the Beretta, so I aimed. Zev hit the ground before my hand leveled. He twisted and flapped. The zombie stayed with him. Now its head raised, flashing a bloodied mouth. A long howl followed. I wasn't sure if it was a cry of triumph or a beckoning.

In seconds, a line of zombies rushed around the corner. Sniveling and growling they lunged at Zev's body. They clawed at him and at each other. Soon there were ten, twenty, maybe fifty. The writhing crowd covered Zev's form. One tried to back away, a severed hand in its mouth. Others pounced on the escaping zombie, viciously biting. More joined. Soon fingers, fists, teeth were everywhere. Zombies tripped and climbed over each other.

I stepped away. Brianna leaned against a rail, pale, trembling hands covering her face. She shook, but wasn't crying.

An uproar of howls sounded from below. I looked down. Several zombies leaped upward. They swiped at the fire escape or at us. I hoped they didn't have the sense to climb ladders. Didn't wait to find out. I dragged Brianna to the roof. What she and Zev were doing became clear. Figured they'd sneak away while everyone else was busy, hunt down a yacht maybe. Probably the best idea they'd ever had. Still didn't make it a good one.

I lowered Brianna onto a box. She sat there. Her hands remained locked over her face. She made tiny gasping sounds. Nothing else.

This is what happens when I make plans. You know better. Go with your gut.

"Stay here," I said. Seemed pointless to say. She didn't acknowledge me.

◆　　◆　　◆

No one was on the fourth floor. Yells came from the stairwell. Lights flashed, and I heard the crash of glass followed by the *whoof* of fire.

With a growing mob of zombies in the building, the Beretta was useless. I kept it anyway, stuffing it into the front of my belt. Then I made my way to the third floor. Hank and Cada had a battleship gray desk balanced on a railing. Half filled bottles with checkered cloth wicks sat along the wall.

"They're trying to come up," Hank grunted.

"What happened on the roof?" Cada asked.

I shook my head. She understood it wasn't the time to mention it.

"Maybe you should go up there," I said to Cada. I didn't want her on the frontlines.

She flashed a brusque look. "I'm needed here."

One floor down, Ryan counted aloud. Metal squealed against concrete, followed by a heavy crash.

"Now!" he yelled.

Flames splashed in the air. Shadows weaved along the walls.

I leaned between Hank and Cada who shared the burden of the desk. An errant thought raced through my head: *Was Freedom Furniture being used as weapons by whoever bought it?*

"Listen," I said, pushing aside the notion. "I need the both of you to get on the fourth floor and haul the conference table to the roof."

Hank looked quizzical. Or as close as he could manage with the fright on his face.

"It's a fallback plan," I said. "In case this doesn't work. Bring the conference table to the roof and barricade the exit. It's big enough to cover the entire doorway. Once you've finished, lean against it and don't let anything through."

Cada looked at Hank. They lowered the desk to the landing. "What do you mean? We're not leaving you—any of you," she said.

"Good," I said. "I want you guys up there blocking the exit. Didn't mean for you to keep the humans out."

"Think that'll work?" Hank asked. His thin hair was haystacked. Or at least it tried.

"Has to," I said. "I'm going to light-up the stairs. Hope it drives them off. If not, everyone can lean against the conference table and maybe hold out the zombies. The stairwell is too narrow for many of them to get good leverage."

Ryan called from the second floor. "Need some help down here. They're coming."

"Don't have time to debate it," I said.

Hank agreed. He headed up the stairs. Cada rubbed a hand against my cheek, then followed him.

CHAPTER

45

"**N**OT LOOKING GOOD," RYAN said.

Flames belched over the hand railing. The combination of wood and flesh formed a harsh, acerbic smoke. I tried breathing through my mouth, but the taste gagged me. Inhaling through my nose stifled me. I kept working on both. Couldn't stop breathing. Not yet.

Natalie tossed Molotov cocktails over the railing. She grabbed bottles and extended their tops to Joey. He left the Zippo burning—had to be hot in his hands by now. Once the shredded cloth blossomed, the bottle went over the side, shattering against the wall. Ryan tossed wood from chairs as well, building the flames.

Long wails and screams spiraled upward with the smoke and stench. Burning zombies squirmed, crawling over each other. With a desk in front and behind, they didn't know which way to go. Flames even waved along the surface of the water.

"Here," Ryan handed me a metal chair leg. "They're the only weapons we have."

I thought about Hank and the Glock. But discharging in a stairwell was risky. I took the chair leg. Not quite a baseball bat.

"Throw everything you have over the side," I said. "We'll move to the third floor and try again."

"I don't think they're going to stop," Natalie said. Her eyes welled. Large tears spilled down her cheeks. I didn't know if it was from the smoke or the situation.

"Maybe not," I said. "Won't know until we try."

She nodded, and started grabbing bottles in pairs, holding them for Joey. He seemed relaxed. Hands not shaking, face smooth, emotionless. Undoubtedly he'd already slipped away from the sane world where all of this was matter-of-fact.

"Meet you up there," Ryan said.

Before I replied, I saw the lighter slip from Joey's hands. It bounced, then glided away, scooting into a corner. He was after it in an instant.

The ride had snuffed the flame, but it was close enough to the stairs for a zombie to spot Joey. In a long bound, it hurled over the desk, scampering up the remaining stairs.

Natalie threw one of the ignited bottles. Flames exploded on the wall, splashing on the zombie and Joey.

"Look out," she yelled.

The zombie ignored the new flames and pounced.

I rounded the corner, gripping the hand rail, kicking with my boot. The zombie slammed against the wall—Joey still in its grip. Natalie bolted toward Joey, slapping at the flames.

"I'm so sorry. I'm sorry." She swatted frantically.

Joey didn't make a sound. Didn't struggle. He curled-up like a worm baking in the sun.

"Get away," I yelled to Natalie. She continued patting Joey and sometimes the zombie.

Another head popped above the desk. The flooded first floor was dousing the flames. It appeared the zombies were learning how to use the water.

Before the new zombie had purchase, I nailed it in the head with my boot. Always wore steel toes.

The zombie's head wrenched back. The body followed, splashing in the water.

The one on Joey ripped clothes, digging for the flesh beneath.

It gnawed on Joey's head, slobbering, unable to anchor its teeth. I swung the chair leg at its skull. Burnt flesh splattered on the wall. Along with it came an even fouler stench.

The zombie ignored the blows. Its clothing had melted into its skin. The thing was bloated. A flaming marshmallow. So I skewered it with the metal leg, ramming it through the back. The leg sank in, sticking in the torso. The zombie lurched up, eyes finding me.

I planted a boot in its face. "Don't give me that fucking look."

It bounced against the wall, hands swiping blindly. In the flickering light, I saw one of its eyes had erupted, and my kick collapsed part of its skull.

Natalie moaned, dropping to her knees, wiping at Joey. Blood jetted from someplace on him. He still remained motionless.

A fresh chorus of cries came from the first floor entrance. As though propelled by an unseen engine, five zombies crawled through the doorway, over the desk and toward the stairs.

Hell was throwing a rave, and everyone had an invite.

"Leave him," I said to Natalie. "Just get up." I nudged her with my boot. Wasn't about to bend down with a group of undead heading toward me. The only thing slowing them was the second desk. That bought seconds at the most.

She didn't look up. Her bloodied hands glided over Joey, trying to find his wound. From the amount of blood, I knew he was already dead.

CHAPTER

46

I KILLED PEOPLE. SAVING THEM wasn't my bag. Ask my mom or the girls in Detroit. Pretty much ask anyone who was with me for the past day. I wasn't the hero type. But with Paul gone, it all landed on me.

Two zombies climbed up the stairs, and the third was wallowing around with a chair leg in its back. Natalie continued her quest to save Joey.

In the back of my mind, I wondered if whatever was inside the zombies jumped to a new body when the old one stopped working. Figured if you crushed their skull, whatever was left of them died.

Keeping my eyes on the zombies, I backed away, reaching out for Natalie. My fingers caught her blouse. I tugged. "Come on. You can't help him."

She jerked away and continued mindlessly trying to staunch the elusive wound. The bleeding had already stopped—no thanks to her.

I pulled the Beretta. Missing a target in this narrow space was risky.

"Natalie! Get upstairs."

"I'm so sorry," she whimpered over and over.

One zombie, then another climbed onto the landing. I fired at the first, going for a head shot. It didn't flinch at the sound of the Beretta, and it didn't go down. At least there was no ricochet.

I gripped my wrist with my other hand, steadying my aim. Squeezed the trigger. This time the zombie did the dead man dance. Its torso twisted, head tilted, and it dropped like a bag of sand.

The second one shambled forward. Perhaps it smelled blood through the stench. I fired again. It rocked backward, then tumbled forward, sprawled on top of Natalie.

She screamed, beating her palms against its head.

The zombie pumped its legs as though it were still trying to walk. Hands clawed left and right. Its head cranked up and down, teeth snapping.

A sullied nail, as though in slow motion, dragged across Natalie's cheek, tearing flesh as it went. Blood welled and spread down her face. The wound was ragged.

Skipping forward, I drove a boot into the zombie's ribs. Flesh and bone gave way, but other than jostling it, there was no effect.

Gray skinned and emaciated, tattered clothes, and covered in grime, it looked as though it had climbed out of the grave.

A second and third kick broke several ribs. But the zombie held to Natalie, tongue snaking about. Finally, its head lowered, mouth sucking the wound on Natalie's cheek. And then came a long, wretched keening as the creature ripped away a mouthful of flesh and muscle.

It lifted up, shaking its head as if it were showing a prize. Then in one gulp, the fleshy meat vanished into the zombie's mouth.

Two more undead mounted the landing, hands balled into fists, bodies swaying left and right.

Turning sideways, I thumped a knee into the zombie pinning Natalie. It wobbled for a moment. I sighted Natalie with the Beretta. Terrified eyes, wild and wide, locked on me. This time my first shot found the mark.

◆ ◆ ◆

"The desk! Throw it!" I charged around the landing to the third floor. Ryan stood ready, one end of the metal desk hanging over the railing. "Do it!"

He huffed, and the desk flipped, clattering against the hand rail, then scraping the wall, and finally crashing on the stairs, sliding down several steps.

Right behind the desk came a bottle. It shattered on the landing.

"Have any matches?" Ryan asked, gasping.

Before I did my last stint in prison, everyone smoked. When I came out, no one did. At least, no one admitted to it. A dirty little secret. Automobile manufacturers even started removing the fucking lighters from their vehicles. Needless to say, I wasn't surprised to learn Ryan didn't have a match. A score of Molotov cocktails, and no way to start the party.

"Just break them. Cover the area." I kicked the bottles, breaking them against the wall.

"Try this." Ryan grabbed two bottles by the neck, one in each hand, and he slammed them against the floor. *So much for my keen insight.*

"Get to the roof," I said. "I'll finish here."

He looked at me, puzzled.

"Cada and Hank are on the roof. They have the exit barricaded. We're going to try to hold out there."

"Sounds better than here," he said. The two bottles in his hands collided against the floor, and he was off.

For a few seconds, the smell of whiskey overwhelmed the fetid pall drifting in the air. Too quickly it vanished. I killed a few more bottles—not the way I normally did it—and then clambered up the stairs.

Huddled around the threshold to the fourth floor were several more half-full cocktails. With a sweeping movement, I pushed them down the stairs and dashed for one of the electric lanterns. Bottles jingled as they rolled behind me. The gurgles and rambling sounds of the undead came in reply.

Next to the lantern was a paper bag with three bottles of Jack Daniel's—all full. The word "Recycled" appeared on the side of the bag. Guessed there'd be a new definition coming with the waking undead on earth.

I grabbed the bag and the lantern. It was a long shot, which meant there was nothing to lose. I tossed the plastic lamp at the puddle of whiskey. It clattered, bounced, and flickered off.

Fuck.

CHAPTER

47

STACKED AROUND THE STAIRWELL leading to the roof were several bundles of newspapers. I dropped the paper bag, and grabbed the newspapers, throwing the bound blocks around the entrance like bales of hay. Then I unscrewed a bottle of Jack, and poured it over the paper. Sure, paper burned well enough, but a little accelerant never hurt. Normally, I was pretty good with fire. But today things refused to go my way. I'd call it a bad day, but it was pretty much like the rest.

Above the partitions, I saw the shadows of flames still dancing in the stairwell leading downstairs. All I needed was one burning zombie. And as if summoned, a zombie appeared—not on fire. It snarled and spun about, seemingly confused by the empty room. *All of this struggle to find no prize. It'd piss me off too.*

I gave up on the bundles of newspaper. I opened another bottle of whiskey, took a swig, and then stuffed it upside down between the bales. Figured I'd let it drain itself.

The sound of undead entering the room told me it was time to leave. Keeping low, I snatched the last bottle of whiskey, and shuffled up the stairs. Just as I'd asked, the conference table blocked the opening. I hammered it twice with my fist.

"It's Rand. Need to let me through. Fast."

Voices spoke on the other side. Long seconds passed. I glanced over my shoulder—nothing there yet.

The table scraped against the doorway as it moved sideways. Once the opening was wide enough, I squeezed through.

"Close it up," I said. "Does *anyone* have a lighter or matches?"

Already knew the answer. It was one of those days.

"Got a Bic." Cada pulled one out of her pocket.

Ryan and Hank were working on the conference table.

"How long have you had that?" I asked.

She offered it. "You want it or not?"

All this time she'd been playing me.

I grabbed the lighter. "Hold up. Got to go back down for a second."

"Are you crazy?" Ryan asked.

Before I spouted my usual answer, Cada interrupted. "Don't be stupid. Just stay up here."

I twisted the cap off the whiskey bottle. "Need one more bottle of Jack in the punch. Only be a minute." Hurriedly, I slipped into the stairwell.

A permeating stench hit me like a solid wall. The air outside, although far from fresh, cleared my lungs. Now the stinging returned, as did the desire to gag.

Down the steps I went. At the bottom, I shook the bottle about, covering the area in quality hard liquor. Then, I thumbed the lighter and touched the nearest stack of papers. Even though all of my plans went astray so far, I hoped this one would work. Ignite the room, drive out the zombies, and if the entire building didn't go up, we'd sit it out on the roof. Or borrow a number from Zev's playbook and try the fire escape.

The blue flame kissed the whiskey soaked papers, and flashed with a *puffing* sound. I dropped the bottle, and made my way back up the stairs.

This time they didn't move the table.

◆   ◆   ◆

"Anytime," I yelled.

Long tongues of fire lapped at the ceiling of the stairwell, blackening the frame and walls, filling the space with dense smoke.

I tried shouldering the door open. It budged, then slammed back. Screams came from the other side.

"Move the fucking table," I yelled. My fist pounded against it.

This time it shifted to the right slightly, then stopped. I wedged my fingers in the opening and pushed it the rest of the way. Smoke filled my lungs. By the time I was through, I was gasping for breath.

The blaze behind illuminated the world before me. It did so in flashes and waves. On the roof I saw four figures. Cada, Ryan, and Hank circled around a stocky zombie. The zombie shifted clumsily, but there was enough movement to tell me it was the living dead.

Along the retaining wall slumped Brianna. Dark blood covered her body, soaking into her shirt.

This is getting out of hand. I went for the Beretta, but it wasn't in my belt.

"Keep wide," Cada yelled. My mind numbed.

From a distant place, I watched as Cada choreographed the fight.

Ryan stepped away, moving toward the back of the building.

Hank fumbled with the Glock, but the zombie didn't give him time to fire. It dove at him. Hank groaned, flying backward under the weight of the creature.

For an instant, I thought about blocking the stairs with the table. No need. The fire was churning. For now it was a good enough barrier. Instead, I ran toward Hank.

Before I reached him, the zombie grabbed Hank's head, pulled it up and bit deep into his throat. A short moan escaped, quickly transforming into a raspy cough. Blood oozed from Hank's mouth. His eyes rolled back. The zombie thrashed in victory. I had no doubt about it now. I'd seen too many killers revel in their work. It was celebrating a kill.

I didn't break stride. With each step, I gained speed. Between the glow of the fire and the pallid heavens, I saw the zombie's face. Paul Harris.

Dead or not, he leaped from Hank.

I went headlong into the air, missing completely. I bounced on the roof. In the dim light, I saw Cada tugging on the Colt's slide. The pistol was old, and probably jammed from lack of cleaning.

Ryan darted forward, thrusting a chair leg at Paul.

Orton had been right. There were some zombies who were exceptional. This one remembered how to climb. And no doubt, folded away in a primal part of its brain, it had a score to settle. While its brethren clashed in the streets, attacking one another, or hunting for living flesh, this zombie was getting revenge.

Like so many other times, I saw what was about to happen clearly. If I remained down, looking vulnerable, then Paul couldn't resist me. So I did that. Made it look like I stumbled climbing to my feet. Taking enough time for him to close on me.

Paul charged. My heart lurched in my chest, climbing up my throat as I watched him speed toward Cada.

"Cada!" I screamed.

"Look out," Ryan warned.

There wasn't time for her to react. Paul's bulk toppled her. She flew backward, collided with the hard roof. His frame covered her entirely. Only her feet were visible, kicking, trying to wrestle free.

Fury exploded inside me. I bolted toward them, willing my legs to move faster.

Cada's small hand reached out, fingers tapping for the gun next to her. Time slowed for me. I heard every beat of my heart. There was nothing else, only the sound of it thudding.

Ryan threw the chair leg. It sailed end over end through the air, hitting Paul on the shoulder, then rattled to the rooftop.

Greenish-blue light twisted in the sky, making the world shimmer in unreal colors. Paul raised up, a handful of Cada's hair in hand, lifting her torso. The second hand wrapped around her face and jerked.

Her scream pushed through my flesh, past my bones and into my soul. The cry lasted forever, anguished and pitiful. In the gloom, I saw Paul clench his trophy, a fist of dangling flesh. His other hand released her hair. Cada's head dropped.

Then, he slipped a hand underneath her throat. In an instant, her

CHAPTER

48

A STAINED GAUZE COVERED CADA'S face. Ryan had inserted a drinking straw into the wound in her throat, allowing her breathe. White bandage tape held it in place.

Paul had ripped most of the throat away. When I lifted her into my arms, Ryan shook his head. He didn't need to.

I'd bundled her in my coat, holding her close. She tried to speak but couldn't. A sound like someone sipping the remains of a milk shake came from the straw each time she inhaled. Her pulse was faint. Skin cold.

"We'll find a place and go back to watching old movies," I whispered. I pressed my face against her head.

With a sudden movement, her hand reached for mine. Damp fingers clasped my hand—not the warm ones from a few hours ago. She squeezed. It was soft, weak.

My head lifted. Our eyes met. Hers were lidded, and beautiful blue, and moist with tears. My lips trembled as I felt my own eyes sting.

"I won't leave you," I said softly. "We'll stay together." I searched for the pistol.

Again, she squeezed my hand faintly. Then a second time.

I laced my fingers around hers.

The bleeding continued. Her body trembled.

"Morphine," I said to Ryan.

"Sure." He shuffled through a red and white case.

Cada squeezed my hand twice. Her eyes were pleading.

"Just enough to reduce the pain," I said.

Two more squeezes.

Ryan kneeled next to her.

"No. Don't," I said.

"You sure?" He looked worried.

"For now."

The gauze covering most of her face and throat glistened in the light. Ryan moved away, giving us some time. There wasn't much left.

Now the night felt cold. I pulled her close. She moved her lips. The straw sputtered.

"Let me do the talking," I said.

A wan smile crossed her lips.

None of this was right. What kind of a world lets a murderer live and destroys a beautiful life? This time, I did pray. I begged for her life. Offered mine instead. If there was a Hell, it was my proper home.

Cold lines ran along my cheeks. Cada shifted her feet and squeezed my hand.

I gazed at her. She slowly shook her head as if to say "no."

"I–I want to–" The words caught in my throat. Not because I couldn't utter them. I didn't know how. I inhaled deeply. "I want to tell you I love you."

A tear streamed from her bloodied eye. She squeezed my hand, still trying to smile.

"I don't know how to love," I continued. "So I don't know what to say."

Round, little tears rolled down her face. Her lips moved, shaping silent words. My heart hammered against my ribs. More tears slipped from my eyes. I gasped. She mouthed, "I love you."

Everything inside welled up. All of the pain, the hate, and the love. I convulsed with every breath. My soul ached.

I said, "I love you." But her eyes were already dead.

CHAPTER
49

THE NIGHT PASSED, MELTING into a hateful new day. Ryan took care of the other bodies, using the Glock first, then pushing them over the wall. The rest of the night he spent sitting against the conference table—no zombies attempted to pass.

I'd held Cada in my arms most of the night, talking to her, speaking of better places and times. Then, I covered her with a blanket I found in a box. I dropped against the rear wall, and slept a couple of hours.

The ugly gaze of the sun stirred me from a dream. It had not been about my dad, or my mom, or any of the other dark things prowling my memories. For one last time, I had been with Cada. We sat on a haggard couch in my apartment, talking, laughing, and watching television. It was *our* Thursday night together. And she'd smiled the entire time. A bright smile only she had.

I stood, sore from the little time I slept. Ryan leaned over the front wall, surveying the world.

"They left," he said as I came alongside.

Empty clothes with missing bodies sloshed on the surface of the impenetrable water. Severed arms and legs drifted as well. I recalled the howls. Throughout the night the zombies clashed with one another, ravaging anything alive or dead. Then they faded into the pale glow of the night.

To the south and east, fires burned. Spiraling columns of smoke dotted Temperance. I was surprised the *Herald* building hadn't gone down in flames.

Ryan must have tuned into my thoughts as I leaned over the wall, examining the soot stained façade.

"The presses were removed years ago," he said. "Otherwise, I don't think we'd be here. Oils and inks and cleaners would have poisoned us if they didn't outright explode."

"Real lucky," I said dully.

◆　　◆　　◆

Ryan knew what I was up to and offered to help. Guess two tours in Iraq taught you how to read people. Not very different from prison.

Together we carried Cada's body into the forest on the north edge of the city. If Ryan was worried about encountering zombies, he never said as much. In fact, he was the one who found a shovel while I wrapped Cada in a second blanket. Now he shared her weight without complaint, shovel strapped to his back with a nylon rope.

We carried her in no particular direction. I simply walked until I found the right place. It was on a lush hilltop next to a towering oak. No marker I manufactured could match the majesty of this tree. And it reminded me of the place I dreamed about when in solitary.

In better times, Cada was fond of walks in the forest, though I never joined her. I hoped this spot pleased her.

"We'll take turns," Ryan said. "Just give the word."

I never gave the word. Didn't say a thing. I worked the shovel in the black soil until there was a deep grave.

In that hole, next to the oak tree on the top of a hill, I rested Cada Finch's body. I offered no words. Everything I had to say I'd already said. Although, my heart sank as I realized I wanted to say them many more times.

From my pocket, I removed Nate's cell phone. I tapped the front.

It displayed the next song ready to play. "Move Along," by a band named All American Rejects. I smiled. Knew I liked the guy.

I pushed play, and tinny music came from the small speaker. I leaned over Cada—blood had soaked through the blanket. Gently, I pulled the covering free, and slipped the phone beneath her laced fingers.

For a moment, I stood there listening, imaging her singing along. *Yes. Move Along.*

Then I removed the Colt from my belt and lowered it over the center of her head.

CHAPTER

50

THERE WAS NO DIRECTION I planned to head. Ryan said he was going to Chicago, so I tagged along. We followed I-94, walking for hours, until we reached a ramshackle Super 8 motel. Looked like a good place to stop for the night. The tangled lines of color were already becoming visible above.

In the parking lot, we found an old Ford Maverick. There had been other vehicles scattered along the Interstate. All of them had computer brains. Didn't know how to rig one of those. But the Maverick was like hearing an old melody. You never forgot it. In minutes, I had the pea-soup green car singing my tune. Satisfied, I killed the engine. Figured it'd be needed in the morning.

The Front Desk was lonely.

"Looks like we have our choice," Ryan said, rummaging through the rack of keys. "Maybe the second floor is best."

Didn't matter. Some zombies knew how to climb.

Throughout the entire day, there were no zombies wandering around. No humans either. None of the Civil Authority vehicles Brianna said the radio had mentioned. Only a few birds hung in the cloudy sky.

Although I'd said nothing about it—wasn't in a talking mood— Ryan had suggested blockades.

"Checkpoints to make bottlenecks," he'd said as we marched along the Interstate. "We used them in Iraq to funnel and control movement. Of course, we also had Red and Green zones."

I'd heard plenty about the zones over the years. Even in prison everyone was talking about the war. Never heard an inmate say he'd trade places, though.

"What day is this?" I asked, returning to the moment.

Ryan checked his watch. "Thursday." He made a sound, a stifled laugh. "Going on the second day, and time's already slipped away."

"They have cable here?" I asked.

He smiled. It quickly faded. "Sure. But they're probably not getting many channels right now." He made a show of looking at the thick shadows inside the entrance as if to remind me there was no power.

"Any room on the second floor works," I said.

He grabbed a key off a hook and tossed it.

"Looks like free food," he said, nodding at the vending machines.

"Think I'll just get some sleep."

He shrugged. "Sure. I'm going to hunt down a crowbar and crack these nuts. In case you change your mind, I'll leave some stuff outside your room."

"Great." I pushed through the door. Before it closed, I halted, facing him. "Might want to set some empty bottles or cans along the top of the stairs. Doubt the zombies have learned stealth yet. Kicking them over might make an alarm."

"Good idea. Did that in Iraq too." He shrugged. "The camps were guarded, but you never knew . . ." The words faded away. "Hey. I'm sorry."

I tilted my head.

"Sorry about Cada," he clarified. "I know we just met and all . . .." He paused as though searching his memory. "What I'm saying is I know what it's like."

"Guess you do," I said.

◆　　◆　　◆

With a wall of pillows against the headboard, I settled in the bed. Wasn't quite the same as my couch, but it'd do. Before me sat a dead television. I gazed at it. *Thursday is our day.* And I tried to let the memories return. They were stubborn, and unwilling to come forth.

I watched the blank screen on the small television until the sun hid from the world. *Move along.* Cada was good at that. It was harder for me. I didn't let things go. Kept them with me, in the dark corners of my mind. Now I had more to hide away.

The night solidified in the room. With the curtains drawn, not even the strange lights in the sky shone through. I pulled the slide on the Colt, loading a round into the receiver. Carefully, I pressed the barrel beneath my chin. *Move along.*

My finger tightened on the trigger. In some remote place, I heard Cada's voice. It was filled with happiness. No troubles or worries. *Just enjoy the ride.*

The room was silent. Ryan had given me plenty of space, respecting my privacy. I pictured Cada's face. Her eyes. Her lips. *Just enjoy the ride.* I lowered the pistol. I hadn't earned it yet. There was a long way to go before I could slip away.